The Firewitch bore dow... so close now that I coul... lumps in its array ...

I stared into the big purple eye, waited for the train wreck, and said, "Crap!"

The eye flashed yellow. Then it burst like a brittle balloon. Then the Firewitch exploded silently into pieces that tumbled in all directions, not least toward me. A metal triangle bigger than a piano pounded my gut, and I began to spin in another direction, twice as fast as I had been tumbling, so I couldn't distinguish what I saw, except alternating dark and blinding brightness.

I thought a voice said, "It's over."

Shadowy, curved pearly wings appeared around me, then slowly enfolded me.

Then there was only darkness.

Praise for the Jason Wander Series:

BOOKS BY ROBERT BUETTNER

Orphanage
Orphan's Destiny
Orphan's Journey
Orphan's Alliance
Orphan's Triumph

ORPHAN'S ALLIANCE

ROBERT BUETTNER

www.orbitbooks.net

New York   London

Copyright © 2008 by Robert Buettner
Excerpt from *Orphan's Triumph* copyright © 2008 by Robert Buettner. All rights reserved. Except as permitted under the U.S. Copyright Act of 1976, no part of this publication may be reproduced, distributed, or transmitted in any form or by any means, or stored in a database or retrieval system, without the prior written permission of the publisher.

Orbit
Hachette Book Group USA
237 Park Avenue
New York, NY 10017
Visit our Web site at www.orbitbooks.net

Orbit is an imprint of Hachette Book Group USA, Inc. The Orbit name and logo is a trademark of Little, Brown Book Group Ltd.

Printed in the United States of America

First Orbit edition: November 2008

10 9 8 7 6 5 4 3 2 1

For Rob and Kim

Nearby Waterloo, I saw a Sergeant of Artillery seated upon his caisson, which the rains had mired in the road ditch. His eye had been shot out, and one of his men, whose leg was off, wept beside him. The Sergeant complained that Prussian cavalry had bypassed them. He said, with some heat, "Our own allies abandoned us like orphans!" I told him straight, "In this hell, better an orphans' alliance than no alliance at all."

> — Remarks at the annual Waterloo
>   Dinner of 1821, attributed to the
>   Duke of Wellington

ORPHAN'S ALLIANCE

ONE

"MOUSETRAP'S VISIBLE NOW, GENERAL." My command sergeant major taps my armored shoulder, points through the *Emerald River*'s forward observation blister, and my heart skips. The two of us float shoulder-to-shoulder in infantry Eternads, like unhelmeted frogs in a gravityless fish bowl. Ord has been a jump ahead of me since he was my drill sergeant in Basic.

With my gauntlet's snot pad, I mop condensed breath off the observation blister's Synquartz, and cold stings through the glove. Fifty thousand frigid miles away spins Mousetrap. In two hours, on my orders, a hundred thousand kids plucked from fourteen worlds will arrive down there, innocent. None will leave innocent. Too many won't leave at all.

The gray pebble Ord points to has just orbited out from a vast orange ball's shadow. In the red sunlight that bathes the gas giant planet and its tiny moon, Mousetrap tumbles as small and as wrinkled as a peach pit.

Ord grunts. "The real estate hardly looks worth the price, does it, sir?"

"Location, location, location, Sergeant Major." Mousetrap is the only habitable rock near the interstellar cross-road that linchpins the Human Union's fourteen planets.

That's why the Union fortified Mousetrap. That's why the Slugs took it away from us. And that's why we arrived here today to take Mousetrap back, or die trying. "We" are history's deadliest armada, carrying history's best army. My army.

I'm Jason Wander, war orphan, high-school dropout, Lieutenant General, Commanding, Third Army of the Human Union. And infantryman until the day I die. That day is now thirty years closer than when I enlisted at the start of the Slug War, in 2037.

Ord and I push back from the observation blister's forward wall, to head aft to our troop transport. I glance at the Time-to-Drop Countdown winking off my wrist 'Puter. In two hours, Ord and I will be aboard a first-wave assault transport when compressed air thumps it out of one of *Emerald River*'s thirty-six launch bays. Kids embarked aboard *Emerald River*, and aboard the fleet's other ships, will go with us.

Ord sighs. "A hundred thousand GIs don't buy what they used to, General."

Whump.

Emerald River's vast hull shudders, tumbling Ord and me against the observation blister's cold curve.

Hssss.

A thousand feet aft from our perch here at *Emerald River*'s bow, thirty-six launch bay hatches reseal as one.

A tin voice from the Bridge crackles in my earpiece. "All elements away."

I turn to Ord, wide eyed. "What the hell, Sergeant Major?"

Ord turns his palms up, shakes his head.

Through ebony space, thirty-six sparks flash past us, from the bays that ring *Emerald River*'s midriff. In a blink, they disperse toward Mousetrap, leaving behind thirty-six silent, red streaks of drifting chemical flame.

For one heartbeat, *Emerald River* forms the hub that anchors those thirty-six fading, translucent wheel spokes. It is as though we spin at the center of a mute, exploding firework. To our port, starboard, dorsal and ventral, identical fireworks blossom, gold, green, blue, purple, as the Fleet's other cruisers launch their own craft, each ship trailing its mothership's tracer color.

I blink at the vanished silhouettes. The Army I command wasn't scheduled to launch for Mousetrap for two hours. We expect that we will take lumps by landing with no aerial prep. And more lumps when we start digging the Slugs out of Mousetrap, one hole at a time. But landing without prep is the only way we can avoid killing the human POWs that the Slugs hold on Mousetrap.

But what I just saw fly by weren't chunky troop transports. They were sleek Scorpions, their bomb racks packed with liquid fire. The ships that made that fireworks display weren't just an aerial prep force. The formations I just saw were powerful enough to incinerate every living thing on Mousetrap, Slug and human alike, three times over.

Before Ord and I paddled up to this observation blister for a final, weightless look at our objective, I inspected every launch bay myself. One of our troop transports filled every bay. But one order from the Bridge could rotate troop transports out of the bays in fifteen minutes, like cartridges in old-fashioned revolvers, and replace them with bombers.

I'm already torpedoing my weightless body hand-over-hand down the rungs that line the cruiser's center tube, back toward the Cruiser's Bridge. "If those bombers fry Mousetrap, our POWs die." Mousetrap's POWs are simple grunts, mostly, and that swells my throat even more.

But Army commanders are supposed to consider the Big Picture, as well as their kids. I shake my head at Ord. "The Outworlds already oppose this war. If this fleet kills Outworld POWs, the Union's dead. If the Union dies, the Slugs will wipe mankind out. Did Mimi lose her mind?"

Ord paddles up alongside me, so fast that the slipstream seems to flatten the gray GI brush he calls hair. He shakes his head. "Admiral Ozawa wouldn't launch bombers, sir. She wouldn't even consider it without consulting you, first. But there is a ranking civilian authority aboard this ship. If he ordered her to do it, she couldn't—"

The two of us tuck our legs, then swing into the first side tube like trapeze artists. Then we 'frog along toward the Bridge, gaining weight as we move away from the rotating Cruiser's centerline.

"I know. But I warned them, Sergeant Major. That Alliance was a deal with the devil." Lieutenant Generals don't have tempers, especially while commanding invasions. But Ord and I are alone in the passage tube, and I'm angry enough that I could punch my fist against the tube's wall until my knuckles bleed.

Not because our allies are cruel and stupid. Thirty years of war have taught me how to beat cruelty and stupidity. I pound out my frustration because my godson has become one of them. Worse, I know my godson is the only officer in this fleet who could be leading those bombers.

Ord closes two hands over my clenched fist. "Sir, Churchill said if Hitler invaded hell, Churchill would at least make a favorable reference to the devil in the House of Commons."

I know the quote. I talked myself into believing Churchill had the right attitude, so I could smile while diplomats pattered their white-gloved hands together, applauding a deal that I should have known would bring us to this. An infantryman's life is talking himself into things that may kill him, or kill others.

Crack.

A side-tube pressure valve releases, like a rifle shot, and my heart skips. Just like it skipped four years ago, when this mess started.

TWO

CRACK.

I flinched, though my head was already a foot below the trench lip as the rifle round screamed yards above us. My mouth went dry. The bullet didn't care that I was a non-combatant observing someone else's war. It didn't care that my Pentagon desk was light-years away from Tressel. It most certainly didn't care that I had already paid my dues as an infantry grunt. But if the bullet knew what its side was in for tomorrow at dawn, it would've kept right on going, out of this theater of operations.

I tripped on a trench floor board, and splashed muddy water over my boots and Plasteel-armored knees.

Alongside me, Brigadier Audace Planck didn't even blink at the tall shot, just rolled his iron-colored eyes beneath prematurely gray brows. "That's one Iridian round that won't hurt anyone."

His shoulders filled the simplified cloth uniform of an army too long at war, while mine hid under Plasteel plates that his planet's armorers wouldn't dream of for a century. "Stay on your feet, Jason. Snipers can't touch us. But that water might kill you."

The Tressel Barrens' water contained plenty to kill a man, even before three years of trench warfare. Tetras, a mixed bag of flat-headed, blubbery reptiles and amphibians bigger than swamp rats and dumber than frogs, populated the Barrens. The tetras' intestinal bacteria, introduced into the brown soup of the great swamp by the usual means, spawned virulent dysentery in humans. However, tetra crap didn't bother the crocodile-sized, aquatic scorpions that patrolled the mangroves, feasting on tetras as they sunned themselves on rotted logs.

The Barrens were a hundred thousand square miles of brackish coastal swamp that had mired the Tressen army when its General Staff tried to maneuver fifty divisions through the Barrens, to outflank the fortification the Iridians called the West Wall. Tressen and Iridian motorized vehicles could barely negotiate the Barrens, bogging down worse than 1900s French caissons and German trucks bogged in the mud of Flanders, a century earlier and light years away.

Now a million stalemated human infantry faced one another, in trenches separated by a hundred yards of shrapnel-scoured mud. The trenches zig-zagged from the north end of the West Wall to the sea, wherever the spongy ground was solid enough for GIs to dig.

Tetras didn't sun often in the Barrens. The dug-in GIs couldn't bail their holes fast enough to keep the daily rains from washing dysenteric slime, their own feces, and the occasional monster scorpion, back into the trenches that sheltered the troops from shrapnel and bullets.

Planck and I pressed ourselves back against the trench wall as a pasty-faced squad, heads down and rifles slung muzzles-down against the rain, limped toward us in sodden boots.

My armor probably puzzled them, but when they glanced up and saw Planck, every kid straightened, bug-eyed, and saluted.

One kid smiled, another waved Planck a weary thumbs up. Planck smiled back, patted each kid on the shoulder as they passed.

I chinned up my audio gain so I could hear them whisper to one another once they got a few yards down the trench.

"Did you see? That was Quicksilver, himself!"

In the war's early days, Audace Planck's Raiders had slipped around and through larger forces like mercury rolling on glass. The silver-haired young officer, whose given name meant "the daring one," was every Field Marshal's darling because he leapt where they wouldn't dare. He was every mudfoot's hero because he stepped alongside them, where they had to. Even to his enemies, "Quicksilver" was as legendary for his grace in victory as for his mercurial brilliance.

"No. Quicksilver in the mud at the front?"

"My brother was a Raider. He said, 'Where you find Planck, there you find the front.'"

Another kid asked, "What was that with Quicksilver, in the crab shell armor?"

"Motherworlder."

"They're real, then?"

Their voices died as the trench zagged them out of sight.

In the seconds while I eavesdropped, Planck had hopped up on the firing step carved into the trench's forward wall, rested his elbows on the lip sandbags, and raised brass field glasses to his eyes. "Let's see whether the Iridians will be as surprised to see us as those boys were."

I mounted the firing step alongside Planck, and wide angled my optics to view the shell-pocked, mined, and concertina-wired mud strip between the trench lines.

Nothing stirred but dirty orange tape, twisting in the wind atop aiming stakes driven crooked into the mud.

Gunners didn't really need the stakes. When either side sent kids over the top, targets were too numerous to miss. And afterward, when the survivors on both sides crept out to retrieve the dead, the gunners held fire. Not from altruism. Bloating corpses attracted scavengers, polluted the water worse, and stank.

Beyond no-man's land lay the Iridian lines. There, sentry's periscope heads swiveled above the opposite trench lips like bored cobras. A slow tune, played on an Iridian bone pipe by some GI, drifted to us.

Under my helmet, hair stood on my neck. The Iridians had no idea. Neither did the Tressens alongside us in these trenches. Outside of the Tressen General Staff and political leadership, only Planck's troops far behind us, Planck, and I, knew that dawn, tomorrow would change this world.

Five years ago, once we deciphered the Slugs' C-drive, Earthlings started dropping out of the sky onto the human populations of the Outworlds like Tressel, where the Slugs had transplanted them from Earth 30,000 years ago. For presumably backward long-lost cousins, the Outworlders took us in stride. In stride compared to the panic you would have expected, if you watched the alien invasion stories that Holowood cranked out in the years before the

Blitz. Of course, after the Blitz, holos about aliens were no longer escapism.

I don't know whether "race memory" is real. But the Cultural Behaviorist Spooks said the Outworlds accepted the truth of a home world their ancestors had left millennia before because the story was already embedded in the Outworlds' myths. And then, as the Spooks put it, our arrivals "validated the myth by empirically verifiable demonstration." I suppose if Jesus landed on the White House lawn, even agnostics like me would accept him as soon as He validated His credentials with a miracle.

At dawn tomorrow, Audace Planck and Tressen would be on the good side of a miracle courtesy of Earth's politicians.

By 2059 Earth standards, Tressel's warring great powers, Iridia and Tressen, were incompetent, despotic, and as benign as rabid pit bulls. And each had its teeth sunk in the other's throat. Earth's policy makers had decided to stop the fight before both of them bled to death. Unfortunately, that meant one dog would get petted while the other got kicked.

Earth needed allies to win the Pseudocephalopod War, and couldn't be picky. If the Slugs flood hell, the politicians will send the devil a bucket.

The daily rain began in a rumble, coursing in instant waterfalls down the already-sodden trench walls. Drops splattered into my helmet through my open faceplate, then ran icy down my neck, and puddled above the neck seal. Aud jumped down off the firing step, motioned me to follow, then sloshed fifteen yards further down the yard-wide trench. He stopped at a canvas flap, black with rot, that hung over a dugout doorway cut in the trench wall. Planck ushered me past him, and I ducked beneath a hand-lettered sign that read, "Infirmary."

We stepped into a leaking, lantern-lit, shoulder-high room. The roots of trees, long-since decapitated, whiskered its mud walls, and it stunk of gangrene, like an open sore on the world. The infirmary contained a camp table, rough racks tall enough to lift a body above the floor's ankle-deep puddles, and nothing else vaguely helpful to the infirm. My eyes dilated to match the flickering light of a single lantern on the table, while they watered at the stench.

Planck breathed through his mouth, then his eyes darted beneath bushy brows below his helmet. "I'm a soldier and a Tressen, Jason. So I appreciate what the Motherworld is doing for Tressen. But if your Motherworld had decided to get these kids out of these holes by tilting toward the Iridians, I might . . ."

Planck stepped to a canvas-bagged field telephone on the table, its cable curling down into the mud, out into the trench, then back two thousand yards to staging clearings. There his infantry waited, behind three hundred tarps that hid three hundred electrobus-sized objects from rain and from prying eyes. He cranked the phone, then spoke into its handset. "Go."

My eyebrows flickered, and my heart skipped. A good adviser knows how much he doesn't know. Aud knew his troops, his enemy, and his planet in ways I never could. So I kept my mouth shut, even though Aud had just launched the offensive that would decide the fate of this planet sixteen hours early. I also kept my mouth shut because it was a brilliant, if risky, stroke. Average generals don't accelerate offensives to jump off during driving rain. That's why average opponents get surprised by generals who aren't average. I sighed. What happened next wasn't going to be miraculous for too many GIs, on both sides of the wire. But it would be a miracle, nonetheless.

By the time the two of us ducked back out into the trench and the drumming rain, a growing drone thrummed behind our trench line like hell's bumblebees.

THREE

WE BOTH SCRAMBLED onto the slick firing step, this time with our backs to no-man's land, and peered toward the Tressen rear. Shapes glided out of the rain no faster than infantry could trot, like black ships parting fog. The Kodiaks' engines shook the ground beneath our boots now, as the Earth-made hovertanks slid toward us.

Audace Planck had lived up to his name again. The daring one was launching the biggest assault in three years when nobody expected it, foregoing artillery prep. His own troops and commanders might be more surprised than their enemy.

I turned to Planck. "I know the rain cover will enhance surprise. But you and I were supposed to be with the lead squadron when the offensive jumped off."

He shrugged. "If subordinate commanders are trained properly, they take appropriate initiative. We'll hitch a ride as your machines pass over this line."

I cocked my head. "Maybe."

Audace Planck had grasped the hovertank's potential like Rommel had grasped Panzers. But he couldn't grasp its nuts and bolts. Aud had seen his first Lockheed Kodiak sixty-one days ago. The ground effects and Nano'Puters that made a Kodiak tick were as black magic to a Tressen like him as the Slugs' starship technologies were to me. Hitching a ride wouldn't be easy.

The Kodiaks slid toward us, riding cushions of down-forced air, oblivious to the varied substrate below them, in this case swamp water, mud, and outcropped rock. Their wedged prow armor dripped rain, which their downdraft beat into ground fog, which swirled around their ventral skirting.

In radar-absorbent midnight black, their cannon-snouted turrets hunting left then right, the hovertanks would seem like ghost elephants to the Iridians. Actually, Tressel's transplanted humans couldn't imagine elephants. Tressel's evolution hadn't yet produced mammals, or even land animals bigger than hogs. That would make bus-sized hovertanks all the more nightmarish to the GIs huddled in the opposing trenches.

Kodiaks were largely overkill here. Iridia had no radar for a Kodiak's outer shell to damp, no smart rounds for its electronic countermeasures to spoof. Tactical Observation Transports flitted above the onrushing formation, like tickbirds flitting above charging rhinos. But the TOTs intercepted no encrypted burst transmissions. Both armies were barely accustomed to the telephone. The Kodiaks brought to this party what armored formations from Hannibal's elephants to Guderian's Panzers brought: shock power and mobility. Here multiplied by a quantum technologic leap that would seem supernatural.

The squad that had passed us sprinted back round the trench corner, eyes wide, pointing back at the oncom-

ing Kodiaks. "General! The Iridians have got behind us
with—"

Planck halted them with a raised palm. "Stand fast.
The Iridians have got nothing. Those are ours."

"Ours? Sir?" They stood, panting.

One kid pointed at me. "They're his!"

Planck shook his head. "Every crewman in those vehicles is as Tressen as you are."

Planck told the truth. A Tressen GI was as tech-illiter-
ate as a World War I Earth doughboy. But once the vehicle
displays were translated and the Kodiak's 'Puters learned
voice commands in Tressen, a Tressen crew could roll and
shoot a Kodiak well enough to whip the World War I-level
army they were facing.

So Earth's strategists had decided to supply weapons,
not soldiers. It would make for more cordial post-war re-
lations with Tressel if us nice guys from the Motherworld
didn't have blood on our hands. At least, that's what the
diplomats told us.

The infantry kids crept onto the quivering firing
step, darting glances first at Planck and me, then at the
hovertanks.

The first Kodiak poked its snout over our trench, like a
cloud across the sun. It blew a hurricane left and right, so
violent that the kids grasped their strapped-on helmets.

I leaned toward Aud and screamed, "Follow me!"
Then I scrambled over the trench lip and sprinted for the
Kodiak.

Lockheed designed the Kodiak so nobody can board
one when it's moving. The outwash from under the skirting will blow a man away like Kleenex. And break his
legs if he isn't wearing armor. But there's a two-foot wide

exhaust duct that exits the armor alongside the rear clamshell doors. It boils the upwash fog, because a Kodiak's
exhaust blows out hot enough to melt lead. But the duct
blocks the outwash a little, and an access ladder is welded
down the duct's side.

Lockheed could have designed in a safety cage to keep
personnel away from the exhaust, but didn't. Sane personnel wouldn't risk third-degree burns and mangling by
trying to board a moving hovertank, just to avoid walking. Would they? Lockheed's designers never met an
infantryman.

In the day, I could spot a Kodiak ten yards, catch it up
in twenty, and swing aboard with one hand, wearing a
day pack.

The Spooks claim Tressel gravity is .99 Earth normal
and the air has more oxygen, but that can't be right. Because after forty yards, I was wheezing and falling behind
the hovertank. I lunged, caught the bottom rung with one
hand, and got dragged through the rain like a fallen water
skier. Finally, I got both hands on the rung, and boarded.
Then I reached back, and pulled Aud up alongside me.

We slipped and slid along the Kodiak's Plasteel spine
until we knelt behind the turret.

Aud tugged goggles over his eyes, against the wind
and rain. His sleeve flapped in smoking, black tatters
where it had brushed the exhaust. Blistered skin showed
on his forearm.

I pointed at his arm and shouted, "You okay?"

He glanced down and shrugged. "S'nothing." Then,
one fist round a handhold, he swung his free hand at the
squadron of five Kodiaks flanking us, then at the Commander's pennant stenciled yellow on our turret's flank.

"You caught us the lead vehicle of the lead element, Jason." He smiled. "Perfect."

I frowned, and peered behind us. "Yeah. Perfect." Our own wire obstacles already lay behind us. Lanes had been cleared through our own wire, so Planck's fresh infantry, advancing through their weary, startled buddies minding the trenches, could trot in the Kodiaks' wakes. To our front, partly obscured by the turret, the Iridian concertina wire trembled in the rain, row stacked on row, like rusted tumbleweed.

Beyond the Iridians' wire lay their minefields, through which the second-wave Kodiaks would clear lanes by dragging lengths of heavy chain as they advanced, to detonate the mines they overflew.

Thump.

An Iridian cannon round screamed by five feet left of us, then burst somewhere in the Tressen rear.

In response, electric motor whine vibrated the deckplates beneath us, as our Kodiak's turret traversed toward the Iridian pillbox from which the round had flashed. The turret twitched, then locked, while the Kodiak's cannon tube depressed.

I chinned down my audio gain as Aud clapped one hand over one ear, while he gripped his handhold tighter with the other.

Foom.

Flame flashed sideways from the brake on our cannon's muzzle like an incandescent mustache, and the Kodiak tried to buck us both off into the mud as it absorbed the cannon's recoil. Before I could blink, the Iridian pillbox disappeared in an orange flash.

A sound like pots and pans clanked beneath us. The

hovertank slid on across the battlefield while it extracted
the spent shell, stored it, selected the type of round its
commander chose for his next shot, and reloaded its
main gun.

Sliders, except for their propulsion system, hadn't
evolved far beyond the tracked main battle tanks of the
early 2000s. Why mess with success? Modern fire control systems demand of the gunner just that he point and
shoot. If he loaded smart rounds, they even homed on
their targets after he fired them. Even Planck's gunners,
who thought gas turbine power was high tech and 'Puters
were witchcraft, routinely got first-round hits.

The squadron flashed across the Iridian forward
trenches, raking them with machine gun fire and flechette
cannon rounds that peppered steel darts into the Iridians
like old fashioned grapeshot.

In all directions, Iridians died, but far more broke and
ran. Which was the idea.

This squadron's commander, unaware that his boss
rode topside, acted like a typical Planck subordinate, aggressive and independent. He knew his job was to split
the Iridian line, and drive into the Iridian rear, disrupting
communication, sowing panic, and igniting a rout. We bypassed and ignored thousands of fleeing Iridian infantry,
who barely glanced up at us as they splashed through the
driving rain. They looked back over their shoulders as they
ran, at orange cannon flashes. They heard the tidal wave
of our main formation, a mix of engine roar and screaming infantry, as it rumbled forward to drown them.

Another Iridian cannon round splattered as harmlessly
as a snowball off the prow armor of the slider on our right.

Harmless to a Kodiak. Shrapnel buzzed around us like hornets and rattled off our slider's turret.

Eternad personal armor stops shrapnel like a roof stops snow. But Aud might as well have been wearing pajamas. In addition to the shrapnel hazard, one Iridian infantryman with the presence of mind to take a potshot at the commander of this offensive could still change this battle and this war.

I pointed at the command hatch, up the turret's sloping side, and shouted to Aud. "The plan was for you to be inside the slider, not on it!"

Aud sniffed. "What would that say to the men about their commander?"

"That he wasn't a fool. Aud, this 'follow me' crap can be overdone."

He frowned, shrugged. "Perhaps."

Before we could rap on the hatch and talk our way inside, our lead element outran the Iridian retreat. We drove thousands of yards beyond the battlefront, so deep into the Iridian rear that we might as well have been Iridians. Around us was just tree-studded swamp, dim and sizzling with late-afternoon rain. The unfriendly fire that had threatened Aud became irrelevant.

But on a battlefield where one side possesses overwhelming superiority, unfriendly fire can be the least of a GI's problems.

FOUR

THE SQUADRON HALTED in a clearing, dispersed, and the sliders sank down on their skirting, rumbling at idle. Aud and I peered back through the rain and listened to the cannon thunder behind us, while he tugged his canteen from his belt and offered it to me. "A toast to victory, I think."

I shook my head. "You save yours. There's a water nipple inside my helmet. But you're right about victory. Your formations will have to regroup, eventually. But I wouldn't advise you to slow down before nightfall."

Planck nodded, smiled. "Your Eisenhower said 'relentless and speedy pursuit is the most profitable action in war.' I enjoyed the books. There is so much we can learn from you about war."

Antique paper books made great gifts for Tressens. FlatReaders creeped them out. "Learn about peace, too, Aud."

His smile faded, and he shook his head. "I'm a soldier. The politicians will make the peace."

"We had a war a lot like this one, a hundred fifty years ago. After it, our politicians made a peace so harsh that we had a second world war twenty years later. It made the first one look like a pie fight. Eisenhower entered politics after that one."

He nodded. "With malice toward none, with charity for all."

"Different president. Different war. Good idea."

A cannon round whistled from the battle behind us, invisible in the low clouds overhead. It struck in the swamp a hundred meters beyond us, geysering tree trunks and brown water.

Aud frowned. "My gunners don't understand your guns. A stray round."

A Kodiak's main gun was typically used for line-of-sight, direct fire, when it fired rounds that pierced other armored vehicles or targets like pillboxes. But a squadron could easily function like an artillery battery, lobbing high-explosive shells like nine-iron shots at unseen target coordinates called to it by a spotter.

I frowned, too. "Or a ranging round."

Hair stood on my neck. Old soldiers survive by seeing things that can't be seen. A neophyte artillery spotter, in the confusion of battle, might phone in wrong map coordinates for a target he was observing. A simple mistake. He might then mistake another, unrelated detonation for the first, ranging round we just witnessed impact a hundred yards to our front. Also simple. He might then direct all five tubes of a Kodiak squadron to drop their aiming point a hundred yards and fire for effect. He would think his adjustment was going to bring the Big Rain on top of the target he was watching. But, in fact, he would be bringing fire down directly on us. Expect the worst from the gods of war, and they will seldom disappoint you.

I flicked my eyes to the sky in time to see a flash of

motion as the rounds rained from the low cloud that ceil-
inged the clearing.

When those high-explosive rounds burst on the ground,
or in the air above us, they might damage the Kodiaks
some. But troops in the open, like Aud, and even me in
hard shell armor, would be concussion-hammered like
flank steak, then shrapnel-gutted like sushi.

"Fu—!" I didn't finish the syllable before I tumbled up
through the clouds, flailing through gray mist.

FIVE

THE BARRAGE'S EXPLOSIONS cartwheeled me up, then tumbled me down, crashing through vine-choked branches. I wound up swinging by one booted foot snared in a vine noose, fifteen feet up a tree.

I groaned. Eternad hard shell protects the wearer from most impacts. And the underlayer absorbs shock. A GI can get stomped like a roach, yet crawl away to fight another day. But under my armor I would be purple and lumpy for a week.

Below me, Aud Planck lay, facedown in the mud and still.

"Aud? You okay?"

Nothing.

I drew my trench knife, fumbled it, then twisted up and sawed the vine that wrapped my trapped foot. I dropped headfirst fifteen feet, splash-landed on one shoulder, then crawled to Aud.

"Aud? You okay?"

He turned his head to me, stared past me.

While he stared, I triaged him. No broken bones or

significant bleeding, so far as I could tell. But, by the blank look in his eyes, his gong had been rung like Big Ben.

Beyond my vision, machine gun and cannon rounds crackled every few seconds, like the last kernels in an ogre's popcorn machine.

I said, "Aud, we gotta move, buddy."

He stared past me, concussion-blank, as I dragged him to his feet. We shuffled, Aud hopping on one foot, leaning against my shoulder, back into the clearing where the Kodiak squadron had been. Aud's left leg wasn't broken, but he winced each time he tried to put weight on the ankle.

We sheltered flat in the weeds, staring at five blackened heaps of gnarled metal as they smoldered under the rain. The last of their cannon and machine gun rounds cooked off as I peered at the hulks. A turret had blown off, and lay tilted upside down in the mud like a bowl filled with burnt bacon.

I smelled burnt hair and flesh, squeezed my eyes shut, and balled my fists. A soldier's lot is to die young and unexpectedly, which is cruel. But for a commander, friendly fire casualties are cruelest, because there's no place to direct your rage but into your own gut.

The odd thing about this incident was that normal battlefield concussion and shrapnel bothers Kodiaks no more than thrown rocks, yet this squadron had been wiped out by five rounds.

I left Aud to sit still in the reeds while I picked around the wrecks, as close as I could get to the metal as it steamed in the rain. A neat hole as wide as a human head was punched in what remained of each Kodiak's dorsal armor, near the turret.

I kicked mud and swore. When the misdirected fire

mission had been called onto us, the distant gunners' tubes had already been loaded with pillbox-clearing smart penetrators. As the five shells dove into the clearing, each had homed on one of the five Kodiaks' mass and heat, penetrated its back armor, then sprayed a jet of molten copper into the Kodiak's gut. Crewmen not immolated instantly got crushed by the blast when the Kodiak's ammunition detonated.

Remaining outside the slider had saved our lives. The smart shell had struck the Command Kodiak's thinner back armor four feet to our right as we knelt on the slider's back. The shell had speared into the Kodiak's guts, then detonated and vaporized everything and everyone inside. But we simply got blown off the slider like leaves.

I held Aud's face between my palms and asked, "What day is it?"

He stared back at me, still concussion symptomatic.

A stray rifle round buzzed through the foliage alongside us. The offensive, and the enemy troops that were being bulldozed ahead of it like angry sand, were closing on us.

Given Aud's injuries, we couldn't outrun the Iridians. The only weapons we carried were trench knives, and Aud's sidearm. I couldn't assume hardened, vengeful Iridians carrying assault rifles would accept a surrender, even from VIPs, when a couple quick head shots made more sense.

In the distance, voices shouted orders. The enemy would be on us within minutes.

SIX

I STAGGERED, shoring Aud up under one arm, to the wrecked slider nearest the clearing's edge. A blackened corpse hung from the blown-out rear-bay hatch. I shoved the corpse aside, shoved Aud into the bay, then tugged the corpse back in behind us to block the hatch. Its hand broke loose at the wrist like charcoal.

"Terrible," Aud muttered, then he slumped against me.

I jostled him. "No sleeping with a concussion."

We huddled in the dark, burned-out bay until I heard footsteps and the rattle of rifle-sling buckles on wooden stocks.

An Iridian-accented voice shouted, "They're slowing behind us, sir!"

"Unless the bastards start pushing forward again, we'll dig in here for the night."

Lucky us.

"Should we inspect these war wagons of theirs? If any of the bastards are still alive . . ." Metal scraped metal as the Iridian GI chambered a round.

I swallowed. These men had spent three years in trench warfare hell, and today the Tressens had made it worse.

Surrender? We would stand a better chance if we surrendered to rattlesnakes.

"Nobody survived inside those. Sketch the wreckage. Maybe intelligence can figure what killed these."

"Sir, I don't—"

"Use ration wrappers, if you don't have a notebook."

Beside me, Aud twitched. "Who are you?"

"Quiet!" I hissed in his ear, and pressed him against the still-warm hull plates.

He elbowed me. "Let me up. I'll be late to Formation."

I jammed my gauntleted palm across his rambling mouth, so hard that he thrashed for breath.

Outside the wreckage, footsteps stopped alongside us.

I held my breath, which just made my heartbeats drum louder in my ears. I was sure they could be heard over the rain.

"Do I need to sketch inside it, too, sir? I mean . . ."

Crap. I felt in the dark for the holster on Aud's belt, then unsnapped its flap.

Rain drummed on the hull.

A sigh. "Let the dead rest, Corporal. First we get the nets up, then you sketch."

The footsteps sloshed away.

By the clock that plodded inside my brain, we huddled in the bay, shielded by our dead sentry, all day. My 'Puter insisted that we lay there for thirty-one minutes.

By then, I had heard no man-made sound, except the distant ring of entrenching tools against rock, for ten minutes. Aud was making sense again. Rainwater funneling through rents in the hull had flooded our hideout six inches deep, and kept rising.

I extended my fingercam, snaked it around the corpse,

and peeked out. The Iridians had moved off sixty yards away from the wrecks, where they were digging in. Their attention was focused on the live Tressen threat to their front, not the dead behind them.

We wormed past the corpse, then ducked behind the wreckage.

Aud said, "Jason, we have to get away from here."

"Sure. We'll cross the open ground after dark."

"Now." Aud drew his pistol in the fading light, then counted his spare magazines by fingering his belt pouch.

I grabbed his wrist, and pointed at the Iridians. "There's at least a company out there!"

He shook his head, tilted it to the sky, then blinked away the falling drops. "The pistol's not for them. We have to get away from these bodies. That's why the Iridians moved off from here to set their night perimeter. But unless we find oilwood before dark, it won't matter."

Well, he knew his planet, and I didn't. Hair stood on my neck, and I swiveled my head. "What should I watch for?"

"My backside. There's no time to educate you. Just follow me closely." Then he double-timed, crouching, through the mud and into the trees, avoiding the gaze of the Iridians and also avoiding any patch of water that looked big enough to hide a bus.

We picked our way back toward the Tressen front lines, which had stabilized for the night, but the light faded while we were still in limbo. Aud slowed to a walk at the edge of a solid clearing ringed with fat, brown brush. He drew a Tressen trench knife as long as a machete, then started hacking down brush bundles and tossing them over his shoulder into the clearing.

My knife was too short to cut brush, and I wouldn't have known which brush to cut anyway. So I stood panting, hands on hips, turned my head inside my helmet, sucked my water bladder dry, then looked around.

The sixty-foot plants that choked and overhung the clearing weren't trees, though they looked like fat, scaly-trunked palms. They threw off spores, not seeds, and resembled what a paleobotanist would call Earthly lycopods. Tressel displayed conditions parallel to conditions on Earth during the upper-middle Paleozoic. No bird chirps echoed through those trees, just as there had been no chirping birds during Earth's Paleozoic. Six-inch long insects droned. They looked like dragonflies, but weren't.

Parallel evolution sounded as linear as geometry, but actually kinked and swirled like a Jackson Pollock painting. Exploring Tressel and the other Earthlike Outworlds was like paging through an old photo album. You turned the page and saw someone who looked like grandma. But when you looked closer, she was just a chimp in a dress.

But whether the Tressen Barrens were an upper-middle Paleozoic swamp, or just a malformed twin, they were no place to honeymoon. There were no flowering plants, so the landscape offered two color choices, spinach green or mud brown. The only home cooking was roast tetra, which tasted like warm dirt. It rained most of every day, and drinking the water turned your colon into a garden hose.

I sighed. Then I sidestepped down to the water's edge, extended the suction tube from my gauntlet's index finger, and squatted so I could dip my finger in the swamp.

I rolled my head on my neck, closed my eyes and

moaned. A guilty pleasure of infantry Eternads is that the water purifier's pump, which nestles between your shoulder blades, whirs you a little back massage while it sucks muddy soup up its intake tube.

When I opened my eyes, I saw, four feet out in the water, a fuzzy, lemon-yellow worm as small as my thumb, rippling the water as it wriggled on the surface.

Probably tetras ate them, snapping them up with their tongues the way frogs did.

I leaned forward and chinned my optics to record a worm snapshot for the exobiologists back home.

At the edges of my vision, another ripple flickered four feet to my left, and another four feet to my right.

Maybe the worms swam in broods, like ducklings.

"Jason!" Aud screamed like my hair was on fire.

SEVEN

AUD STARTLED ME so that I rocked back on my heels.

In the same instant, the ripples to my right and left exploded. From the spray, two rigid, segmented black arms, as big as oak limbs, each ending in a two-foot long lobster claw, scissored me chest-high.

If it hadn't been for Aud's yell, my helmet would have been crushed like a hammered olive. As it was, the stress register on my helmet display flashed yellow. My torso shell would crack within thirty seconds if the squeeze continued.

The beast that held me lifted its head out of the water, flat and black and bigger than a manhole cover. From the manhole's top bulged two serving-bowl sized gray eyes, each faceted with compound lenses like a split beehive. The yellow lure that had wiggled in front of me wobbled on a fleshy stalk that rose between the large eyes, and was flanked by two round simple eyes like glistening black stones. This monster had hunted me like snapping turtles with worm-shaped tongues hunted back on Earth, but it was no turtle.

With me pincered, the scorpion swam backward, dragging me toward deep water.

I dug in my heels, but they slid down the muddy bank. When the scorpion undulated, its spade-shaped tail fluke broke the surface. Its tail and head were fifteen feet apart.

Water lapped around my chestplate as I tore at one pincer with both hands, and failed to budge it. I kicked the head, and something caught on my foot. Probably the monster's open jaw.

The water beneath me deepened, so I no longer could feel the muddy bank with my feet or fingers.

Brown water closed over my faceplate.

Bang.

The scorpion half-rolled, and my head came up out of the water for an instant.

Bang. Bang. Bang.

The scorpion's grip loosened, then re-tightened, with each shot.

Bang. Bang.

My armor's stress indicator faded back to green, and the pincers slipped away. I thrashed to the surface. Aud, smoking pistol in one hand, reached with his other hand and dragged me by my backpack loop onto the bank. Then he waded back out, grabbed the dead scorpion's tail fluke, and wrestled it until the beast's eight rear limbs lay anchored on the mud bank.

I sat, arms on my knees, in the mud, popped my faceplate and sucked air in ripping sobs.

Aud staggered up next to me, sat and gasped, too.

Five minutes later, I croaked. "Thanks."

"S'nothing."

"Nothing?" I ran my eyes from the flat tail fluke down the segmented tail. Out in the shallows, the scorpion's pincers poked above the water like giant broken-toothed combs.

Aud shrugged. "Just a sixth-molt female. No reason for you to know that the yellow wiggler means 'run away.' But every Tressen child knows it from the time his parents start telling bedtime stories."

"Why did you drag the body back up here?"

Aud waded out alongside the carcass, knee deep. Grunting, he heaved the tail section up like a rolled carpet, hacked at the beast with his trench knife, then stood and smiled. In one hand he raised what looked like a sack of translucent ping pong balls. "Egg roast tonight!"

Rain pattered the sodden vegetation again.

"Aud, we can't make a fire."

He pointed at his brush pile. "We can. Oilwood will burn even in a full rain barrel."

Especially on Tressen. Like on late-Paleozoic Earth, Tressen's swamp plants cranked out so much oxygen that the atmosphere was fire-friendly. I pointed back in the direction from which we had come. "I mean Iridians will spot a fire. I'd rather be a cold fugitive than a dead POW."

"Jason, Iridians are our least worry." Aud pointed at the carcass. "You saw the enormous eyes on that beast. Scorpions hunt submerged during daylight. At night, they hunt onshore." He fingered his ammunition pouch. "I can wound perhaps two more. Without a fire's light to discourage them, we'll attract a dozen before the sun's two hours down. How many can you wrestle?"

I rubbed the new row of dents in my chestplate, and swallowed.

Then I scooped an armload of brush onto Aud's pile. "I'll take my eggs over easy."

An hour later I sat elbows-on-knees in the dark, with my back to our fire. Oilwood cracked and sizzled like bacon, while warmth soaked through my armor's backplates.

Facing away from the fire, I chinned my optics to night passive and zoomed on the object on the bank, twenty yards away. The Barrens linked to the sea, and the outgoing tide had now completely exposed the scorpion that had nearly killed me. It slumped in the mud like a flattened lobster fifteen feet long. Longer if someone tugged its forelimbs out in front of it, like Superman holding pliers. I shuddered inside my armor. That someone wasn't going to be me.

Aud tossed a pebble at the scorpion carcass. "Do you have these in your home?"

I wiggled my index finger. "Our biggest scorpions are this long."

He poked me in my side, grinning. "And sergeants serve privates breakfast in bed."

"No, really." I tapped my earpiece. "I think there's a translation problem. Our big scorpions are extinct. Actually, barely relatives of our little modern scorpions. Closer related to what we call horseshoe crabs."

My earpiece ticked as the translator program hunted, then continued. Tressen had a word for "shoe," of course, but not for "horse," because horses were millions of years down Tressel's evolution trail.

"We'd call scorpions like yours pterygotid eurypterids. Ours were big, but not *that* big." This time, my translator didn't tick. Most of the time, the translator worked so fast that you just talked and listened.

I said, "Today, reptiles—animals like tetras, but bigger—have replaced eurypterids in the swamp predator niche."

"Tiny scorpions. Ferocious tetras!" He shook his head and chuckled. "I needed a laugh."

"We call them crocodiles. I can show you pictures. I wouldn't lie to you, Aud."

He turned his head to the sky, as a sprinkle of stars winked through a break in the clouds, then he stopped chuckling. "You would lie to me, if it was your duty, Jason." He turned, and poked the fire with a stick. "You brought your machines to us across the stars. A great favor to Tressen. But every favor has a price." It wasn't a question, but a statement.

"Aud, now it's my turn to defer to the politicians."

"I'm not asking the price. Haggling is for politicians and pimps. I just don't understand why a world so different that its scorpions are as small as pickles cares about Tressel." He pointed at the scorpion he had killed to save my life. "You owe me that much truth."

"I do." I nodded, scooped a handful of pebbles, and tossed them in my palm. "The Slugs brought your ancestors from Earth to Tressel because some of the rocks here on Tressel fell from the stars. More accurately, they fell from the boundary layer where this universe ends and another begins."

"This Cavorite your friends spoke about."

"A name we borrowed from an old bedtime story about men who flew to our moon. Cavorite let the Slugs, and now lets us, fly to the stars. Cavorite's poison to the Slugs, but not to humans. Thirty thousand years ago, the Slugs realized that. So they exported Earthlings to mine it for them. When the Slugs exhausted the meteoric Cavorite from Tressel, they didn't need to use your planet or your ancestors any more."

Aud frowned. "Now it's the Motherworld's turn to use us?"

I let out a breath, "It's not like—"

Out in the water, a black shape rose, glistening, and ghosted toward us. The eurypterid spidered onto the bank, water coursing silver off eight rear limbs, while its front limbs arced above its carapace like tree boughs. The beast's forward-most mandibles probed the body of its dead cousin, and paused. Then it slithered up over the corpse like a pulled scarf. Twenty feet long if it was an inch.

Click. Aud cocked his pistol.

My heart pounded.

The big predator curled around, then grasped, the carcass in the mud. The dead female weighed easily a ton, but within three heartbeats, the bigger one had dragged it back into the water like a laundry bag, leaving behind only furrows in the mud.

I gulped, then turned to Aud. "Tell you what. Let's build a bigger fire."

EIGHT

OVER THE NEXT SIX HOURS, eight scorpions cruised around our clearing, just beyond the firelight. One rushed us, forelimbs flailing. Aud pumped six rounds into the monster, until it staggered away, then collapsed into a shadowed heap just beyond the fire's glow.

Aud fingered his empty ammunition pouch. "That meat will distract them for a few hours, but I only have two rounds left. Jason, we won't last the night."

Even on Earth, the firewood-per-night rule of thumb is figure all that you think you need, then gather five times that much. An hour before dawn, we had hacked and burned all the oilwood we could reach, and the fire had burned low enough that we could hear monsters respirating just beyond the firelight.

A chugging noise echoed in the distance, and swelled. Then we heard shots, and shouts.

With my night passive, I saw them before they saw us. "Aud, it's a tracked vehicle with Iridian markings." It lurched, slow and clumsy even for an Iridian vehicle, and it clanged and rattled like a frontier tinker's wagon. "I can see three crew."

He smiled. "I don't have to see. I can hear. Pots and pans banging. It's an Iridian field kitchen transporter. The company messes were so far in the Iridian rear that their own infantry ran right by them. The field kitchen crawlers are so slow that these stragglers are just getting to us now. The Iridians assign new recruits as cooks. Not blooded infantry."

A yellow flash bloomed, a rifle crack echoed through the lycopods, then somebody swore.

I raised my eyebrows. "They sound blooded to me."

"Probably a scorpion wandered close to the crawler. Veterans wouldn't waste a bullet. They know a crawler's big enough, and loud enough, that scorpions won't bother it."

Ten minutes later, the crawler had clanked within shouting distance.

"Hello the fire! Friend or foe?"

Aud called back, "We wish to negotiate."

Pause.

I upped my magnification. A kid stood on the crawler's deck, in stained cook's whites. He steadied himself with one hand against a rack hung with pots that swung back and forth to the chug of the crawler's engine. A white headcover, probably a bunched chef's toque, peeked out beneath his crooked helmet. I could see him, but he couldn't see me.

He cupped his hands around his mouth. "Negotiate what?"

Aud yelled, "Your surrender. I'm Brigadier Audace Planck, Acting Commander of the First Expeditionary Army of Tressen."

The crawler stopped, and chugged at idle, fifty yards

from us. The kid laughed and called, "Quicksilver himself? Here in the mud? Then I'm the Brigadier of the Sixty-Eighth Iridian Fusiliers! *You* surrender, or we'll surround your position and bombard it."

"You're a single unarmed crawler. Not one of the three of you has ever fired a round in combat, you're lost, and you're running for your lives. By noon tomorrow the Tressen offensive will roll over you and blow you and that crawler to bits." Aud handed me his pistol, and whispered. "I can't see them, but can you put one round on their front plate?"

Rank and experience aside, we were two middle-aged men sharing one pistol and two bullets. We were facing an armored vehicle, and three enemy soldiers with rifles. Yet Audace Planck was demanding their surrender. The daring one indeed.

I dialed up my optics, sighted, then squeezed one off. The bullet struck the iron crawler one foot below the kid's boots, and spit an orange spark as it sang off into the night. Now we were down to one bullet.

The kid grabbed his helmet with one hand as he leapt down inside the crawler, swearing.

Pause. Whispering.

From inside the crawler, the kid yelled, "What if we do surrender?"

"Lay your rifles on the top deck where we can see them. We'll board your crawler and wait out the night with you. When my troops overtake us tomorrow, you'll be treated well. You have my word."

"You're really him? Quicksilver?"

Beyond the firelight, a huge, multi-legged shadow lumbered. Too close.

I shouted, "It's him. Hurry up."

"Who are you?"

I turned to Aud and shrugged. Officially, I didn't exist, but the fiction wasn't going to survive any better than we would if we didn't get inside that crawler in the next ten minutes. I called out into the darkness. "I'm the marksman who put a round one foot below your boots. The next shot goes one foot below that white hat you're wearing under your helmet."

A half hour later, Aud and I sat inside a rattling iron box with three pimply teenagers. Occasional scorpion tines scraped the crawler's hull plates, but the monsters seemed disinclined to pick on something their own size.

The ranking corporal, the negotiator, removed his helmet, fluffed his toque, and held out a bread loaf to his captors. "Go ahead. One thing we have is food."

Planck tore off a chunk, chewed, then smiled. "Extraordinary!"

The kid shrugged. "My family are bakers."

Planck raised his eyebrows and smiled. "Where?"

"Veblen."

"Oh. I'm sorry."

"My father lost his leg in the shelling. If I don't come home, my mother won't be able to rebuild the shop alone."

Planck reached across the crawler, and patted the kid's knee, "Don't worry. This war's over for you. This war will be over for everyone in a month."

By twenty minutes after sunrise the next morning, the scorpions had retreated to deep water, or so Aud assured me. We ran a white cook's apron up the crawler's signal mast, then we all hid twenty yards away, in the weeds, in case some Kodiak plinked the crawler anyway.

Thirty minutes later, a surprised Kodiak squadron commander saluted the hell out of Planck, then detached one of his sliders to speed Planck, me, and our prisoners to Planck's constantly-displacing HQ.

We rejoined Planck's staff outside a quick-pitched canvas tent, sides rolled up, which sheltered map tables and signals gear. There were smiles and handshakes all around. Then the staff officers got back to the business of winning the war.

Erdec, Planck's command sergeant major, who was as gray, leathery, and professional as Ord, stayed with us and with the three kid cooks. So did an Intel captain.

The captain, dark-eyed, intense, and, by his service ribbons combat-blooded, waved his sidearm at the kids. "What about these three, General?"

Planck hardly glanced up from the morning reports his sergeant major handed him, drawing his index finger across a line here and there as he read. "No need to interrogate cooks, Captain. But get their bread recipe. Then this war's over for them."

Once the captain marched the three kids away, I said to Planck, "Last night, you didn't say much when that kid said he was from Veblen."

Planck's sergeant major, Erdec, said, "Veblen sits on an island bounded by two rivers. Every war over the past three centuries, the winner took Veblen. And Vebleners changed citizenship. My grandmother called herself Iridian. My parents called themselves Tressen. But when the war started, Veblen was part of Iridia."

I said, "But you're in the Tressen army."

Erdec shrugged, smiled. "I'm a soldier. I'm a Veblener. For a Veblener, nations come and go." He sighed. "One night, six months into the war, Tressen rolled 6,000 artillery pieces up on the plain outside Veblen, then pounded the town to rubble while the residents slept in their beds. The idea was to break the will of the Iridian people. And to retaliate for Iridian atrocities."

"Oh."

Planck said, "What you said, Jason—that we have to learn to keep a peace? It starts here. Now. This has been a dirty war."

"They all are," I said.

Planck nodded. "Those boys, and prisoners like them, can break the cycle. If we send them home with memories of decent treatment." He shrugged. "That's my contribution to politics."

Planck handed the morning reports back to Erdec, and their fingers touched. The older man whispered, "I thought we had lost you, sir."

Planck clapped his sergeant major on the shoulder, and grinned. "Me, lost? I bet you thought so. You told us in basic training that the most dangerous thing in the army is an officer with a map."

Erdec smiled. "That was long ago, General."

Three pistol shots rang close by.

Planck's brow furrowed.

Sergeant Major Erdec's brow furrowed, too.

Then Planck's eyes widened, he spun, and dashed around the command tent.

I followed, as Erdec, limping like the old soldier he was, followed me.

The dark-eyed intelligence captain stood fifty yards

from us, alongside a shallow ditch, staring down at three piles of white cloth. He held his pistol down at his side, and it smoked.

When I got closer, I recognized, sprawled on the ground, the baker's boy from Veblen, and his two friends. Cheek-down in the mud, each boy's eyes stared, and each bled from a bullet hole in the back of his head.

Planck reached the captain first. "What did you do? What the hell did you do?"

The captain stared at Planck. "What you told me to. End their war—"

Planck lunged at the captain, and twisted the pistol from the man's hand.

The captain stiffened. "We're moving too fast to process prisoners! They were just cooks."

Planck grabbed the captain by his lapel, pulled him nose-to-nose, then stabbed the pistol barrel into the captain's cheek. "They were children!"

The captain's eyes widened.

Erdec shook his head, and reached toward Planck. "General—"

Rain ran down the captain's forehead, into his eyes, until he blinked.

Planck's gun hand quivered, and so did the captain.

Planck shoved him away, flung the captain's pistol to the mud next to the three dead cooks, and stared down at them. "Sergeant Major, republish the General Order regarding humane treatment of prisoners." Planck looked up at the captain, and his gray eyes burned into the man. "Place the captain, here, under arrest. Confine him. Advise the Advocate General to prepare charges."

"Yes, sir. I'll arrange a burial detail, as well."

When Aud Planck and I stood alone again, he rubbed his forehead. "We leveled this dead boy's hometown and we didn't bat an eye. Yesterday, we cremated a whole squadron of our own troops and to their families all I will be able to write is that I'm sorry. Is what that captain just did really so much more wrong?"

"It is where I come from, Aud."

He sighed. "I suppose you're looking forward to going home, Jason."

It was my turn to sigh. "Not exactly."

NINE

TWO MONTHS OF SWAMP-CROSSING, two hours of surface-to-orbit blasting and one day of .66 light-speed cruising later, I tidied up the paperless paperwork alongside the two members of the Tressel expedition I knew best.

Another part of the expedition was the four hundred armor-branch techs beneath us, scurrying over the hovertanks' hulls like camouflaged ants. The techs had performed all maintenance the Tressens couldn't. The last part of the expedition, which remained behind on Tressel, was twenty State Department civilians, ten each in the Tressen and Iridian capitals, who were to establish consulates, and four contract security guards.

My Command Sergeant Major, my Intelligence Liaison, aka my resident Spook, and I sat in a bubble-shaped clear plex cab that hung from ceiling tracks as it rolled twenty feet above two hundred seventy-six gently pre-owned Lockheed Kodiaks. The hovertanks were packed hull-to-hull in the football-field long centerline bay of U.S. Space Force Heavy Cruiser *Dwight David Eisenhower*. The Kodiaks looked like factory-fresh Electrovans, aboard a wet-bottom freighter bound from China to the Port of Houston, rather than aboard a warship.

Semantically, the *Ike* was no warship. She was rechristened Human Union Consular Vessel *Charity* for the duration of the Tressel Expedition. The diplomats we left behind on Tressel notwithstanding, bludgeoning the Tressens and the Iridians to Armistice at cannon point had involved nothing consular and little charity.

As we glided above each Kodiak in the loadmaster's pod, the pod's downlooking sensor recorded the ID code of the hovertank, which was etched into its turret top.

Ord pointed at the running tally winking on the pod's screen. "Two lost to enemy action. Five to friendly fire."

I looked away and blinked.

Ord continued, "The remaining sixteen units couldn't be recovered, due to operator error or mechanical fault, and were verified to have been destroyed in place, per orders."

"So my pension remains intact, Sergeant Major?"

Ord smiled. "As long as all of these get back home with us."

An officer's most solemn responsibility is his mission. As solemn, though barely in second place, is his responsibility to his soldiers. But an officer is also directly responsible to the army, and indirectly to the taxpayers, for hardware under his command. Even a modern infantry platoon's equipment costs more than its lieutenant could earn in three lifetimes. For me, just handwriting the total MSRP of the stuff I've signed for over the years would cramp my hand.

In the pod's jump seat behind us, Howard Hibble leaned forward, sucking nicotine out of a stop-smoking lollipop until his wrinkled cheeks cupped inward like deflated balloons. "Actually, we'll get home before them."

I gritted my teeth. "You set up a pony? And didn't tell me?" Howard's rank was colonel, because the army didn't have a rank of witch doctor. We had served together since the Blitz, when I was infantry's most expendable trainee and he was an extraterrestrial intelligence professor turned intelligence captain.

Now I outranked Howard, but he didn't report to me. He reported up through the Spook chain of command until it disappeared from public view somewhere around the National Security Adviser level. That gave him the back-channel clout of a Washington lobbyist, coupled with a weasel streak most lobbyists envied.

Howard shrugged. "I thought you'd be pleased. It beats the Local."

"The Local" was how most soldiers, goods, services, and people traveled among the planets of the Human Union. The Local was slow. If you could call travel at two-thirds the speed of light slow.

Mankind had reverse-engineered enough Slug technology to build starships that could jump Temporal Fabric Insertion Points just like a Slug Firewitch. But even a Firewitch had to heal itself after the structural stress of slingshotting past a collapsed star whose gravity was strong enough to tack folded space together.

A Firewitch could heal in hours after a jump, if it could ground on a planet that had a few basics like oxygen and liquid water. However, human-engineered ships still needed month-long overhauls, orbiting above massive ground-based shipyards, after every jump. And Outworlds like Tressel lay five jumps away.

Each single jump took days or weeks getting to, then away from, the jump. Even at speeds close enough to light speed that onboard clocks lost a few ticks relative to Earth normal. In short, single-ship interstellar travel, also known as "the Local," was slower than sailing Spanish galleons around Tierra del Fuego.

But with coordination and at great cost, small volumes of high-priority cargo could travel faster. The pony process took its name from Pony Express postal riders of the American West, and it was pretty simple. At each layover, the high priority cargo—in this case, Howard, Ord, and me—switched from a fatigued ship to a fresh one, with just hours spent transferring between ships. As simple as changing horses.

Simple, maybe, but hard on the high-priority cargo. A TFIP jump is basically diving a spaceship at an object the size of an invisible golf ball, into which is squeezed the mass of the Sun. The golf ball is invisible because its gravity is so strong that it sucks in even light. Gravity that strong also tacks together points that are light years apart in conventional space.

Howard says those with limited aptitude for non-Newtonian physics, meaning pretty much everybody but the Slugs and Howard, can best visualize this by imagining the universe as a folded newspaper page. But "folded" means crumpled into a ball, then glued together at random points where the paper touches. The glue being the intense gravity of collapsed stars. Jumping across at a glued-together point could take you all the way from the page's upper right corner all the way to its lower left corner. Or the jump could take you from the "5" in a sports page score only as far as to the "2" right alongside it.

Whatever. If the dive is sufficiently precise and fast

and dodgy, the ship pops out in new space, light years away, without traveling the long way across the newspaper page. Otherwise, everybody dies.

The gravity cocoon woven by Slug technology insulates the ship's interior, more or less, but even a single jump beats human passengers like veal hammered into schnitzel. Back-to-back-to-back jumps wear humans down like the old Pony Express wore down the kid messengers who rode it. Recruiting ads for Pony Express riders specified "orphans preferred."

On the voyage back from Tressel, we three left the Kodiaks behind after Jump One. We changed ponies three more grueling times. By our last pony switch point we were so Jump Thumped that even Howard had the presence of mind to schedule us for an overnight, which happened to be on Bren.

The State Department profile about Bren highlights four things.

One, Bren is the first-discovered Outworld. It is the place where modern man learned that, about the time our human ancestors learned to use stone tools, the Slugs had shipped Earth humans across the Milky Way, like Africans to the New World. Our species infested some planets that the Slugs visited, like rats that escaped down the conquistadors' anchor hawsers.

Two, Bren is the sole remaining source of propulsion-grade Cavorite known to mankind.

Three, Bren resembles Earth at the end of the Cretaceous period, but with bigger dinosaurs.

Four, the Expulsion of the Pseudocephalopod Hegemony from Bren sparked the formation of the Human Union.

With Tressel in my memory, and explaining it all at the Pentagon looming in my future, all I wanted from my layover was to forget everything for a night.

I had a minor role in kicking the Slugs off Bren. Therefore, I could have spent my overnight layover relaxing with old friends in high places. But I'm infantry enough that I relax better with old friends in low places.

A GI can forget plenty during one night on the Marinus waterfront, for a price. Part of the price is the morning after.

Therefore, after I changed and shaved, I was late for the upship. The ship squatted like a droop-winged manta ray out of water, in a cleared field next to a carriage depot.

Carriages behind teams of duckbilled dinosaurs stood ranked alongside boarding platforms crowded with travelers. A dozen years before that morning, no human on Bren imagined ships that flew, much less ships that flew among the stars. Now, only the children on the platforms stared at the upship.

I overtipped my cabbie, patted his team as I passed them, then jogged the hundred yards toward the upship.

The upship's pilot, in powder-blue Space Force Utilities, paced back and forth near the boarding ladder, glancing down at a wrist 'Puter, head shaking. Another head, on uniformed shoulders, poked out of the hatch at the top of the ladder.

As I got close enough to identify the poking head as Howard's, I realized that the pilot was a head shorter than me, with raven hair cut helmet-short, and she wore Rear Admiral's shoulder boards.

I slowed to a walk, and groaned.

TEN

THE PILOT DIDN'T turn around as I stopped at the foot of the ladder. She crossed her arms, then studied the upship's belly tiles. "You're late. We missed the docking window. You know the cost of turning a *Metzger*-class Cruiser for an extra orbit, Jason?"

I stretched a smile. "Pleasure to see you again, too, Mimi."

Actually, Mimi Ozawa in a pilot's unitard *was* a pleasure to see. The view even improved when she faced me. Women of a certain age just get more attractive, at least to men of a certain age. Mimi still had porcelain skin and brown eyes I could fall into.

"Since when does a Cruiser Commander fly shuttle milk runs?" My question was rhetorical. Mimi was a fighter jock who got kicked upstairs to command a capital ship that was steered by committee. She never missed a chance to grasp the yoke of anything she could fly by herself.

"You're always late," she said.

"You always wait."

"I haven't had a choice, yet."

I scuffed the ground with my boot toe. "I'm sorry. It's been a tough few months. So last night I had a few."

She sniffed. "A few what?"

The Marinus waterfront resembles Gomorrah, with tighter alleys and looser women.

"Meads," I said. Bren's Highland Casunis export three commodities; Cavorite, fortified wine, and mayhem. All three give me headaches.

Mimi and I had never shared a hug, much less a bed. But I swear her posture softened. "Oh." She nodded toward the ladder. "Get aboard."

"I'd be just as happy to follow you."

She rolled her eyes. "Move. Pretend you've outgrown puberty."

I wormed into the seat alongside Howard, and strapped in.

He said, "Did you notice that was Mimi Ozawa?"

"I noticed."

"She's commanding the *Emerald River* now." Howard wrinkled his nose. "What did you do last night? You smell like grain alcohol."

"She noticed. What did *you* do last night?"

"Worked on my draft report." Radio waves could no more transit a Temporal Fabric Insertion Point than light could. They moved through normal space at the speed of light. Therefore, phoning home from an Outworld a hundred light years from Earth would take exactly one hundred years. Once a ship made its last Jump, it could send data ahead of it that would beat the ship to its destination by a little bit. But, for practical purposes, Howard and I would be bringing our commanders the first report of our mission to Tressel, like human carrier pigeons.

Howard shook his head. "Before we know it, we'll be trying to make sense of this to the Washington people."

I stared at the flatscreen on the bulkhead forward of us, which showed the cockpit view over Mimi's shoulder, as her fingers flew over changing touchscreen panels.

Hydraulics whined behind us, as the transport levered onto its tail.

I closed my eyes against the cabin lights and belched up the taste of stale wine. "All of whom know so little about what we do out here that they think the Easter Bunny brings Cavorite. Why do you think I got drunk?"

ELEVEN

"PULL OFF HERE." I pointed as the Staff Pool four-door sped toward the Potomac Tunnel, three feet behind the sedan in the Guidelane in front of us. The car said, "Last exit before Virginia. Manual Guidance required one half mile after exit."

The private on my left cocked his head, and pointed down the Guideway as it descended beneath the river. "But sir, the Pentagon's straight—"

"I need to make a stop."

"Yes, sir." He punched us off, then held his hands above the wheel while the Happi slid itself across three lanes of buzzing traffic and into the off-ramp.

The kid had been puzzled enough at a two-star who was young enough to be his brother, didn't ride in the back, and didn't make him hold the door open. He was more puzzled when we pulled up in front of a cluster of wooden buildings, which had been "temporary" since World War II.

I hopped out before he could dash around to open my door, then turned back to him. "I'll be an hour. Grab a coffee or a nap."

He smiled. "Yes, sir."

I didn't need a nap. I had spent my first night back on Earth sleeping off five jumps in as many weeks, and I had two hours before I reported to my boss at the Pentagon, just across the Potomac from this place, which was the Army Officers Personnel Directorate.

AOPD didn't take walk-ins, to discourage officers from dropping in to wheedle and lobby for better assignments. But stopping by to greet an old friend was just GI courtesy.

I hadn't seen Lieutenant Colonel Druwan Parker since he and I bunked together in Basic, during the Blitz. He set a half-eaten doughnut back on a paper plate, then lifted a cane from the chair alongside his desk. He motioned me to sit in the chair, while he laid the cane, which had forced him behind desks throughout his career, alongside it. Tall metal drawered boxes, the kind that held paper files, lined the walls. The place even smelled of real paper.

I pointed at his leg. "They can fix that now."

"Soldiers with low IQs and two good legs get dangerous jobs. Look at you." He grinned, teeth white against his skin.

I leaned forward. "That's what I dropped by here to talk about."

"What a surprise. Most officers just drop by here for the doughnuts." He punched up my file on a manual keyboard that looked as old as the building, and stared into the pages as the images flickered in the air between us. "You're up for rotation next month."

I nodded. "I was thinking, you know, something close to home."

Parker wrinkled his nose. "The Pentagon? You hate paper pushing."

"Not a staff job."

He punched through pages. "Your Officer Efficiency Reports say you're suited for unconventional ops. Why do you want to stay home all of a sudden?"

"Family matters."

"You're an unmarried orphan."

"The Army's my family. Can you get me a division?"

Parker snorted. "Dream on. Every two-star in the Army wants his own division."

"Every two-star in the Army didn't bunk with you, Druwan."

Parker sighed, leaned back in his chair, then swiveled it and squinted into his back screen. "Jason, if you wanted your own division, you should've got your ticket punched right. You've ridden dinosaurs. But you've never overseen a staff preparing for an annual three six-three dash five."

"What's a three six-three dash five?"

"I rest my case. Compare that to Stump Peavey. He angled for the right jobs. He got commanders to write him fat OERs, for ten years. All so he could get the Third Infantry Division at Fort Stewart, when that slot opens up next month. Last posting before he retires down there, close to home."

"Stump's earned it. He's a good officer."

"Was. He had a mild stroke two days ago. This morning he elected early retirement. Nobody knows it yet, but Third I.D.'s unexpectedly looking for a two-star to command it."

I rocked back and frowned. Stump, like every other general in my class at the War College, was old enough to be my uncle. His wife sent me cookies every Christmas, like a favorite aunt, and I sent them a fifth of Jack Daniel's. "I didn't know. How is he?"

"Hundred percent recovery projected. But somebody's gonna have to fill that slot right away."

I stared into my hands. Waiting wouldn't help Stump. "So I'm first on the list to request it."

"You know it isn't that simple."

"Do what you can."

Parker nodded, then screwed up his face as he punched in data. "Family matters, huh?"

"It does."

Fifty minutes later, I sat down across a Pentagon desk from my boss. Behind him on standards hung the streamered colors of the units he had commanded, and the place smelled of coffee and old leather.

Lieutenant General Nathan M. Cobb had been my boss off and on since I was a Specialist Fourth Class and he commanded the Ganymede Expeditionary Force.

He said, "You look good, Jason." He always told visitors they looked good, to put them at ease. Even the ones like me who already knew he could see better with Virtulenses than naturally sighted people with glasses. Then he adjusted the humming Virtulenses on his spare cheekbones. He waved at his desk reader. "Got your report this morning."

"Yes, sir."

"Tell me more about this General Planck."

"His troops love him. Tactically and strategically brilliant. Even the Iridians respect him."

Nat Cobb nodded, waved his hand. "You'll get to elaborate later."

"Sir? I can go into detail now if—"

"Jason, why do you want to command the Third Infantry Division?"

I rocked back in my chair. "Sir? How did you—"

He waved a hand as thin as a rooster claw. "A blind man survives in Washington by seeing more than other people. Well?"

"I dunno." That didn't sound like the response of a leader who deserved to command ten thousand soldiers and a military reservation as big as Liechtenstein. "My career portfolio has to be broadened to maximize my value to the Army. And—"

General Cobb covered his ears with his palms. "Save the moose shit. Jason, commanding a Division in garrison is mostly lunch speeches to the local Lions Club. And persuading troops that a five-percent increase in mechanized equipment upchecks is important."

"Those things *are* important!"

"Knowing things are important doesn't make an officer good at doing them. Commanders like Stump Peavey actually find assignments like that fun. Tell me you do and you're a liar."

I stared down at the floor. "If I wanted fun, I wouldn't have stayed in the infantry. I commanded a half million troops and saved a planet. But I can't handle the Lions Club?"

"Jason, when things go wrong, there's no soldier I've ever commanded that I trust more than you to make them right. But if you don't like the window you're looking into, your eyes wander." General Cobb slapped his palms on his knees and sighed. "Alright. Assuming, which you shouldn't for one minute, that I might let you break your pick attempting a job that fits you like garters fit a goat, tell me why you want to try."

I squirmed in my chair. "You know Sharia Munshara Metzger and I served together."

He turned his face to the ceiling. "The Munchkin. Shorter than her machine gun, but that gal could shoot the ass off a flea at six hundred yards."

I smiled. Nat Cobb was a GI's general, who remembered every soldier he ever commanded, or so the story went. Of course, it was easier for a general to remember a soldier who now held a seat on the House Armed Services Committee.

"Munchkin's son is my godson. His father was my best friend."

Nat Cobb nodded. "Jude's had his problems. Most ex-POWs do."

"I'm getting too old to call the Army my only family. I've spent most of my career overseas or Extra-T. I'd like to spend some time around my godson."

"Separation from family comes with this job, Jason." He walked around his desk, then rested a hand on my shoulder. He stood still for ten heartbeats, then nodded. "But maybe we can squash two toads with the same rock. When we get to the Tank this afternoon—"

"The Tank?" Hair stood on my neck. The Tank was the Chairman of the Joint Chiefs of Staff's Conference Room. In two prior Pentagon tours, I'd spent nine whole minutes in the Tank.

"You think I'm the only person in Washington who read your report? Anyway, after you finish your presentation, just behave out of character for once." He wagged his finger in my direction. "Meaning you shut your pie hole, except to follow my lead."

Nat Cobb fumbled behind himself until he found the edge of his desk, then leaned back against it.

I sighed. I was back in Washington. Where there was nothing odd about following the lead of a blind man.

TWELVE

PEOPLE EXPECT THE Tank to be some subterranean Bat-cave, with 360-degree flatscreen animated wall maps, and battalions of field-grade officers pointing at holos of every trouble spot on Earth, and, lately, off it.

Actually, the Tank in 2061 was what it had been, on and off, for a century: a large, soundproofed conference room on the first floor of the Pentagon, just inside the Potomac River entrance. In the Tank's center stood a mahogany conference table that dated back one hundred years, now with a holo gen carpentered into its center. Military-subject oil paintings, which got changed out to suit the taste of the current chairman, hung on the walls. By tradition, one, a rendering of Eisenhower being knighted at Westminster Abbey, never changed.

Batcave or not, with all the brass in the room, the armpits of my uniform shirt were damp by the time the chairman finished introducing the others whose elbows touched the mahogany. On my prior visit to the Tank, I had occupied a horse holder's chair along the wall.

Much in the room would have surprised Eisenhower. The holo gen, of course. And the addition to the Joint

Chiefs of the Admiral commanding the United Nations Space Force, which was for practical purposes a branch-level U.S. outfit eye-to-eye with the Air Force and Navy.

But Ike, who coined the phrase "military-industrial complex," would have understood the makeup of the table's placeholders for this meeting. The chief of each service branch got a seat, and the chairman, of course.

A Defense undersecretary, who had been a lobbyist for Lockheed, the Kodiaks' manufacturer, filled one seat.

In another seat sat an undersecretary from the State Department, who had dreamed up the Kodiaks-for-Peace scheme in the first place. State had then negotiated with the United Nations to borrow the U.N. name for the mission. In return for which the U.S. would quietly bear the entire cost, and would take all the blame if things went wrong, for the "multinational effort." But the U.N. would reap all praise and honors if the mission succeeded. If I can ever sell a used car to a State Department negotiator, I'll be able to retire on the overpayment.

In the three remaining chairs at the table sat the Headline Act: Howard Hibble, General Cobb, and me.

When I finished my brief, the undersecretary of Defense asked me, "This operation has proved that Outworlders can be trained to operate modern weapons systems?"

I cocked my head. "Depends on the Outworlders and the weapons systems. The Tressens are familiar with motor vehicles. A tank's a tank, especially when it does the thinking, and we do the maintenance for them. But, say, aircraft, remotely piloted or manned? Too radical. Tressens haven't even seen birds."

"But the advanced Outworlds can handle advanced weapons?" the undersecretary pressed. He had a law degree, and he was leading his witness. But witnesses can't object.

"The advanced Outworlds, yes." The sad truth about the grandiose-sounding Human Union was that most of the Outworlds' orphan humans, as my first grade teacher told my mother when they considered flunking me, needed "the gift of time to mature." Lots of time.

For example, Weichsel was a planet that the Slugs had abandoned millennia ago, leaving behind human strays. We stumbled across Weichsel three jumps out. Weichsel resembled Earth about 10,000 BC, complete with ice and mastodons, and its humans hadn't progressed much beyond fire. The humans didn't have a name for their place. They barely had names for fire and mastodons, so we called their planet after the Weichselan glaciation in Scandinavia. The Weichselans didn't actually sign the Human Union Charter. The State Department sort of assumed they wanted to join the Union because nobody threw sticks at the survey ship.

I said, "Tressens, and to a lesser extent, the Bren, are teachable, and some contemporary machines don't spook them. But they don't have the infrastructure or technology to maintain, much less copy, hovertanks. Much less hurt one another with discarded ones."

The undersecretary nodded.

I said, "If you don't mind my opinion, after the Armistice, we should have left the Kodiaks on Tressel to rust in the rain. They're expensive hardware. Shipping them to Tressel was even more expensive. But instead of re-orbiting two hundred thousand tons of vehicles, support equipment, and fuel, we would have saved the taxpayers a fortune if we had destroyed the equipment in place. And now the taxpayers are footing the additional bill to ship them the rest of the way home."

Somebody asked, "Who said anything about shipping them back here?"

Before I had time to decipher that question, the commandant of the Marine Corps asked, "What kind of Officer Efficiency Report would you write for Planck, if you had to?"

"Promote ahead of contemporaries. Tops. He grasped the Kodiaks' potential to reshape the battlefield faster and better than the Tressen General Staff."

I stopped short of saying, "You know how General Staffs are." But a few of the brass still scowled.

"How so?" the marine asked.

"The Tressen General Staff wanted to array the Kodiaks against the Iridian West Wall, as glorified artillery. That would have wasted their mobility. Planck realized that hovertanks have a disproportionate mobility advantage over terrain like the Barrens. He planned, organized, and executed a wheeling maneuver through the Barrens and around the West Wall, with the Kodiaks punching through like Panzers. Frankly, the German assaults through the Low Countries and around the Maginot Line in World Wars I and II weren't done as well. The offensive ended a stalemated war in a month. Most Iridian units got pocketed, and surrendered. They weren't slaughtered. That minimized Tressen casualties, too."

"So he's an intuitive tank jockey," somebody grunted.

I shook my head. "I think he's more. He was a junior officer when we arrived, so he had to sell his plan, too. A lot of battlefield geniuses lack that tact. On the other hand, he's no politician. Long on courage and integrity, short on blarney."

The State Department guy furrowed his brow. "But could a leader like Planck stabilize the new government?"

I've spent enough time in this puzzle palace that I've learned to smirk invisibly. But these people in Washington really did think the Easter Bunny brought Cavorite. "Mr. Undersecretary, the Armistice was barely signed when the *Ike* deorbited Tressel. I don't know that there is a new government. I don't know that it needs stabilizing. And I certainly don't know whether Audace Planck has a role in it. Later news from our Consulates has to make its way through five jumps and layovers. It travels almost as slowly as the *Ike* and those Kodiaks have to."

The State Department guy raised his eyebrows, then turned to the chairman, while he pointed at me. "He doesn't know about the Mousetrap?"

The chairman scowled at Howard. "You didn't tell him?"

Howard shrugged. "He didn't need to know."

The chairman said, "He does now."

THIRTEEN

I SAT THERE feeling my face burn. Howard was a professorial geek, but once the Army commissioned him as a Spook, he burrowed into the Intel need-to-know mentality like a beetle into dung. And, as always, the result for me was that I was the slow kid in class.

Howard shrank inside his uniform like a turtle, then cleared his throat. "Jason, we're discovering new Temporal Fabric Insertion Points all the time, nowadays."

I nodded. That much everybody knew. "Wormholes" or "black holes" are examples of TFIPs, though most of them lead nowhere, and some of them even drift around. But not all TFIPs are even as detectable as wormholes or black holes. Before a captured Slug ship spit us through the first TFIP, astronomers identified black holes as distant and almost theoretical rarities in the vastness of space. Turns out TFIPs are neither distant nor rare.

Howard said it was like looking at the Pacific Ocean through a telescope from space. If you didn't know there were ping pong balls floating in the ocean, because you didn't even know ping pong balls existed, much less what they looked like, you wouldn't notice them. Now, the

astronomers knew what to look for, and they were iden-
tifying TFIPs as fast as floating ping pong balls. But if a
particular TFIP didn't lead to a populated outworld, or at
least a habitable layover planet, it was as useless to us as
a ping pong ball.

I said, "I remember that."

"Well, you probably should forget most of what I'm
about to tell you." Howard popped the table's holo, and the
image of a little metal spider appeared, floating alongside
a cruiser for scale. "For the past three years, we've been
inserting expendable drones like this one across newly identified TFIPs. The drones were programmed to survey their
exit points, then return with the data. A TFIP's a stressful en-
vironment. Most of the drones didn't return. But two years
ago, astronomers at the Mount Evans observatory identified
a TFIP a week's normal-space travel from the Solar System. The survey drone we sent across returned. On the other
side, it found a *cluster* of other TFIPs just days' travel from
the first one. I had a hunch, so we funneled every drone we
had through that TFIP. Then we sent the drones on ahead,
through the other TFIPs beyond the new one."

"You built drones that can survive two jumps out, and
two jumps back?" I whistled.

"It was a little pricy."

I covered my mouth to stifle a snort. When he was
spending tax dollars, Howard thought a thirty dollar coffee was a little pricy. Someday that would come back to
haunt him.

Howard sawed the air in front of him with his palms.
"Jason, at the Mousetrap we found TFIPs that link Earth
to every Outworld within a single Jump."

I whistled again, even as I fought the impulse to leap

across the table and wring Howard's scrawny, mendacious neck. I wouldn't have told me, either. The Mousetrap's importance, and the need to keep its location secret, was as obvious as the derivation of its name. The Mousetrap had been a high-traffic freeway junction in Old Denver, east of the Mount Evans observatory. It had also been Ground Zero for the Denver Projectile. If the Slugs ever found this new Mousetrap, they could plaster it, too.

The State Department guy said, "So, that's why we have fresher news than you have, General. We can transmit high-priority data to a drone outside the Mousetrap, the drone jumps, travels across the Mousetrap, jumps again, then retransmits as it falls apart. We can communicate in weeks, not months."

Howard nodded. "In days, between some worlds."

I said to Howard, "But the real jackpot would be a layover planet."

Howard shook his head. "There's one planetary system within useful range. But the system consists of one gas giant planet. We can no more establish a layover base on that planet than we could on the surface of Jupiter."

The chairman said to me, "But there *is* a workable layover base within the Mousetrap crossroads. Not a planet. A small, airless moon orbiting the gas giant that Colonel Hibble just mentioned. We call the moon Mousetrap, too."

Howard said, "As a commercial and military waypoint, that moon's Gibraltar, Pearl Harbor, Hong Kong, and the Port of New York all in one place."

The chairman frowned. "There are problems. Developing Mousetrap will be the most massive civil engineering project in human history. The shipping required to build and utilize it, and the fleet to defend it, are beyond the industrial and military capacities of all the nations on Earth, combined."

I nodded. The slow kid was coming up to speed. "But there are nations off Earth, too, now. Tressel at peace can afford to contribute."

The State Department guy leaned forward. "And the military phase—your part—went brilliantly. But since the Armistice, the situation is deteriorating."

"Now there's a surprise!" I bit my tongue too late, and the chairman frowned. But the fact was that U.S. nation-building historically resembled Halloween. Military phase, treat. Reconstruction, trick.

Howard said, "There's an additional complication."

I sighed. "With you, there always is."

Howard said, "Cavorite."

I turned up one palm. "Bren exports more than we can use."

"Not anymore." The State Department guy said, "The Marini, Tassini, and Casuni kept Cavorite flowing to the Pseudocephalopod Hegemony for thirty thousand years. When they, as you say, kicked the Slugs off Bren, we became the Unified Clans' new buyer. Tidy."

"Sure."

"Until three months ago. While you were tidying things up on Tressel, the Casuni and Tassini started intercepting the Stone Hills caravans. We're going to need a ten-fold production *increase* to supply Mousetrap's construction, commercial, and defense traffic. But what we have today is disunified Clans at war again, and zero exports."

I sighed. "The Clans hated each other for centuries. Can we broker a peace?"

"We can't wait for that. Marin's receptive to assistance."

I narrowed my eyes. "That's why the Kodiaks aren't coming home? They're going to Bren, to rig another war? You're going to give them to the Marini, to flog the Casuni and the Tassini."

"Not us, General. You."

I shook my head. "I rode with Tassini scouts. I lit the funeral pyres of Casuni sergeants. Fight against troops I led in combat? Against allies? Is that what you expect me to do?"

"Advise against, not fight against. Alliances change. Policies change. What we expect you to do is follow lawful orders, General."

I would never vote for that policy. But this wasn't a democracy. If I was going to air my disagreement at all, it wouldn't be after thirty seconds' consideration, in the middle of the Tank. I said, "Yes, sir." Then I folded my chippad.

The chairman raised his palm. "We aren't finished, General. Tressel owes us a favor, thanks to you. But Tressel won't be sharing any external burdens with us if it dissolves into anarchy."

I turned my palms up. "Sir?"

The undersecretary of State said, "Our Consulates have identified General Planck as a potential unifier. Just as you have. They say you've bonded with him personally. That makes you the perfect choice to encourage him to enter politics. So on your way to Bren, you'll stop by Tressel, and pay your respects to General Planck."

The chairman's aide interrupted the meeting to get the chairman to thumb documents, and we broke for five minutes. I leaned toward General Cobb and whispered, "Sir, I understand why I'm getting the Bren advisory assignment, even if I don't like it. But I'm the last person I'd send to advise Aud Planck, or anybody else, about politics. I stink at diplomacy."

"Jason, there are two kinds of diplomacy. The kind you stink at is the tea-party stuff, like pretending the shape of the negotiating table matters. Parties resort to that stuff if they don't trust each other. The best diplomacy is based on trust. Trust is based on personal relationships. Planck trusts you and you trust him."

Still, I almost guffawed. The State Department trusted me to jigger intragalactic politics. But Nat Cobb wouldn't let me talk to the Lions Club. Until that moment, I had forgotten my earlier discussion with my boss. This tour meant I would be bouncing around outer space again, for years. I was due for rotation in one lousy month. Just hours before, I had specifically asked General Cobb for a non-separation tour. My heart rate sped up.

I had never ducked a dirty job. But now I had asked for just one dirtside assignment, and this was the thanks I got? I just wanted to spend time with Jude, before I bought the farm. It was the one lousy thing I had ever asked of the Army, after all it had asked of me. Who could say I wouldn't have a stroke tomorrow, like Stump Peavey? The hell with Washington. Maybe I'd retire early, too, like Stump.

I felt the adrenaline pump, the chairman reconvened the meeting, and I started to stand. Then, below the table, I felt General Cobb's hand tug me back down by my jacket hem.

He had told me, before the meeting, to shut my pie hole if it came to this.

But, like he said, I stink at that kind of diplomacy.

FOURTEEN

BEFORE I COULD insert boot in mouth, the Air Force Chief of Staff cleared his throat and smiled. "I can see General Wander's upset. No living officer has sacrificed more over the years. If I were in his shoes, I'd prefer a dirtside tour. The Air Force would·be willing to dig in and handle these missions."

I was grateful to him for his remarks. For a nanosecond. He was calling me a crybaby. Besides, what could the Air Force do, other than bomb Tressel and Bren back to the Stone Age? Which was ridiculous because they were already halfway there.

All he was doing was grabbing at a piece of the Outworld pie for his service, which the Air Force had been trying to do for years. I sat back and swallowed a smirk. In the Tank, nobody would tell him he was wrong, of course. I waited for somebody to thank him for his suggestion, and take it under advisement, which was Washingtonese for calling him an idiot.

General Cobb said to the idiot, "Burt, you're right."

I turned to Nat Cobb and gaped.

General Cobb tapped his fist on the mahogany table.

"Fine idea. But Jason, here, knows the ground. What if we expand the delegation to two. Jason and an Air Force representative?"

The Zoomie rocked back in his chair. He had got half of what he wanted, and twice what he deserved, without a fight. He felt for the hook, but couldn't find it. So he nodded, and took the bait. "Makes sense, Nat."

The chairman, who earned his chair by never looking a compromise in the mouth, nodded, too, and said, "Done."

Wait a minute. General Cobb had told me to shut my pie hole. I had. The result was still that I was going off-world for years, which I didn't want. Only now I would have to travel in the company of some Zoomie.

I breathed harder. Nat Cobb had never jobbed me before, but there was a first time for everything.

General Cobb tapped a message into his chippad, then slid it across the table. The chairman spun it so he could read the screen, then smiled and nodded. "Well, he's only a captain, but he's got off-world experience. His pedigree will impress the hosts. And Captain Metzger's current assignment ends in a few days."

My jaw dropped. Then I hid a smile behind my hand.

The Zoomie general crossed his arms, and pressed his lips together so hard they turned white. He felt the hook, now that it was set. Nat Cobb could have arm-twisted and plucked a junior officer from another service from a sensitive assignment, and shoehorned him into an equally sensitive mission, just to solve my personal problem. But that would have meant Nat would owe the Zoomies a favor, for doing what they should do anyway. Instead, Nat had manipulated Jude's boss to insist on doing it.

You don't have to be blind to get around Washington, but it helps.

The chairman said to me, "Your delegation leaves in two days."

"Yes, sir." I cocked my head. "But two days? Is Earth suddenly more desperate for cheap company than a sailor on liberty?" I smiled at the Chief of Naval Operations.

He didn't smile back. Squids take a joke even worse than Zoomies.

Howard said, "Well, there's another thing."

The chairman raised his palm at Howard. The chairman glanced around the room, at the array of horse holders seated along the walls, then at his wrist 'Puter. "We're out of time."

Hair rose on my neck. The chairman's glance told me that Howard's "thing" was so sensitive that the horse holders couldn't be trusted to hear it. Even though the horse holders were all so senior that they could be trusted to deploy nuclear weapons.

Washington keeps two kinds of secrets, secrets from its enemies and secrets from its friends.

What Washington kept secret from its enemies was often good news for the U.S. An atomic bomb that would win the war, a code cracked. Mousetrap was that kind of secret, so we kept it from the Slugs. Howard said the Slugs probably didn't bother to spy on us, any more than we spied on wasps. But we couldn't assume that.

What Washington kept secret from its friends was usually bad news. Like torture to preserve, in the estimation of the torturers, civil rights. Or like ballot boxes stuffed to save democracy.

But sometimes Washington kept secrets from its friends

because the truth was too awful, the way a parent might not tell a child about terminal cancer.

The chairman shared Mousetrap with his horse holders, but not Howard's "thing." Therefore, Howard's "thing" was almost certainly the second, bad kind of secret. Or worse, it was the last kind. And that was why a cold knot now swelled in my gut.

The chairman adjourned the meeting, and as we all stood to leave, I leaned toward General Cobb. "Sir, this idea with the Kodiaks."

General Cobb whispered, "Take it up with Howard. They're buried inside his budget. He'll explain the 'thing' to you, too, on the trip out."

"Sir?"

"Howard's going, too. And Ord. And enjoy your time with Jude."

Howard stepped alongside us. I said to both of them, "Thanks. For laying the ground work."

Both of them shrugged. Duplicity was legal tender in Washington, but insiders kept their mouths shut when they spent some.

General Cobb patted my shoulder, then excused himself.

As Howard and I watched him walk away, I shook my head and chuckled. "Speaking of ground work. When you told Munchkin you were messing with her only child, did she howl like a scalded cougar?"

We stepped out of the Tank into the bustling corridor, as Howard studied his fingernails. "Actually, we left it for you to break the news to Congresswoman Metzger."

FIFTEEN

SIX HOURS AFTER I left Howard at the Pentagon, and one hundred thirty-three years after Charles Lindbergh landed at Paris Le Bourget, I landed there, too.

Lindbergh's flight from the U.S. took thirty-three hours, via propellor-driven aeroplane. My flight took one hour and thirty-three minutes, via VIP scavenging combustion ramjet, funded by Howard.

Lindbergh came to Paris to become a hero. I came to the Paris Air Show to pet a scalded cougar who might bite my head off.

Munchkin was working the Paris Air Show as a celebrity spokesperson because she was a decorated veteran of the Ganymede campaign, a member of the U.S. House of Representatives, who served on the House Armed Services Committee, and most of her constituents worked for or supplied Lockheed.

Lockheed had chosen the Paris Air Show to debut to the aerospace industry a vehicle rumored to make scramjets more obsolete than scramjets had made propellor aeroplanes.

I say "rumored" because what Lockheed called Scorpion

was one of those good news secrets. Scorpion was the closest-held U.S. aircraft program since Lockheed rolled the Stealth Fighter out of the Skunk Works almost a century before.

After my plane landed at Le Bourget, a gratuitously pretty hostess electricarted me across a runway, weaving through crowds who circulated among displayed jets, helicopters, and associated implements of destruction. The Paris Air Show had been the world's premier aerospace bazaar since 1908. I had attended the show once before, as a celebrity greeter peddling U.S. fire control systems to third-world dictators, who needed them like pigs needed Peugeots.

My hostess deposited me at Lockheed's hospitality pavilion, which was a circus tent, with *foie gras* where the cotton candy should have been.

Beneath the Big Top, Munchkin sat on a raised dais, behind a skirted table. A wireless mike the size of a raisin clung to the lapel of her lipstick-red suit, which set off her olive skin and gray-streaked raven hair like Chanel had sewn it just for her. Behind her on the dais, a holo of Lockheed's Scorpion, sleek and prototype-pearlescent white, rotated in the air like a party balloon. In front of her, a dozen adults elbowed and waved like a kindergarten class.

I listened as Munchkin pointed out a reporter, then leaned forward, finger behind one ear, to listen to a question in French. I stood watching and listening with my arms folded, and my chest puffed a little, watching my former foxhole mate take charge. French was Munchkin's third language. Napoleon occupied Egypt for three years. The language he left behind occupied Egypt's prep schools ever since.

She answered first in French, then in Arabic, then said in English, "I won't quote you performance numbers. Scorpion will speak for itself in a few minutes."

Munchkin had just blown off the guy's question, but he smiled broadly. Most males did in Munchkin's presence.

The next question came from a Brit. "Congresswoman Metzger, if this C-drive is so reliable, why is Scorpion also equipped with a jet motor?"

Munchkin the politician had dropped her hyphenated last name, "Munshara-Metzger," at the insistence of the poll trolls. Munchkin was as sentimental as any daughter, but as pragmatic as any ex-machine gunner when traveling from point A to point B. If excess baggage jeopardized the mission, out it went. I told myself that Munchkin got elected for her smarts, hard work, and her own military record. But carrying the name of the hero who saved the human race had to have been worth a few votes.

"It isn't equipped with a jet." Munchkin shook her head at the reporter, and smiled. She swiveled in her chair, toward the rotating Scorpion image. The Scorpion was flat and streamlined, a ceramic watermelon seed, tapering to a kicked-up rear boom like a scorpion tail, hence its name. It looked nothing like the image of the slightly smaller, conventionally-winged Lockheed fighter-bomber that turned with it, to show scale.

Munchkin pointed at Scorpion's tail boom. "The prototype mounted a jet engine in the stinger housing during testing. The jet kept it flying while its test pilot stopped and restarted the C-drive. For today's demonstration, the stinger pod's fitted with display pyrotechnics. Normally, the stinger pod will deploy weapons rearward, like a conventional combat aircraft deploys flares and radar chaff. Even when Scorpion's operating in the mid-range of its performance envelope, it outruns conventional weapons like cannon rounds and missiles fired forward. It could literally shoot itself down."

The reporter smiled. "Faster than a speeding bullet. That's why Superman is the test pilot, then?"

The group laughed.

A female reporter asked, "Are you nervous to have Captain Metzger at the controls?"

Another reason Munchkin was in Paris was because Scorpion was going to be flown above Le Bourget by the best pilot on Earth, at least the best since his father had died saving Earth. Who happened to be Munchkin's only child.

Munchkin smiled again. "I'm as proud of my son as any mother."

Nicely sidestepped. Jude was the world to Munchkin. A son may mean more to a widow because he is all that's left of his father, too. Of course she was nervous. As Jude's godfather, I was nervous, too.

The reporter waved her Stenobot for a follow-up question. "I meant nervous in light of the Captain's mental difficulties. He tried to crash the prototype once, already."

Munchkin turned away from the reporter, as though she hadn't heard the question, and her eyes found mine. Munchkin flicked me a smile, glanced at her 'Puter, then said to her audience, first in French, then in Arabic, finally in English, "We'll have to cut this off. It's showtime." She pointed to her right. "At the bar, Claire has a pair of Zeiss MacroLenses for each of you, compliments of Lockheed and the United States, to help you enjoy the demonstration."

Munchkin wove through the crowd, hugged me, and said, "Welcome home!" Then she led me to the bar.

Claire, who was more gratuitously pretty than my electricart driver, gifted me with a Zeiss set, in a glove leather presentation box, a glass of champagne, and earplugs. I tapped the champagne flute. Plastic. Maybe Lockheed had blown the entertainment budget on the binoculars.

I glanced around at the champagne-lubricated arms dealers, reporters, and foreign military, then asked Munchkin, "Home. That's what you call this carnival?"

She shrugged. "I call this carnival good for the U.S. taxpayer, and better for the people I represent. The U.S. won't sell C-drive technology, even to our allies, for years. But what Scorpion is about to do for Lockheed's reputation is going to keep it exporting conventional aircraft 'til you retire."

I hefted the Zeiss case. "I could retire on what these cost the taxpayer."

She snorted. "At least our swag's presentation-related. ChinAir's handing out tennis bracelets set with Weichselan diamonds. Besides, if we get just one foreign fighter-bomber contract out of this party, that buys my constituents job security for a decade."

A live orchestra at the tent's end, beneath a stadium-sized flatscreen, struck a fanfare. The tent's roof canvas rolled back, exposing blue sky. It was the brightest, clearest day I had seen on Earth since before the Blitz. Of course, I've spent a lot of those days off Earth.

The orchestra, and the crowd, hushed. Everybody screwed in their earplugs, craned their necks skyward, and pressed their zooty MacroLenses to their eyes, as if they were glass refraction binoculars.

A red spark flashed in the sky, just left of the tent center pole. My lenses' display ranged the distance to the spark as nine miles high. I zoomed on the spark and saw it was a red smoke plume, trailing behind a speck shadowed black by the sun.

Two heartbeats later, the speck had flashed down faster than an object could fall, five thousand miles per hour according to the lenses, was one mile dead-center above me, and was still accelerating. Someone screamed, and the person alongside me gasped.

I death gripped my lenses, and held my breath. I'm no physicist, but the Blitz had taught me plenty about kinetic energy. Scorpion was no bigger than an airliner. But if my godson suicided it into this crowd at five thousand miles per hour, the impact would obliterate Le Bourget, and wag the Eiffel Tower like a wheat stalk.

SIXTEEN

TWO HUNDRED FEET above the tent peak, Scorpion froze nose-down in mid-air, as silent and silky white as a toe-pointed ballet slipper.

Whoom!

Air displaced by Scorpion's nine-mile dive hurricaned down on the crowd, flapping ties and scarves, as Scorpion's sonic boom caught up with it. Earplugs or not, people winced. From somewhere beyond the tent, I heard shattered glass tinkle.

I squeezed my unshattered plastic champagne flute and smiled. Jude wasn't grandstanding or suicidal. He was following Lockheed's script.

It was a risky and expensive script. Lockheed's bill for this blockbuster opening was going to include reglazing half the windows in Northeast Paris.

The Brit reporter whispered, "I've wet myself!" Then he chuckled. "Fine bloody theatre, though!"

Two hundred feet above us, Scorpion somersaulted silently in place, tail over nose.

The stinger pod's smoke generator shifted from squirting red smoke to red, white, and blue. But rearranged

French tricolor style, as *bleu*, *blanc*, *et rouge*. Then Scorpion spelled out, in smoke script, with precision so effortless that it floated back and dotted the "i"s, "*Bienvenue à Paris*. Welcome to Paris. Lockheed introduces the future of aerospace flight."

Actually, Scorpion didn't fly, at least not in the way that Lindbergh's aeroplane, or even a scramjet, flew. Scorpion didn't fight Earth's gravity by thrusting a bird-wing airfoil forward through the atmosphere to generate lift.

Howard, who was privy to every secret dating back to the Kennedy assassinations, had clued me in about Scorpion before he VIP-jetted me to Paris. Scorpion's C-drive was unfamiliar to this crowd, but was really no more exotic than the Cavorite drive of a *Metzger*-class cruiser like the *Eisenhower*. Scorpion was just streamlined and strengthened, so it could fly not only in vacuum, but also in atmosphere. Scorpion had to withstand getting pulled forward, or sideways, or backward, by the gravitational pull of one side of the universe, when the Cavorite it carried absorbed the gravity on the opposite side.

Scorpion's accelerations and decelerations within an atmospheric envelope were limited only by its airframe's ability to endure heat generated by atmospheric friction, to absorb mechanical stress, and by the fragility of Scorpion's cargo.

The human cargo of the *Eisenhower*, by comparison, rode inside a Slug-technology gravity cocoon that we had learned to mimic, but not yet to understand. So the *Ike* could slingshot human cargo through black hole gravity at 120,000 miles per second, undamaged except for a few bloodshot eyeballs.

But Scorpion compromised cocooning for lower cost, higher mobility, and manageable size, and had to fly slower as a result. Sort of *Eisenhower* lite. Scorpion protected a human pilot from gravity at the relatively low speeds Scorpion could endure in atmosphere without melting itself, or frying its pilot. Maneuvering at twenty thousand miles per hour, the shielded pilot had to endure maximum loads of "only" six gees, which were "manageable." And once Scorpion reached space's vacuum, it could ramp up to enormously faster speeds.

Scorpion sped up to six hundred miles per hour, faster than an airliner, slow enough to break no more windows. Then, without slowing, it turned right-angle corners like a caroming billiard ball. It left L-shaped smoke signatures drifting across the sky, to prove its path to those spectators who couldn't believe their eyes. Which was all of them.

One of Lockheed's top-of-the-line contemporary fighters joined Scorpion above the runway. The jet swooped and thundered through aerobatic paces that had drawn oohs and aahs in past years. Scorpion literally flew silent rings around the jet every step of the way. Then Scorpion shot straight up and disappeared.

Two minutes later, the big flatscreen above the orchestra lit up with a live feed beamed down from New Moon, orbiting twenty-three thousand miles in space.

Scorpion appeared, a teardrop pearl flashing up from below, against the blue and white crescent of Earth. It flipped and barrel rolled around and through the space station's rings, then shot back down toward Earth.

Three minutes later, it floated again above Le Bourget's runway, as though it had traveled no farther than downtown, circled the Eiffel Tower, and returned.

Every sentient human being at the Paris Air Show stared up at Scorpion, silent and slack-jawed.

The ship drifted down like an ermine leaf, until it hovered a foot above the runway, then it stopped, and a hatch clamshelled open. Scorpion extended no landing gear, because it didn't land, it just hovered. After its tear through the atmosphere, its skin would have melted the runway asphalt if it touched down.

Jude climbed out, down an extended ladder that whined out of the hatch, and kept him from touching the hull, which was so hot that the air shimmered above it. He hopped off the bottom rung onto the runway's asphalt, and stood slender and relaxed, muscular beneath a silver gee suit, helmet tucked in the crook of his arm.

Thirty thousand people stood rooted to the runway, as if Scorpion *had* melted the asphalt, amid suddenly antique jets and missiles. But the only sound was breeze that fluttered the tent canopies and ruffled Jude's strawberry-blond hair.

I hadn't seen my godson in two years. Over the years I hadn't seen him often enough since I delivered him, because we were short of medics, in a cave on Jupiter's largest moon. As Jude grew up, my mind's eye always measured him against my memories of his father, who had been my best friend since childhood. Jude had now grown older than his father had been on the day he died. From today forward, I could build only one set of memories. I swallowed against the lump in my throat.

The skeptical reporter that had sharpshot Munchkin about Jude's mental problems stood next to me, now, eyes bulging. She shook her head, slowly, and whispered into her Stenobot, "—Flying saucer. I'm standing here looking at a flying saucer come true. And next to it, the man from Mars."

I wiped my eyes, leaned toward her with a lump in my throat, and whispered, "From Ganymede, actually."

SEVENTEEN

TWO VANS CAREENED out to Scorpion. A chipboard-and-Mediprobe bunch scrambled out of one, surrounded Jude, then hustled him back into their van for debriefing. Uniformed security piled out of the other van, and cordoned off Scorpion from the crowds that surged toward it.

Munchkin tapped my shoulder. "They'll be debriefing Jude 'til midnight. Lockheed prepaid a two-top dinner in Paris for their CEO, but he 'cancelled.' They want to know if I want to use the table. It's swag, but you don't get out enough. *Le Tour d'Argent.* Top-shelf place."

"The taxpayers will eat that bill one way or the other."

"You're right. Let's just find a cafe on the Left Bank. My treat."

"Dutch."

"Done."

After a cab ride as exciting as a Scorpion flight, we sat outdoors at a café a block south of the Seine, sipping house red and wolfing bread without butter. A brass plaque in the sidewalk claimed DeGaulle had stopped there when the Allies liberated Paris during World War II.

I said, "Best meal I've had in years."

Munchkin smiled across the table. "Best company I've had in years, for sure."

I rolled my eyes. "How do you stand Washington?"

"I can't. I didn't stand for reelection. I'm out next year."

"You? Get fat lobbying?"

She rolled her eyes. "Out, not back in through the other side of the revolving door. Maybe I'd do a blue-ribbon panel, if it was interesting." As Nat Cobb might have said, Munchkin got tired of looking into any one window. Unless somebody told her she couldn't. Egyptian women couldn't serve in the infantry. Small female soldiers couldn't handle machine guns. Non-native-born Americans couldn't get elected to Congress. So, naturally, she had done all those things.

"Why were you ever in? You don't suffer fools gladly."

She shrugged. "Because my son and you—whatever you are, I dunno, surrogate brother—deserted me to fly into space."

"Presumed dead isn't exactly desertion."

"I never presumed either of you were dead. The only thing I could do to get you both back was to persuade the world to accelerate the space program. That meant politics. I'd suffer fools for Jude. Even for you."

People say mothers have lifted trucks to save their children who were pinned beneath them. I had no doubt that Munchkin, all four feet ten of her, could and would lift the U.S.S. *Nimitz* if Jude was pinned beneath its keel. She might even lift a dinghy for me.

"I promised I'd bring Jude back to you. I kept my promise."

She nodded, raised her glass and toasted me. "To promises kept. A rarity in politics."

I shrugged. "You're too cynical. Since the Blitz, the world's changed faster than it did in World War II."

"Accidents accelerate change. Politicians chase it. Cavorite. Human civilizations we could reach in months. Proof that the Slugs are still lurking out there. That's why things changed so much so fast."

I shrugged at the other café tables where people laughed and drank, and at people walking dogs beneath the street lamps. "Nobody here looks motivated to change."

Munchkin tipped our emptied bread basket toward the waiter. *"Encore?"* Then she said, "Appetite motivates. An *average* Weichselan diamond is two carats, flawless, and a child can dig up a cupful in an hour. And trade means export, not just import. Space exploration used to mean traveling for years, just to reach uninhabitable rocks. So we paid geeks to send robots. Today, entrepreneurs see virgin populations, just months away. Ripe for consumer goods, entertainment, franchising."

"Franchising?" I snorted. "Weichselans will love drive-through. As soon as they invent the wheel."

She shrugged. "Neocolonialism's overhyped. Weichselan diamonds are literally just flash. But serious people understand the Slugs won't go away. Especially since we've taken over their Cavorite."

"Howard thinks the Slugs may not care. That they have additional sources. Something got them to Bren and Earth in the first place."

Munchkin made a close-mouthed smile, then stared up at the stars. "Howard. One of too many people I haven't thought about in too long."

"Speaking of. I ran into Mimi Ozawa on the way back here."

Munchkin dabbed her lips with a napkin, as her eyebrows shot up. "And?"

"Forget the matchmaking. She still thinks I'm a puerile slacker."

"You are. But women like a challenge. I should fix you up when she gets back."

"Let's order." I waved the waiter over, to change the subject. I wouldn't be here when Mimi got back, and neither would Munchkin's son. Worse, our conversation was closing too fast on the fact that both Munchkin and I lost the great loves of our lives to war, and neither of us had been whole since.

When the food came, I said, "We need to talk about Jude."

Munchkin pushed *pommes allumettes* around with her fork while she stared at them. "The French still sear these in beef lard. That's why they taste good."

"Don't weasel. Was that reporter right, today? Is Jude suicidal?"

Munchkin shrugged. "Nobody can be sure Jude would have crashed the prototype. Scorpion has failsafes that stopped the dive. But he's quick enough that he could have overridden them. Either way, the shrinks say his depression's not improving. They haven't been able to medicate him because it might slow his reflexes. Until now, he's been the only pilot quick enough to trust with Scorpion."

"Change of routine, change of scene. That can be therapeutic to treat depression." Like a trip to Tressel.

"Maybe. Piloting a flying saucer's not routine. And

here we are in Paris, but all Jude's seen is the inside of a briefing van. Geography doesn't solve people problems, Jason. People do." Munchkin set down her fork, and stared at me. "You know you're the closest thing to a father he has. You've got months of unused leave. Would you do something together with him? A trip? Anything."

I reached across the table and took her hand. "Look. I flew over here to tell you something about Jude. And now you're going to think I manipulated the whole thing."

She wrinkled her forehead as she laid her other hand over mine. "Whatever it is, you're the only person on Earth I trust like a brother. It's fine. Besides, you couldn't manipulate a pound of lard."

"Remember you said that." I gritted my teeth and told her.

EIGHTEEN

ONE WEEK AFTER Jude and I left Paris, I convened a meeting of Howard, Ord, and me around a Plasteel mess table in the wardroom of the *Kabul*, bound for the first jump of the latest pony string Howard had rigged. Howard had justified the cost of this pony because we had to get to Tressel, do our business, then arrive at Bren in time to rendezvous with the slow-boat *Eisenhower*, which was still en route from Tressel loaded with our hovertanks and their technicians.

I asked Ord, "What's the latest from Tressel, Sergeant Major?"

Howard answered before Ord. "Nothing. We can't spare the drones. We'll be lucky to know anything before we land."

I sipped coffee from a thermcup. "Good. We finally have nothing else to talk about except the 'thing.'"

Howard squirmed. He gave up secrets as easily as Japan gave up Iwo Jima. "Maybe we should wait. Isn't Jude cleared to hear this, too?"

"He is. But I sent him to the launch bays. So you

couldn't argue that he *wasn't* cleared. Which you would have. Cough it up."

Howard sighed. "Okay. Can I begin at the beginning?"

"Stall as long as you want. You're gonna have to end at the end."

Howard sniffed. Then he said, "We like to think of the worlds of the Union as equal contributors. But except for Earth, Bren, and Tressel, the populations compare to Earth's from the Bronze Age to the Middle Ages. The primitive Outworlds' greatest contribution to the Union will be as defensive buffers. We assume the Pseudocephalopod entered this area thirty thousand years ago, via jumps near the primitive Outworlds. It would re-enter by the same jumps."

I nodded. "If the Slugs come back, the Outworlds will be our speed bumps."

"Let's say tripwires. Speed bumps actually slow something down, and the primitive Outworlds won't." Howard said, "Earth can never have enough equipment or manpower to defend all the avenues of approach simultaneously."

Ord nodded. "But if we base a force in the Mousetrap, we can meet a threat wherever it appears."

I said, "Sure. But Howard, a crash program? What if the Slugs only swing through this corner of the galaxy once every thirty thousand years? And they just left."

Howard frowned. "That's the thing, Jason."

I narrowed my eyes. "What?"

Howard tapped the table in front of him, and its holo gen popped. It showed an overhead image of a frozen river snaking down a snow white valley. Something black and rumpled stuck up from a bar in the stream's middle.

Howard said, "This image was gathered on Weichsel. A De Beers mining operation."

I squinted at the black object. "That's a diamond mine?"

Howard shook his head. "That's a pilot project to dredge bort—industrial-grade diamond slag. Or what's left of the project. When the cruiser that De Beers chartered returned to retrieve the survey party, it found the camp destroyed. No survivors."

I shook my head, too. "Survey parties are armed. Weichselans can barely spear mastodons. And they've never bothered us."

"It wasn't Weichselans." Howard zoomed on the scene.

I shuddered, then squinted at the black object. It was the scorched, twisted carcass of a massive barge, stern-upturned on a sandbar in an iced-over river. Around it were familiar craters. Made by Slug Heavys, projectiles the size of wall safes. A wolf trotted away from the wreckage, dragging a human thigh.

Howard said, "While the cruiser recovered the remains, its Tactical Observation Transports flew Weichsel, pole-to-pole. Every native encampment had been hit. The Pseudocephalopod effectively wiped the human race off the planet."

The Slugs did the same thing to my mother. And to sixty million other Earthlings in the Blitz. I swallowed hard, and shook my head. "But why Weichsel?"

"My hunch?" Howard said.

Ord and I leaned forward and stared at Howard. The Army put up with him because his hunches about the Slugs were usually right.

Howard shrugged. "The Pseudocephalopod doesn't differentiate among humans any more than we differentiate among strep bacteria. When we expelled the Pseudocephalopod from Bren, It would have taken the event as evidence that a superbug strain has cross-bred. A strain capable of hurting It. It will destroy humans wherever It encounters them, even primitives."

"Is this an isolated incident?"

Howard said, "Well, the cruiser didn't find any remaining Pseudocephalopod activity as of when it left Weichsel. That was eighty-six days ago. The cruiser just got back last week."

Ord shook his head. "If the cruiser could have come via the Mousetrap, we would have known months ago."

Howard said, "Weichsel's just a tickle. It's winding up for the punch."

If you understood the Slugs, and Howard did, genocidal carpet bombing was just a tickle.

Ord asked Howard, "When and where next, Colonel?"

Howard unwrapped a lollipop, sucked on it, then cut the holo. Then he shrugged again. "Weichsel, presumably. This looks like a probe. But it could be a feint. When? My hunch, based on the interval between the Expulsion and this first reaction, is that the big push starts within three standard years from now."

I said, "Weichsel's one jump from Mousetrap. Mousetrap's one jump from everywhere. Especially from Earth."

"You can see why we haven't told anybody before we have a plan."

The Slug Blitz traumatized Earth like no war or natural disaster ever had. At the low point, Las Vegas odds were five-to-one against mankind surviving four more years. When the Slugs attacked Bren, that quainter society suffered misery of biblical scope. And neither of those attacks represented a fraction of the Slugs' apparent destructive capacity. When word got out, widespread panic would understate the reaction. Fourteen planets. Three years. Impossible.

I said, "Have a plan? Howard, how can you plan to eat a rhino?"

Howard shrugged. "One bite at a time."

I pushed back my chair and stood.

Howard asked, "Where are you going?"

I turned and walked toward the launch bays, one hundred yards aft. "To take my first bite."

NINETEEN

FIVE MINUTES LATER, I reached the hangar deck, amid-ships. I found Jude, in blue flight coveralls, climbing, thirty feet up one of a pair of inspection ladders that par-alleled the fuselage of one of the *Kabul*'s troop transports. *Kabul* was the third of the *Bastogne*-class cruisers to be-come operational. The B-class were the first operational vessels advanced enough to rely solely on Cavorite drive for propulsion, as elegant as a Slug Firewitch.

I cupped my hands, and called up to him, my voice echoing in the bay, which was one of thirty-six on *Kabul*, each as large as a dirtside aircraft hangar. "Getting a workout?"

The stolen Slug-tech gravity cocoon that kept a Cruis-er's cargo from getting squashed had no effect inside the cocoon. Humans had to rely on *Kabul*'s rotation, as it au-gured through space, to stick us feet-outward, to the deck. We weighed more at the faster-rotating outer shell, where the launch bays were, than closer to the centerline.

Jude looked down at me, and just shrugged.

I said, "This is a big improvement over *Hope*."

United Nations Space Ship *Hope* had carried me and

ten thousand others, including Jude's parents, to war in response to the Slug Blitz. Mankind's first space warship had burned chemical fuel, so it took nearly two years just to reach the orbit of Jupiter. Its troop transports had been unpowered gliders.

I drew a breath, then followed Jude up the companion ladder, shaking from wrists to ankles. I didn't look down, and I wheezed, from acrophobia, not exertion.

I caught up with him, and said, "On *Hope*, the drop ship inner hulls were scavenged airliner fuselages. The drop ships were just tethered outside the mothership, for hours. The bouncing around made everybody airsick. We actually looked forward to landing on Ganymede, just to get away from the vomit."

Jude swung onto the scaffold that led to the transport's open belly hatch, with the athletic grace his father had displayed. "So Mom tells me. About twice every month."

I followed him through the hatch. "Sorry."

On the way forward, Jude paused in the dim troop bay, hands on hips, and sighed. "No. Jason, I'm sorry. I've always liked the stories. You're my window to my father." He stared down at the deckplates. "It's not that I don't care about that. I don't care about anything."

I laid a hand on his shoulder. "So let's talk about all the things you don't care about."

He shrugged it off. "I didn't need this so-called therapeutic scene change. I didn't try to crash the prototype. That was bullshit."

"I never believed you did. And if the shrinks really thought you did, you would never have gotten near the prototype again."

He shrugged. "I don't have to. Test cycle's done. Now any decent pilot can fly Scorpion."

We walked ahead, to the troop transport's flight deck, and looked through the windscreen. "You miss flying? Did you climb into this tub because you want to fly us down to Tressel when we get there?"

He shook his head. "Just browsing. I'm not rated to fly these cattle cars. I'll be as much a passenger as you will." He leaned forward and pointed through the windscreen, up and out. The troop transport was loaded back-to-back with a sleeker fighter, in a two-slot scaffold that could be rotated, so either slot could engage with the exterior lock that opened to space.

Jude said, "I can fly a Starfire if we need one. But you need me here playing diplomat? That's bullshit, too."

I said, "We may need pilots more than diplomats."

Starships were grandly called cruisers, but were interplanetary boxcars, too. They had to be. Building and operating one cruiser absorbed more resources than a turn-of-the-century U.S. aircraft carrier battle group, with its cruisers, destroyers, subs, aircraft, and support ships.

So a *Metzger*-class or *Bastogne*-class cruiser could stand off and launch munitions ship-to-ship, or ship-to-surface, like a wet navy cruiser or battleship. A cruiser could also embark an infantry division, with its equipment, and thirty-six transports to drop it all onto a planet's surface, the way a wet navy troopship sent troops ashore in landing craft. And cruisers hauled everything else that moved among planets, from Cavorite to diamond miners.

Mostly, though, a cruiser was to war in space what an aircraft carrier was to wet navy war. It projected power via thirty-six Starfire fighter bombers, capable of defending

Kabul in space, attacking other ships, and bombing targets on a planet's surface, by descending into at least the upper reaches of the atmosphere.

The trouble, if the Slugs were coming back, was that a cruiser was one basket holding too many eggs. After the Blitz, the Slug Armada had destroyed *Hope*'s sister ship, *Excalibur*, and all save one of *Excalibur*'s rudimentary fighter aircraft, in an hour.

I leaned forward, so I could stare at the stub-winged, chemical-fueled Starfire across from us. It wasn't much advanced from the crates that the Slugs had swept aside to get at *Excalibur*. I compared the Starfire to my mental picture of the pearlescent watermelon seed that had flashed above Le Bourget. With Scorpion, we would stand a chance. "What will it take to refit the revolvers to launch Scorpions?"

He shrugged. "Scorpion was designed from day one to fit a B-class hangar deck revolver. But it's a bullshit question."

"Is everything bullshit with you?"

He sighed. "No. Seriously. As of today there's exactly one Scorpion. It only got built because Howard's Spooks buried the prototype program. Mom's Congressional buddies will never scare up appropriations for more."

"Scaring may be no problem." I gestured at the pilot's seat, while I sank into the co-pilot's seat. "Sit down, and let me tell you where we're going and why."

After I briefed him in, we sat in the parked troop transport for another hour, just talking. Like, the shrinks would have said, a father and son. Jude started spending less time in his bunk, and more time with us in the wardroom.

The next time we boarded the troop transport was five

pony jumps later, when its crew delivered Howard, Ord, Jude, and me from orbit to Tressel's surface. The crew reconfigured the cattle car rear compartment to VIP four-across seating, to make our entrance a bit grander. *Kabul*, which would have made a grand entrance indeed, would remain in orbit.

Kabul, like all cruisers, was assembled in zero gravity, in Earth or lunar orbit. Cruisers were designed to live and, eventually, die, in weightless vacuum, never leaving space. So cruisers were built with the structural strength of Dixie cups, and aerodynamics to match.

B-class cruisers like *Kabul*, because they manipulated gravity, weren't confined to space by their lack of aerodynamics. They could theoretically sink gently and majestically down through the atmosphere, and land on a planet's surface, like a bigger, fireproof version of the *Hindenburg*.

But a cruiser costs more than the gross domestic product of Peru. Therefore, the starship designers didn't really want to test whether something as big and complex as a B-class was strong enough to sit on the ground without collapsing under its own weight like a wet Dixie cup.

However, our arrival on Tressel resembled the *Hindenburg*'s anyway.

TWENTY

JUDE, who was our only stranger to Tressel, sat in the window seat beside me, peering down as our transport overflew the Tressen capital at forty thousand feet, then banked and descended.

Jude blinked and turned away from the window. "That's really how we're getting landing instructions?"

Mankind could now navigate light years across the stars, but when it came to navigating the last few miles down from orbit to an Outworld's surface, Alaskan bush piloting was more sophisticated.

Tressel had no aircraft, and so no runways, so we were to land in an unimproved field somewhere outside the city. That was no problem. Transports are built tough. But the only radios on Tressel were the two that Earth's consulates used to talk to one another, and to send signals out toward loitering drone receivers, for relay home. Diplomats make lousy air traffic controllers. Therefore, our pilots were being guided down by morse-style messages flashed by a Tressen heliograph, a hinged mirror on a tripod, operated by a Tressen Signals officer.

Howard leaned across the aisle and touched Jude's arm. "Lack of necessity is the mother of non-invention."

Jude wrinkled his forehead.

After decades with Howard, I spoke fluent Hibble. He meant that Tressel's continental interiors, like what we were now overflying, differed from its coastal swamps. The young ground was mostly bald rock, flatter than Kansas and dryer than Chad. Grasses, which would break rock into soil, and real trees, which would block men from seeing out to the horizon, lay millions of years in Tressel's future.

Inland from the Barrens' swamps, line-of-sight communication worked fine on most days, and over long distances. In this world on which Tressen and Iridian civilization developed, men communicated better by heliograph than Teddy Roosevelt had been able to communicate by telegraph. What Howard meant was that Tressel probably had people smart enough to invent the wireless, it just had no people with a burning need to invent it.

Ord, seated next to Howard, watched out his window through old-fashioned field glasses, and frowned. "We're receiving flash from two locations, two miles apart."

The pilot intercommed us from the flight deck. "Sirs, are there two LZs?"

Ord said, "Flash 'em back with your landing lights. Ask what's up."

The intercom said, "Sergeant Major, tactical aircraft haven't mounted landing lights since before the Blitz. We can listen, but we can't talk back."

Combat aircraft didn't advertise, when their pilots could see by ambient starlight like it was noon. I suppose there was a flashlight clipped to a bulkhead, somewhere.

I said, "Can you make a pass low enough to see what's going on?"

"Roger."

Two heartbeats later my stomach tried to crawl up to my tonsils as my seat tried to drop out from under me, and my lap pressed up against my lap belt. "Crap."

Jude grinned at me. "He's hardly even diving. Barely tactical."

I death gripped my seat arm. "I've ridden plenty of tactical. That doesn't mean I have to like it."

We swooped low and slow, five hundred feet above the first of the two signal points, a rock clump. I leaned across Jude and looked down.

As I watched, a forest of lights popped and twinkled below us among the rocks.

"Christ!" The pilot's voice exploded over the intercom, and suddenly I was looking down but seeing the sky.

The transport's airframe screamed as the pilot cranked it into a tactical, evasive barrel roll. Something thumped behind us, and the engines coughed. The pilot said, in a voice as flat as Death Valley, "Hang on. Somebody just shot us down."

TWENTY-ONE

———

IT DOESN'T TAKE long to fall five hundred feet, but it feels like forever.

I splayed my arm across Jude's chest to restrain him, probably the most futile gesture in parenting but among the most frequent.

The pilot kept us level, and did whatever pilots do to cut our speed, which I imagine is more difficult upside down. The transport's roof thundered as we skipped across Tressel's rocky surface at two hundred miles per hour, screeching like the world's worst adjusted brakes.

The Tressen high desert looks flat from forty thousand feet, but after a mere thousand yards the transport's nose caught a boulder and we cartwheeled, throwing off sparking metal bits and pieces like a Mardi Gras float.

Somewhere, Howard said, "Holy moly."

TWENTY-TWO

I SMELLED HOT METAL, and I tasted blood, trickling from my chin into my mouth, which seemed wrong.

I looked up, and saw black rock above my head, bulging through a rent in the transport's dorsal plates. I hung upside down, seatbelted into place in the inverted wreck.

Ord said, "Sir?" Then I felt him sawing at the belt with a jagged hull spar, and I dropped shoulder first onto the ceiling. Jude knelt there, wrapping a bandage around Howard's arm.

Ord peered at my chin, then wiped away blood and dressed the cut. "Scratch."

A knot swelled above his right eye.

My neck was stiff, so I rotated my body toward the flight deck as I asked Ord, "The pilots?"

He shook his head.

I smelled the kerosene stink of RP9, and stiffened. "We have to get out—"

"Yes, sir. But you've been unconscious for six minutes. If the fuel was going to go up, it probably would have happened before now."

The fuselage gaped where the right wing had torn free, and the four of us scrambled out into daylight.

Three Tressen Army lorries chugged toward us, lurching over the desert pavement at twenty miles per hour. Tressen motor vehicles were Model-T boxy, and their internal combustion engines pocketa-pocked along on biofuel that was distilled from algae scraped off rocks and seemed to burn barely hot enough to boil water. But a goggled machine gunner waist-deep in the roof hatch of each truck trained his gun in our direction as they approached.

Jude asked, "Are those the bad guys?"

The first truck was a hundred yards from us when its gunner opened fire.

"Crap!" I turned to fling Jude to the ground, but he tackled me first.

I lay facedown on hot rock and realized that ricochets weren't sparking all around us. I looked behind us. Two more trucks, these unmarked, and half-again as far from us as the Tressen Army lorries, raced toward us, armed men hanging off the running boards, firing rifles at the Tressens. The Tressen machine gunners were firing back, and their rounds were buzzing ten feet above our heads.

I shouted to Jude over the gunfire, "We slid a mile from where those guys behind us shot us down. We wound up closer to these good guys than those bad guys."

The two unmarked lorries burst into flame under fire, two hundred yards from us.

The troops in the Army lorries cheered as they squealed to a stop beside us.

A Tressen major wearing Signals collar brass dismounted,

ran to me, and saluted. "General Wander. Sir, are you alright?"

I tried to shake my head, but had to swivel my shoulders. "Our pilots—drivers—dead."

The major's face fell and he muttered, "Bastards!"

I asked him, "What the hell happened?"

"We were to mark your landing place. By the time we saw them, it was too late."

"What was their problem with us?"

"You sided with Tressen. They were Iridian separatists."

"Iridia was already separate when I left here, at the Armistice."

"General Planck said you'd be surprised. He extends his welcome." The officer winced. "Such as it is."

Jude limped to the wreck, hefted a twisted, loose strut, and began to pry blackened ultratanium skin back from the flight deck, to recover the bodies of his fellow pilots. He called to the soldiers in the lorries, his translator restating his words in idiomatic Tressen, "Little help, here?"

I turned, stared at the black smoke roiling into the clear sky as the separatists' trucks burned, and sighed. It was going to take more than a little help to sort out this mess. Winning the war on Tressel had been easy. Winning the peace appeared to be a bitch.

TWENTY-THREE

THE SMOKE PLUMES and gunfire must've alerted the good citizens of Tressia of our arrival, but when our convoy of trucks and ambulances rumbled through the capital's suburban villages, no heads showed in the windows, no kids ran out to dash alongside the trucks and beg the GIs for sweets.

I rode in the cab of the second lorry in line, alongside the Signals Major, and said, "Your truck's not taking point. There's a reason for that. Convoys get ambushed?"

He shrugged. "Out here in the villages, pretty safe. Once we get inside the old city's walls, where the streets are narrow, one in three take fire."

"Got a spare rifle?"

He reached behind our seatback, and tugged out a Tressen bolt action that looked like a 1903 Springfield, but with a stock the color and texture of potato skin where the hardwood should have been. He also fished out a helmet for me. He said, "I told the other drivers to give the other members of your party helmets, as well. If the separatists explode a building onto us, though, neither the helmet nor the rifle will help much."

Just drop in on Planck, Jason. Chat him up to run for office, Jason. Take your godson along for the ride. Piece of cake, Jason. I swore under my breath.

In the event, we made it to the Human Union Consulate without incident. By without incident, I don't just mean we didn't get blown up. I mean not a soul risked looking out their window to watch us drive by. Maybe the separatists didn't blow down a building on us because they couldn't find one close to us within the old city that hadn't been reduced to a brick heap already.

The Human Union Consulate had been a bank, by the sign carved into its stone façade. It rose three stories, behind an iron fence twelve feet tall and a dead, brown front garden as deep and wide as a three-car garage. Tressen privates in dress uniforms strode the street in front of the fence gate, with their rifles carried across their bodies at port arms, while their heads swiveled to investigate every flicker of movement or sound.

Behind the gate, flanking the old bank's heavy door, two contract guys in last-year's model Eternad armor, carrying law enforcement rapid fires, stood guard.

I swore again, because my armor was two hundred miles above me, ghosting past every fifty-eight minutes, snug and polished, in *Kabul*'s armory. The diplomats had recommended we land in civvies, so as not to, heaven forbid, scare the citizens.

I thanked the Signals major for the lift, and as the convoy pulled out, he saluted me. I returned it, and called to him, "See you around."

As I stepped through the Consulate door, an explosion

a block away shook the building hard enough to shake rock dust out of the ceiling.

I never saw that major around.

But inside the Consulate I did see somebody I knew.

TWENTY-FOUR

AUD PLANCK DIDN'T smile when he saw us. He wore Tressen gray Class-A uniform, with a high-collared jacket and black-striped uniform trousers. Aud eyed my bandaged chin, and shook his head. "I'm sorry, my friend. We plan. The separatists counterplan. But as your Moltke wrote, 'no plan survives contact with the enemy.'"

Jude, Ord, and Howard stood alongside Aud and me. We stood in the building's chandeliered foyer. Its street-side windows were sandbagged, but the offices that opened off on three sides were finished with polished granite.

I shook Aud's hand as I muttered, "We have met the enemy, and they are us."

Aud cocked his head. "Moltke wrote this?"

"Aud, what happened? When I left here six months ago, the war was won. People on both sides were tired of fighting. Hopeful."

"The war was won too well. Iridia was made to cede the Plain of Veblen."

"Erdec said that always happens."

"This time it went further. Extensive additional territories were occupied. Even the former capital of Iridia is now part of Tressen. Reparations are to be paid for Iridian crimes."

"Iridian crimes? Are the Tressens paying for Veblen, too?"

Aud glanced at his Tressen aide, who was writing in a notepad, out of earshot. Aud said, "The Tressens didn't lose. In the Occupied Territories, everyone associated with the old Iridian government was turned out in every town. Not a bad thing. The Iridian party hacks are worse than the Tressen ones. But no one was left to collect trash or operate the water works."

"Threw the Nazis out with the bath water," Howard said.

Ord shot him the kind of look that only a senior non-comm can give an officer and get away with it. Howard looked down and fiddled with papers on a table.

The Human Union Consul stepped out of his office, in pressed white shirt sleeves and a red silk tic, all peeking out beneath a woven Plastek flak vest. He was thin, and his white hair puffed out around his head so he looked like a Q-tip on feet. He shook hands all around. "There are only ten of us. There wasn't much we could have done."

"You could have told us to bring our body armor."

"At least we told you to land here. It's worse over in Iridia."

"So I heard. No indoor plumbing."

Q-tip sighed. "And no jobs. No wages. No bread. No feeling of self worth for the breadwinners. Starve a man and he'll hate you. Starve his children and he'll kill you."

I turned to Aud. "Where do you fit in to this bus wreck?"

Aud shrugged. "Where a good soldier always fits in. Wherever civilian authority tells him to. Today, that means I'm to invite your party to attend a ceremony with me."

"For what?"

"Reconciliation. Both sides will dedicate a memorial to the war dead. Iridian and Tressen."

I eyed Q-tip's flak vest. "Is that safe in this town?"

Aud shook his head. "No. That's why the ceremony isn't in town. The memorial will be at the site where the battle that ended the war began. Between the trench lines on the Barrens."

Jude furrowed his brow. "The Barrens?"

I retrieved my luggage, all dress uniforms, medals, and nothing vaguely protective, and sighed. "It's not as great as it sounds."

TWENTY-FIVE

PART OF THE MONUMENT project was to include a paved highway out into the Barrens, but we rode out on the same gravel paths that had served during the war. So it took a week to return to the vicinity of the Barrens trench lines by crawler caravan. Then it took hours after that to identify the trenches with precision.

War's bones get picked clean quickly. In the six months since the war's end, tetra trappers passing through, scavengers, and souvenir hunters made short work of iron gun mounts that had been bolted to concrete pillbox floors, of copper field telephone wire, of brass shell casings, of discarded rucksacks, even of the bracing and planking that had shored up the trench systems against the eternal rain.

Already, the trenches themselves were vanishing into soft-edged puddles, except in the survivors' nightmares.

And the scorpions had left few bodies to bury.

The government had erected a tent village for the ceremony participants, netted off from scorpions, leveed against the swamp.

The evening before the ceremony, there was a dinner

for fifty, hosted in one long tent by the Prime Ministers of triumphant Tressen and of diminished Iridia.

A model of the memorial, all heroic marble statues and somber brass plaques, centerpieced the banquet table. Considering the precarious states of the governments present, the conviviality was surprising. There was much toasting to the competence and bravery of this general, and of that one. Also to the wisdom and compassion of each statesman's staff, and to the politicians of his party.

Long after the formal dinner broke up, Planck, Erdec, Ord, Jude, and I remained clustered in our chairs at one end of the now-bare banquet table, defending the last, low-burning candle. We also defended four now-empty bottles, and two full ones, of Iridian red. The serving staff had tried to recapture them, but eventually abandoned us to do what soldiers with wine do.

Erdec topped off glasses all around, lastly Ord's and his own, as two a.m. rain drummed the tent roof. Ordinarily, officers and non-comms might have one drink together, then, for the sake of propriety, adjourn and get slobbering only in company of equivalent rank. But these were not ordinary times, and Ord and Erdec were not ordinary sergeants.

Erdec burped, said, "The Iridians caused half this mess. But we Tressens forced an unjust peace."

Ord turned to his new friend, and said, "I thought you were four-eighths Iridian, Walder."

"Alright, Arthur, Iridia gets one-fourth of the blame."

After four bottles, who did math?

I asked Planck, "The prime ministers—are they getting anything done?"

Planck shrugged. "Everything *I* am told to do gets done."

"Is that much?"

"There's not much left to work with. We're managing scarcity."

"First it was 'I.' Now it's 'we.' But you're not part of the government."

Aud lifted his glass to me. "Thanks for small favors."

"You won't reconsider what we talked about on the trip out?"

Aud shook his head. "If I'm not part of the government, I'm not part of the problem."

I sighed. There was some rejoinder to Aud's argument that involved being part of the solution. Two bottles ago I could have articulated it.

Jude, who had been quiet since we crashed, stood, swayed, and raised his own glass. There were times when he seemed to withdraw into himself, remembering, I supposed, the loss of his own soldiers, and his own captivity, during the Expulsion. He bore no external scars from his ordeal.

Jude said, "Gentlemen. Tonight we have heard toasts to generals. We have heard toasts to ministers. We have heard toasts to battles . . ." He steadied himself against his chair back. "But we have not heard a toast to the man without whom your war could not have been won."

Planck frowned. Erdec smiled at his commanding officer. It was true. Every brass hat who survived the war, which was most of them, had been toasted, except Audace Planck. His charisma—I would have said his common sense—threatened the politicians as well as the generals who were trying to rebuild this dysfunctional, divided society.

Jude said, "It's always the same, on every world, in every war. I propose a toast to the one man nobody ever toasts. The common foot soldier."

Ord looked around at all of us, then at Jude, then he raised his glass, too. "God damn shame on the rest of us that it took you to remind us, Captain."

Erdec said, "Here, here!"

Aud raised his glass, too. "Well said, Sergeant Major. And Captain Metzger." Aud's eyes glistened in the candlelight. Mine were moist, too.

The next morning was mercifully dry, and given over to dress uniforms and more speeches. There was security— Planck's Sergeant of the Guard was so old-school that he made Ord swoon—with some of them today doing double duty, decked out as an Honor Guard.

Aud may have been a threat to the politicians, but even on Tressel, where photography had advanced barely past Mathew Brady, they knew war heroes made great photo opportunities. And an apolitical general ruffled fewer feathers in either camp than the politicians jockeying for position.

As scripted, General Planck, the legendary Quicksilver, was to lay a wreath at the just-begun foundation of the Tressen Barrens Battlefield Monument. The foundation stones rose from the end of a land spit surrounded by silent swamp, and today even the swamp water seemed still and silver.

The Tressen and Iridian military bands struck up a slow piece, to which Aud was to march out the spit, past a line composed of alternating, decorated Iridian and Tressen veterans drawn up at attention, and lay the wreath. The press would watch, photographic flash powder would pop. The Honor Guard would fire off a rifle salute, its rounds arcing out above the water.

Aud grasped the wreath off its tripod stand with white gloved hands, and turned toward the monument foundation. As he began to walk along the line of veterans, Planck paused and turned to Erdec. He whispered something, then tugged his old mentor out of line to walk beside him.

Some men are theatric by design. Theatrics came instinctively to Audace Planck. Sergeant Major Erdec wore a chestful of decorations, was half Iridian and half Tressen, and walked with enough of a limp that his pace was statesmanlike. Jude had pointed out the problem with this ceremony, the night before. It was about generals and politicians who started wars, and not about the soldiers like Erdec who fought them and died in them. Aud had just fixed the problem.

I smiled. Erdec deserved the honor. His mixed blood symbolized reconciliation. And the gesture wouldn't slow Aud's rising star, either.

Jude and I stood side-by-side at the end of the dignitary line, alongside the honor guards. Jude whispered out of the corner of his mouth. "I like Planck."

The bright young general and his aging mentor reached the monument, and the music stopped. Rifle bolts crackled as the honor guard shouldered and elevated its rifles to the sky.

I swallowed as a lump filled my throat.

Aud and Erdec knelt beside the water to lay the wreath.

Water geysered in front of the two of them.

The scorpion was enormous and glistening black. Its spinose forelimbs flashed and dripped as they closed around Aud and old Erdec.

Before anyone could react, someone did.

Jude was born with the fastest reflexes on Earth. Because he wasn't born on Earth. He was the first human being conceived in space, aboard an unshielded troop transport halfway between the orbits of Earth and Jupiter. A heavy metal ion straying through space had sliced an embryonic DNA strand in the best possible place, or so the geneticists supposed.

Before most of the crowd processed enough information to scream, Jude had snatched the rifle of the Honor Guard beside him and pumped a magazine into the scorpion.

I followed Jude as he ran toward Aud and Erdec.

The beast twitched and, from somewhere behind us, another volley tore into its body, as the rest of the Honor Guards reacted.

By the time Jude reached the water's edge, the scorpion lay still, its monstrous tail twitching in the shallows.

A bloodied, black spine as thick as a man's wrist thrust a foot out of Erdec's chest, spreading apart the medals on his lapel. Erdec's eyes were wide and his mouth agape.

I turned to Aud.

He stared at Erdec, gasping, eyes wide. I felt Aud's torso and chest. Except for a spine that had grazed his right wrist, he was untouched, physically.

People mobbed us, shouting and tugging.

An hour later, Jude and I stood alongside Aud in a field

hospital tent. He sat bare-chested, on a white-sheeted examining table while a medic bandaged his forearm.

The diplomats were in another tent, being hounded by the press, and displaying suitable shock and sadness.

Erdec's body lay ten feet away, beneath a bloody sheet, and Aud stared at it. He shook his head and whispered. "Why? Why did I do it?"

"Aud, you didn't do anything except make an appropriate gesture."

He shook his head. "How could I have failed to see the lure? How could the Sergeant Major have failed to see it?"

"I didn't see the lure when you and I were stranded out here last trip."

Planck shook his head, as the medic held out a clean uniform shirt. "Jason, you saw the lure. You just didn't know what it was. Every schoolchild here knows that flash of yellow. We react to it by reflex."

"It was the last thing on your mind. On anyone's mind."

The Sergeant of the Guard stepped into the tent, braced at attention, and saluted Planck. The Sergeant hesitated, frowning. "If you're well enough, General, there's something you should see."

TWENTY-SIX

WE FOLLOWED THE sergeant out of the tent as he turned toward the monument foundation.

Planck asked him, "How did it get through the nets?"

"A hawser had worn through, sir. At least that's what we thought."

A rifleman joined us as we walked out onto the spit. His eyes never left the water, and he kept his rifle's muzzle tracking where he looked.

The scorpion's carcass had been rolled up onto the bank, two armored tons of spine-crusted evil.

Jude's eyes widened. "Jason, you told me about these. But I never really understood . . ."

Aud pointed out into the swamp, where two GIs were looping a braided cable that arced up out of the water, as thick as a forearm, around a scaly lycopod trunk three feet in diameter. "The nets are sound now?"

The sergeant nodded. "Yes, sir. But that's not what I wanted you to see." He walked around the carcass' shoreward side, stepping over the scorpion's splayed rearmost paddle, then its middle limbs, like they were downed trees. The spiked pincer was too big to step over, so he walked around it.

Six punctures, from Jude's shots, snaked across the dead beast's smooth, black head. One shot had struck one compound eye, so it looked like a shattered punch bowl. Shards of torn carapace, a half inch thick, curled up around the bullet holes. It reminded me of the hood of a shot-up limousine from a period-piece gangster holopic.

The sergeant pointed with his pistol between the two compound eyes. "This one's lure's gone."

Planck nodded. "Shot away. I should have seen it, though."

The sergeant knelt in the mud, and grabbed a fleshy stalk that rose from between the scorpion's eyes, and pointed at its clean-sliced tip. "No, sir. The lure was cut off, here. Before this thing ever came at you."

Planck narrowed his eyes. "What are you saying?"

"Sir, I grew up on the coast. On the edge of the Barrens. When we were kids, scorpion pups would get caught in the family nets. Pups can only bruise you. We'd cut off the lures, just like this, then let the pups sneak up on other kids. Scared them to death."

"You're saying this was deliberate?"

"I'm saying you and Sergeant Major Erdec didn't see this scorpion's lure before it struck you because this scorpion had no lure to see. We found kitchen garbage in the water, sir. Scorpions swim to chum faster than Iridians steal. The cooks know that. They never throw garbage out in the Barrens."

Planck ran his eyes from the beast's head to its tail. "Someone made a gap in the nets, then attracted this beast? Improbable. But then they got in the water with this monster, and cut off its lure? Impossible!"

The sergeant reached into his pocket, drew out a coil of field telephone wire, and pinched a loop in it between two fingers. "Sir, we were fishermen's kids, but we weren't stupid enough to get in the water, even with a pup. Once we netted a scorpion, we just stood on the bank, lassoed the lure with a leader-wire loop, then pulled it tight until it cut through the stalk."

Aud stood with his boots planted shoulder-width apart on the bank, his bandaged arm and his other crossed over his bare chest. "You're saying someone deliberately killed Sergeant Major Erdec."

The Sergeant shook his head. "No, sir. The only person scheduled to go near the water was you. It was you they wanted to kill." The sergeant pointed at Jude. "And if the Captain, here, was a heartbeat slower on the trigger, they would have. And that male would have backswum you into the swamp in another heartbeat and disappeared. And it would all have been an unfortunate accident."

Aud closed his eyes and rubbed his temples. "Yes, I suppose it could be. But where would that leave us? Was it separatist infiltrators? Some demented corporal I may have disciplined years ago? The prime minister himself?" Aud shook his head. "No. There's no proof. Sergeant, this was no more than a frayed hawser, sloppy KP, and a hungry scorpion that got its lure shot off after the fact."

"I'd agree, General. Except for this." The sergeant straddled the scorpion's flipper, reached down with both hands, and lifted it like a soggy log.

Tangled around the flipper leg's middle segment was

something like kinked thread. I bent, looked closer, and a shiver shot up my spine. The thread was copper field telephone wire. From a small noose twisted into the wire's end dangled a dripping, fleshy mass. It was bright yellow.

TWENTY-SEVEN

THE NEXT DAY, Aud and I sat on the rear-facing personnel bench of a Tressen crawler bound away from the Barrens, leaning with our forearms on the crawler's iron tailgate. Jude rode behind us.

Aud stared back at the crawler lurching along behind us, which served as the hearse bearing Sergeant Major Erdec home. "Erdec trained me, you know. I was younger than Jude is when I first made the sergeant major's acquaintance."

I nodded. "I made Ord's acquaintance the same way. Nobody forgets their Drill Sergeant."

Aud stretched a thin smile, then frowned. "What do I do now, Jason?"

"Find out who did it?"

He shook his head. "Separatist infiltrators, almost certainly. But it doesn't matter. I can counterattack an army that attacks me. But this? I can't make war on smoke."

"Clausewitz said war is politics continued by other means. Make politics your war, continued by other means."

"Me? A warlord?"

I shook my head. "Nobody said form a banana republic."

My translator stumbled over "banana," as I realized that people like Aud don't resort to politics just because people tell them to. They go there only if their inner compass turns to point them there. My advice wouldn't make Aud's compass twitch, but Erdec's death might.

Aud turned to Jude, and touched his shoulder with his bandaged hand. "I owe you my life."

Jude shrugged. "You owe me nothing. I just reacted." He leaned forward on his elbows. "But Jason's right, sir. About politics. You have a chance to change this world for the better. You may not trust people, General, but people trust you. I barely know you, but already I trust you."

In Jude's life he had known plenty of admirable people who inspired trust, not least his mother. But I suppose heroes are easier to see minus the fog of familiarity. There was light in Jude's eyes, like I hadn't seen in too long.

The rest of the crawler ride was just another week in mechanized-infantry paradise. We threw a track in the midday heat. The crawler in front of us, which mounted a forward-facing cannon, lurched into a narrow stream bed, and stuck its gun tube in the opposite bank. The lead vehicle took a wrong turn. The trail vehicle took a wrong turn, and we had to double back, chain it up, and drag it out of a mudhole. Everything was sharp-edged iron and oily. Unless it was muddy. Either way, as you lurched along, what didn't cut you bruised you.

But every time we hit a snag, Jude was out in front of the problem, pulling, hauling, leading, joking with the tankers, and with Aud.

We reentered the capital after sunset. The street lamps

were dark, but the crawlers were able to steer by the light of fires mobs had set in the streets. By the time the convoy dropped us off at the Consulate, I was never so glad for the opportunity to flop on a camp bed in a sandbagged cellar masquerading as Bachelor Officers' Quarters.

Q-tip, the consul, met us in the foyer, wearing his flak jacket and pajama bottoms. "The city's going to hell out there. Worse in Iridia. The only person people aren't mad at is your friend Planck. The assassination attempt's made him Elvis. Immortality's a draw these days."

A half hour later, Jude lay on the bunk next to me, hands behind his head, staring at the ceiling beams. "That was fun, wasn't it, Jason? Not what happened to Erdec. Not the riots. The rest of it."

"No, it wasn't fun. Getting paid to drive a flying saucer is fun."

"I can't make a difference doing that." I smiled in the lamplight. Jude's gifts made him look like Superman to us mere mortals, but in the mirror he saw someone who wasn't making a difference.

Jude said, "Planck is going to change this world for the better."

"He's decided to go into politics? How do you know?"

"He told me. That day when I rode up front with him. He says he needs people around him who aren't burdened by old allegiances. Jason, this is a frontier."

"You're saying you want to stay here?"

"The only thing back home for me is Mom."

"That's a big thing."

"It is. But so is changing the world." Jude rolled onto

one elbow, and blew out the oil lantern on the low table that separated us.

I lay awake, staring up into the dark for a long time, smiling, but at the same time my heart swelled in my chest like a stone.

The next day, Ord and I took our morning run along the bank of the canal that wound through the capital. Every minute or so, a distant rifle shot echoed off the stone apartment walls that rose on both sides of us. Ord had borrowed Plastek flak vests and steel toed boots for us. That made things as uncomfortable as practicable for me, which had been Ord's mission in life since he was my drill sergeant in infantry basic.

As we ran, I scanned the shrapnel-scarred rooftops of the riverside tenements for snipers. "You really think this is a good idea, Sergeant Major?"

"During the seige of Kabul, our Platoon softball team was two and six without flak vests, undefeated with."

I looked over at him, his eyes twinkled, and he shook his head. "I checked with the Consul, sir. He jogs this route every day. No problems."

"You think if Planck went into politics he could reverse this mess, the way we reversed the Second Afghan?"

"The general's an aggressive commander. He wouldn't be afraid to change things."

"Jude seems to think change is what this place needs."

"Of course he does, sir. If a man is twenty and not a liberal, he has no heart. If he's forty and not a conservative, he has no brain."

I said, "Planck's offered Jude a position on his personal staff."

We slowed to a walk, the cobblestone path to our front

wiped out by a shell crater. The crater made a half-bowl filled in by the river.

Ord said, "If the general will permit me a personal observation that will be hard on Congresswoman Metzger."

"It will be hard on *me*. I thought I had lost Jude on Bren. I was just getting him back again. Now this."

On the canal, a canopied barge chugged by. Its wake pushed waves that lapped into the crater, then receded. Ord pointed down at the water. "The relation between parent and child is like waves on a shore, sir. Adolescence, marriage, more children, perhaps divorce. A constant cycle of pulling away, then returning."

The barge moved on, and the waves diminished, then vanished.

I said, "But the cycle ends, eventually."

"Always, sir. In the meantime all we can do is stay afloat."

A week later, a general strike shut down the capital of Tressen, and a bomb destroyed a wing of the Iridian parliament building. Ten days later, the Iridian currency collapsed, and paramilitary gangs made up of unemployed veterans warred openly in the streets of Tressen's largest port. Three days later, the Iridian prime minister was lynched from a lamp post by a mob.

Eleven days after that, the Imperator of Tressen and the Regent of Iridia met in the Tressen capital. The following afternoon, the monarchs summoned the Acting Iridian Prime Minister, as well as the sitting Tressen P.M., and accepted their resignations with extreme regret.

At eight o'clock that evening, their majesties received their choice to fill the vacancies. At nine o'clock, General Audace Planck was sworn in as one of three generals serving as a joint Prime Ministrate, with plenipotentiary powers, and charged by the unified monarchy to form a cabinet and restore order.

At midnight the same evening, ten minutes before the last moment we could lift to the *Kabul* and still meet the *Eisenhower* on schedule, Howard, Ord, and I strapped in to a fresh transport.

Jude remained behind, newly appointed to Planck's personal staff. Jude couldn't come to see us off, but he sent a runner with a note for me that ended, "Love, Jude."

I chose a window seat, and stared out into the darkness all the way up, so Howard and Ord couldn't see the sheen on my eyes.

Four weeks later, the same transport transferred us from the *Kabul* to the *Eisenhower* as they matched orbits above Bren.

Until and unless we made something out of Mouse-trap, Bren was a waypoint between Tressel and Earth anyway. Earth needed help from Bren to develop Mousetrap almost as much as Earth needed Bren's Cavorite.

So, if I believed what Nat Cobb had said about the importance of personal relationships and trust counting for more in diplomacy than protocol, I belonged here now.

When I had overnighted on Bren while I returned from my previous visit to Tressel, I passed the night with old friends in low places. When Howard, Ord, and I climbed down the disembarkation ladder from the transport, its cold skin's crackle echoing in one of the *Ike*'s launch bays, one of those old friends was waiting for us.

TWENTY-EIGHT

THE HUMAN UNION ASSOCIATE CONSUL to the Court of Her Majesty Marenna the Fourth, Deliverer of the Stones, Protector of the Clans of Marin, and Sovereign of the Near Seas, was a duck.

Actually, Eric Muscovy's lips just stuck out a little, and he walked splay-footed. But that was plenty for his classmates, from grade school through the Harvard Center for Asian Studies.

I hugged him, then held him at arm's length and grinned. "Why'd you burn fuel to come up here, Duck?"

The Duck's eyes twinkled as he shook Howard's hand. "I shouldn't have. Howard tacked on a fuel surcharge last quarter. But I could bury our bar bill from your last visit in Spook travel expenses."

I rubbed my forehead. The memory of my most recent evening with the Duck still made my head ache.

Ord smiled at the Duck, and stuck out his hand. "DeArthur Ord, Consul. We met in Tibet."

The Duck shook Ord's hand, nodded, and smiled. "I'd never forget *that*."

If it hadn't been for Ord, the Duck, and a bamboo ladder, I would have rotted in the infirmary of a Chinese prison, with two broken femurs and a collapsed lung.

Duck's smile faded as he waddled to the bay's exit hatch with us in tow. "I met you up here because I just heard you left a bad situation on Tressel."

"It should improve."

Duck nodded. "So I thought I'd relieve your anxiety about this situation. This one's a done deal."

I shook my head. "I don't like it. I doubt that Bassin does, either."

"Bassin has no say about it. His mother's the monarch. He's the spare heir. Bassin's mother and my boss ironed out the details last night. We deliver two hundred seventy-six Kodiaks, plus trainers and technicians. Marin personnel will operate them to secure the Cavorite caravan routes against Casuni and Tassini raids. In exchange, Marin will deliver, and replenish as needed, sixty thousand trainable workers, plus civil engineering cadre, until Mousetrap is completed."

I spun in the corridor, and grabbed Howard by the shoulders. "Exchange? The Marini are gonna build Mousetrap?"

"It's a fair trade. Mousetrap enhances Bren's security as much as Earth's and Tressel's."

"And you get to bury the project off the Spook balance sheet. This is hideous."

Howard pouted. "It's just bookkeeping. You always overreact."

"I'm not talking about money. Trainable workers? They're *slaves*, Howard! Replenished means that when overwork kills one, Marin will send another."

The Duck spun me away from Howard, and pointed

a finger at my chest. "I don't like it either. But I don't make policy, and neither do you. And neither does your old friend Bassin, the abolitionist. So right now he's on his way back to Marinus from the front, because a good Crown Prince supports his mom's decisions. Just like you're going to support your chain of command's decisions."

I crossed my arms and huffed. Then I asked, "So. What are Bassin and I supposed to do tomorrow?"

"Shut up while she signs. Smile. Wear your medals. It sucks, but I've had to do it for years."

"Except without the medals." It was a dirty shot, and I knew it even as the words left my lips.

The corners of Duck's mouth turned down, then he cocked his head at the ribbons on my chest. "How many GIs got replenished so you could get those medals?"

I balled my fists as we faced each other. The Duck had saved my life, and I knew he was still just an Associate Consul because he had objected too often to inhumane host-country policies. But if we had both been fifteen years younger I would have decked him.

Besides, the Duck was half right. If I came to a fork in the road where the army and I had to part company, I could resign. But meanwhile, I had to follow orders just like I had when I was a Spec 4. Aud Planck had come to such a fork. Maybe I was approaching one. But I didn't have to choose, yet.

So I took a deep breath, then asked the Duck, "What time's the signing ceremony tomorrow?"

"High noon. Don't keep the old girl waiting."

TWENTY-NINE

THE NEXT MORNING ORD, Howard, and I met the Duck at the town gate to the Summer Palace two hours early. One hour of that cushion was because it takes an hour to get from the gate to the Hall of Mirrors, where Her Majesty and the Duck's boss would sign the Kodiaks-for-slaves deal. The Summer Palace has more square footage than the Pentagon. The other hour was because the Duck wasn't kidding about not keeping the old girl waiting.

With time to spare, the captain of the queen's house-holders escorted us not to the Hall of Mirrors, but to Bassin's apartments.

As crown prince, Bassin had no authority, but lots of room in which to exercise it. The "parlor" where he received us was a gilded, dome-ceilinged rotunda bigger than most U.S. state capitols'.

He strode across the room's marble floor wearing the unadorned, brown uniform of a colonel of engineers. Like every other grown man who still lived in his mom's house, Bassin was stuck with her decor. But he could have taken any rank he chose. For that matter, he could have invented one, and some cape-and-plume uniform to match. But an engineer, a brick-and-mortar builder, was what he was, and with Bassin what you saw was what you got.

Unless he was masquerading as a prospector, to spy on the slave trade he despised. That misadventure had cost him an eye, and a leg. And his mother's good will, which may have wounded him worse.

I started to kneel, but he pulled me up straight and gave me a shoulder-pat hug, and another to Howard, to Ord, and even to the Duck.

Bassin frowned. "I had looked forward to seeing Jude again."

"He stayed on Tressel. He thinks he has to save the world."

Bassin wrinkled his forehead above his eyepatch. "Wasn't saving this one costly enough?"

"You should talk."

Bassin turned to the Duck, stiffly. "Consul Muscovy, please understand Marin's gratitude for the Motherworld's generous offer."

The Duck bowed about a half inch. "And please understand Earth's gratitude to Her Majesty for accepting it. How are things at the front, sir?"

The Duck knew exactly how things were at the front. Tactical Observation Transports loitering above the caravan routes relayed real-time overhead intelligence to our Consulate all twenty-four point two Earth hours of every Bren day. The TOTs showed that things stunk at the front for Marin, so badly that Bassin's convoy had been ambushed by Casunis. He had only arrived at the palace an hour before we had. It was the Duck's way of reminding Bassin why his mom had made this deal.

"I'd say not bad enough to export slaves. But it isn't

up to me, Consul." Bassin turned to me. "We have an hour before the ceremony, Jason. I know Mother would love to share a social moment with her son and her former commander-in-chief." It was Bassin's turn to make a half-ass bow, as he extended his palm toward a door that opened into the corridor to the queen's apartments.

I glanced at the Duck and shrugged.

He fingered his blue cummerbund. He knew Bassin was going to lobby his mother to kill the deal, and I was being carted along like an apple for the teacher. The Duck didn't like it, but associate consuls couldn't argue with royalty. Neither could high school dropout generals.

As our escort's polished armor rattled and echoed in the hallway, which was so big that I expected to see a train headlight coming at us, I asked Bassin, "How's your mother?"

"I haven't seen her since her birthday party, eight months ago."

The queen was pushing eighty by now, which was impressive, given the state of medicine on Bren. I had worn out combat boots that weren't as tough as Marenna the Fourth. The first time I met her, the queen had been seventy-two and prickly. She said then that her temperament didn't improve with age. She had aged, so I swallowed at the prospect of another audience.

Bassin shrugged. "She's grumpier than ever, I suppose. But don't worry. She's always liked you."

Bassin was kidding himself if he thought his mother would change her mind because that nice young man from Earth was visiting again.

The escort admitted us to the queen's sitting room, then backed out as he pulled the double doors shut.

The queen's parlor was bigger than Bassin's, with better ceiling art, rimming a clear crystal dome through which cloud-patched blue showed. Her Majesty reclined on a divan centered below the dome, which matched the silver of her gown. She had her back to us, her head upturned toward the ceiling.

Bassin said, "Mother, it's me. I was delayed."

She didn't say a word. We had arrived an *extra* hour early because Her Majesty genuinely didn't tolerate tardiness any better than she tolerated barbarians at her gates.

Bassin muttered under his breath, then he walked to her, his heels clattering on the marble floor.

I stood fast. I'm no diplomat, but I've been at this long enough to know that a commoner doesn't approach a queen unless bidden. Especially this queen.

Bassin said to her, "Don't be like that. There's still time to discuss this."

Bassin reached the divan, stopped, hands on hips, and looked down at his mother.

His jaw slackened, his eyes widened. "Mother?"

He dropped to one knee, and touched her cheek. Then he started to shake, and tears welled in his eye.

I ran to the divan.

The queen, as slight and as brittle as ever, lay still with her eyes wide and staring to the sky.

I breached protocol, and laid my fingers on the royal cheek.

It was as cold as marble.

Bassin lay across his mother's body, sobbing.

I breached protocol again, and patted my friend's royal shoulder.

Only now he wasn't just my friend. He was king.

THIRTY

Night had fallen as Ord, Howard, the Duck, and I slumped in a half circle of chairs upholstered in ochre dinosaur feathers, in Bassin's parlor. A clock that looked like a calliope ticked, and the tick echoed off the dome above us. Beyond the palace, muffled bells chimed from every steeple in the city.

The royal physician, leather bag in hand, stepped out of Bassin's bed chamber and we all stood. The doctor whispered something to the valet who sat in a straight backed chair outside Bassin's door, patted his shoulder, then walked to me. "I've given His Majesty something to help him sleep. I've treated Bassin since he was four. Strong boy. He'll be fine, tomorrow. Physically."

"What happened to his mother?"

He tapped the back of his head, behind his ear. "There is a vessel, at the base of the brain. Increasingly fragile with age." He snapped his fingers. "Gone like that."

I nodded. "We call it a stroke."

"Painless. A blessing." He shook his head. "But for Marin . . ."

The Duck rubbed his eyes. "What do you mean?"

"Most of us have never known Marin without Her Majesty. And with the war, I don't know . . ."

The doctor shook each of our hands, then left us.

The Duck shook his head, as he crossed his arms. "Well, I know. When Bassin wakes up, our deal's as dead as his mother." Then the Duck looked over at Howard, who was sucking on a nicotine-substitute lollipop, and said, "Colonel, if you expect to build a better Mousetrap, I suggest you bring your own shovel."

Howard tugged the lollipop out of his mouth, and it made a little *poink* that echoed up to the parlor ceiling. "We still need the Cavorite, though. We'll just give Bassin the Kodiaks, anyway."

The Duck said, "No, we won't. Our negotiating sideboards were very narrow. The Kodiaks may be buried in your budget, but State is in charge of treaties. We can't cut a new deal to support hostilities. The Constitution reposits the war power with Congress, not you, and not with the rest of us here. Jason learned that lesson in Tibet."

"Duck's right, Howard."

Howard studied his lollipop, then sighed. "The scourge of the universe is preparing to eradicate the human race, our new ally is collapsing into anarchy, our old allies are killing each other, our fleet is running out of gas, and our only fortress is a rock we can't improve."

The Duck sat with his elbows on his knees, chin cupped in his hands. "Thanks for cheering me up."

Outside, the muffled bells rang in the dark. Howard said, "Well, I hear the funeral will be a show. Nobody on Bren would miss it."

The Duck sat up straight, cocked his head, and stared at the tapestries hung on the parlor's distant wall. "There is that."

THIRTY-ONE

THE STATE FUNERAL of Marenna the Fourth was the first of its magnitude in nearly a century, but the royal household took it in stride. The trappings and protocols would replicate those for her mother's funeral, and those for the funerals of every sovereign of Marin for two thousand years. But the Clans cremate their dead, and the timber for the royal pyre, which would resemble a small Egyptian pyramid, had to be gathered. And the dignitaries needed time to travel to Marinus.

So, it was a cool, cloudy morning a week after Bassin's mother died that she would finally ascend to heaven as oily smoke. I stood in the second row of the halted cortège, behind the royal bier.

The royal bier was a gilded wagon with ten-foot tall, jewel encrusted wheels that had borne every monarch's remains for a thousand years. The route never varied, from the Summer Palace, three miles down the Grand Boulevard of Marinus, lined today with four million mourners, to the royal pyre.

The first row of walking mourners behind the bier was

reserved for family, which, because Marenna had outlived so many people, was Bassin.

The second row was heads of state. By skullduggery, that included me, instead of the Duck's boss, who got bumped back to row four.

Behind the dignitaries would march the Palace Household Guard, followed by striped-pants Halberdiers, bands dismounted and mounted, artillery, cavalry, infantry, militia, police and firemen, game wardens, child ballerinas, then the navy. I kind of liked that last part.

As a big wheel, I was full-dressed out like Captain Hook, down to my sword and sash. But in that second row I looked like a Cub Scout.

The Chief of the Council of Headmen of the Hundred Encampments of the Tassini wore a pavement-length, hooded purple cloak that matched the indigo tint of his face and hands.

His sword's scabbard and belt weren't encrusted with ordinary jewels, but with Cavorite Stones the size of walnuts. Raw, Stone Hills meteoric Cavorite doesn't eat gravity, though a Stone is as light as a ping pong ball. A Stone is a translucent, insulating rind that this universe grows around a stray sliver of a universe next door. The sliver isn't matter, at least not as matter exists in the four dimensions of this universe. Harkening back to Howard Hibble's visualization of this universe as one sheet of newspaper, Cavorite is a piece of the preceding page that lays up against this page, and they both got balled up together.

Physics aside, even one Stone glows red, so the Tassini Chief looked like a neon beer sign walking.

Yes, even heads of states at war with Marin attended,

under truce. The Casuni and the Tassini shared a sovereign with Marin the way Canada and Australia shared a sovereign with England. But less chummy.

"May the Bitch burn in hell for eternity!" Casus, ruler of the Casuni, bent toward me and whispered, so close that I could smell the groundfruit crumbs in his black beard. Casus was nearly as tall, nearly as broad, and half as hairy, as a grizzly.

I whispered back, "We wouldn't have won the war without her, Casus."

Casus grinned, and slapped my back so hard that I bounced off the Tassini Headman, who stumbled, then scowled at both of us.

Casus said, "Now, there was a war! When the Emerald River runs with your enemy's blood, you know it's going to be a good day!" He wore a gold helmet with a nose guard, and a stiff, red-plumed crest on its centerline. His metal breastplate and gauntlets matched his helmet, and his breeches, cape, and gold-spurred boots were black. His four pistol holsters, two on his belt and two at his pectorals, were empty in deference to the occasion, but he wore a sword as broad as a canoe paddle.

The Queen's cold, uncasketed body lay atop the bier, elevated on a solid silver catafalque, dressed in a silver tiara, and a gown of feathers, each hammered from silver. Bassin's mother, who in life might have weighed a hundred pounds after dessert, couldn't have stood in the dress.

A whip cracked, and the bier inched forward, then began to roll smoothly on the Queen's final, three-mile journey, "the Miles," as it was called. For all its gold and silver, the bier's mass scarcely fazed the team that pulled it.

A strock looks a lot like a Styracosaur, which looks like a size quintuple-x rhino, with a frill of multiple, rear-pointing horns, as though it were wearing one of those in-dian-chief headdresses. Marini farmers that plow behind strocks file down their nose horn and frill horns, because a bull's neck muscles are so strong that its horn can punch through an armored wagon.

The six matched pairs of ebony bull strocks that drew the queen's bier needed all those neck muscles. The face, frill, and curving horns of each bull were masked behind a concave gold helmet, piped in silver, that must have out-weighed a brick pallette.

Behind us, the massed bands began a dirge.

As we walked, Casus said to me, "I suppose you're right about her. I should pull the long face today. But the truth? I'd dance the Miles barefoot."

Because the Clans cremated their dead, their language had no idiom for dancing on someone's grave.

Casus had stated the equivalent Casuni idiom. We didn't all walk directly behind the royal bier. We all walked be-hind, but fifteen feet to the right of, the bier. A dozen adult strock take in nearly three tons of water and dietary fiber every day. The thrust of the idiom was that you'd have to be really, really happy that someone was dead to walk directly behind their bier barefoot for three miles.

The Duck had bribed the cortège director to diagram me lined up next to Casus, because Casus and I had an-other of those combat-bonded personal relationships that diplomats love to leverage. Walking three miles with the commander of Marin's enemy was a SNO, which was a diplomatic idiom, unrelated to poop. A Serendipitous Negotiation Opportunity was one created without investment of negotiating capital. Neither side had to yield about the shape of the negotiating table, or give in by requesting the meeting. The parties, apparently thrown together by circumstance, just talked. Women understood this technique since the first one dropped her handkerchief. It took men four years at Harvard to figure it out.

As we walked, me taking two steps to Casus' one, I asked, "If the Slug war was good, why is this war bad?"

"We gain nothing from it. We can't eat the Stones we capture. We can't sell them to you, because the Marini control the ports."

"Then why did you start it?"

"The Bitch," he darted his eyes around, then continued, "—God praise her memory, and so forth—unilaterally cut our take by eight percent."

"Do you know why?"

"Some lie about fuel surcharge."

I closed my eyes and sighed. Howard. "Did you talk to her about it?"

"I said when the last war ended that I'd talk to her again if we met in hell. Jason, I have lost sons in this war."

I patted his forearm, but not too hard. Casus grieved for every son he had lost. But he would have been devastated if any of them chose a low-mortality profession, say, retail, instead of pillaging. And at last count he had sired over six hundred of them.

Along the route, a weeping Marini freewoman in housemaid's robes broke from the crowd, and hurled a clothes iron at Casus. "That's for my son! Burn in hell, you ogre!"

The iron bounced off Casus' breastplate like a pebble, and he stared back over his shoulder as guards wrestled the woman to the pavement.

The rest of the Miles passed uneventfully. Women held infants above their heads, to witness the Queen's passage. Men wept. The bier's wheels creaked.

Isolated raindrops plocked the Boulevard's cobbles as the bier halted at the stair that stretched up the royal pyre.

It took twenty of the Queen's Household Guard thirty minutes to march the Queen's silver catafalque up the two hundred steps to the pyre's apex.

Bassin, bareheaded, in black armor, followed them with a lit, upraised torch. Marini artificial limbs were more torture implements than they were modern organic pros- thetics, but after three miles on only one real leg, Bassin betrayed neither a limp nor a twitch of discomfort.

Casus said, "Her son's as tough as she was. He could almost pass for Casuni."

"Would you talk to *him* then?"

"About what?"

"Patching up the alliance. You've lost sons. The Marini and the Tassini have lost sons. My world and yours could lose more than that if the Slugs return. So at least talk, that's all I'm suggesting."

The pallbearers rested Her Majesty atop the pyre, then retreated, and left Bassin alone above the throng. He raised the torch, and the crowd replied to the gesture, speaking with one voice the last toast made at all Clan funerals, "May paradise spare you from allies!"

Bassin knelt, lit the kindling beneath the catafalque, then returned down the stairway, as the flames spread, and the temperature soared until molten silver coursed down troughs that bordered the stairway alongside him.

The thundering, growing fire seared my cheeks, as Casus shrugged. "In paradise, we need no allies. But apparently I'm going to hell."

THIRTY-TWO

THAT EVENING, I cornered the Duck at the wake, an intimate gathering for six thousand, held in the Summer Palace inner court. The skies had cleared, and Bren's second moon, the red one, sped north to south above us. It was a pretty thing, but I never could understand why Howard spent so much time studying it. It didn't even affect the tides, the way a proper moon should.

"It was the Spooks' goddam fuel surcharge!"

"What?"

"That's what set Casus off."

The Duck grimaced, and pumped his fist. "Damn! How could we have known?"

"You could have asked him. Duck, all diplomats do is talk to each other."

"Jason, the Casuni have no diplomats. They have no embassy. Casus lives in a yurt and follows migrating dinosaurs. We would have had to retask an overhead 'Bot just to find him."

A servant passed us silver mead goblets. I sipped, then said, "Anyway, he's willing to talk to Bassin."

The Duck smiled, and tinged his goblet against mine.

"I think we can end this war cheap. We reverse the surcharge—"

"That just gets Casus back to where he was. He's lost sons."

The Duck raised his palm. "Let me finish. If we strip the weapons systems off one Kodiak, we can make Casus a present of it, without exceeding our authority."

I bugged my eyes. "A cheap bribe?"

The Duck frowned so hard that his lips made a beak. "A gesture of respect and shared humanity. In 1945, Roosevelt made the King of Saudi Arabia a present of an airliner and Roosevelt's spare wheelchair. The 'special relationship' between the U.S. and Saudi Arabia held into this century. Would the death of even one more parent's son be cheaper?"

Five weeks later, Howard, Ord, the Duck, and I watched from our Consulate's roof, as a transport carrying the first Cavorite cargo to leave Bren in months lifted off.

The Duck turned to a holo gen, and keyed up a real-time overhead image with audio, from a TOT operating over the Casuni Highlands. Snow patched the grassland, and a herd of thousands of grazing duckbills drifted across the rolling landscape.

As we watched, duckbills at the herd margin raised their heads, and stared in the direction of distant thunder. They began to trot, then the herd stampeded, a living tsunami that shook the ground.

A Kodiak, painted in purple and yellow stripes, with a sawed off stub protruding from the turret's cannon housing, fishtailed across the plain at fifty miles per hour. It roared toward the stampeding herd, trailing a dust plume behind its skirting. Waist deep in the commander's hatch atop the turret, his hands gripping the bare gun mount ring, swayed Casus. He wore tanker's goggles under his plumed helmet, and his beard and cape snapped in the slipstream. The Kodiak roared in among the duckbills, spun doughnuts, and they scattered, honking. Casus threw his head back, and yodeled.

Ord stood with his arms crossed, shaking his head.

I smiled at him. "Not a regulation paint job, is it, Sergeant Major?"

"Hardly, sir. But I know many dead men who would love to see it." Ord clapped the Duck on the shoulder. "Peace well made, Mr. Muscovy."

The Duck and I walked to the brick wall that rimmed the Consulate roof, rested our forearms on its cool, tile rail, and looked out across the city. The Summer Palace, granite pink and spired, loomed to our left, the onion towers of the Great Library rose to our right. The four-story Consulate nestled among stuccoed villas of the wealthy, amid tree-lined streets.

We peered down into the gardened courtyards of two villas, side by side. The Duck pointed at an orange pennant, hung alongside the servant's entrance of the left-hand villa. "Well, at least one slaveholder agrees with Bassin."

Marin's new monarch had embraced peace with the Casuni and Tassini for its own sake, but also to free his nation to remake itself. However, change is hard, especially change for the better.

Marini, Casuni, and even Tassini, custom had always allowed an owner to emancipate a slave. Longevity in service, acts of heroism, even the declining ability of the owner to support his household, were common reasons.

And there was a small class of freemen and freewomen who filled similar jobs to those slaves held, mostly doing laundry.

Bassin the First had the absolute power to simply abolish slavery. But the vile thread of man owned by man had been woven into the Clans' fabric for millennia. By comparison, the United States' Emancipation Proclamation after "only" a few hundred years of slavery had been overdue, but its aftermath hadn't exactly been smooth sailing. Bassin the First was wise enough to take it slow, because Bassin the Assassinated couldn't accomplish much.

The first token of Bassin's administration was to encourage slave holders to replace their slaves by hiring freemen and freewomen. An orange pennant by the door meant the household was hiring. We could see a hundred villas. We saw one pennant.

In each courtyard below us a robed gardener bent, tending flowers. The man on the right wore the yellow bracelet of indenture. The man on the left didn't. He was a freeman. Both lived with their families in modest quarters behind the big house. Both sweated dawn to dark. Both were paid less in a month than their master or boss paid for wine in a week.

The Duck said, "You could argue there's no practical difference."

"You wouldn't. I wouldn't. Bassin wouldn't."

"Then tomorrow should go great."

THIRTY-THREE

THE NEXT DAY, Bassin became the first Clansman to see his planet from space, unless you counted his ancestors, who the Slugs had brought to Bren from Earth as slaves thirty thousand years before.

Marini were more worldly than a plains nomad like Casus, but getting an average Marini citizen to climb into a claustrophobic tin box that fell straight up would have resembled kidnapping. Bassin wasn't average.

He rapped his knuckles against the four-inch thick quartz window beside his seat, then traced the joining between it and the hull's plating. "The pressure differential is that great?"

The Loadmaster nodded, then leaned across Bassin, and pointed to the planet four hundred miles below. "You can make out Marinus, below. Where the cloud breaks, and the river joins the coast, sir. Your Highness."

The transport slid cleanly into the empty bay it had left on *Ike*. The swabbies fitted Bassin with complimentary blue coveralls, with "H.M. Bassin I" sewn above the breast pocket, and a red baseball cap with an *MCC-3 D.D. Eisenhower* patch on the peak. Baseball was hardly the only thing new to Bassin here, but he sponged up every detail. *Ike*'s skipper, himself, gave Bassin a tour, then the new king sat together with Howard, the Duck, and me in *Ike*'s wardroom.

Duck pitched the general idea, which was that Marin should want to move toward the more advanced reality that the *Eisenhower* represented. Then the Duck pitched the specific idea that, with Bassin's nation unexpectedly at peace thanks to us, Bren could and should commit its considerable non-slave civil engineering capacity to Mousetrap. Of course, our Spooks bungled Bren into the war in the first place, but the Duck skipped over that.

Bassin gazed at the bulkheads. "The Stones move this mass?"

Howard splayed his fingers, and waggled his hand, palm down. "More or less. They allow gravity to move it."

Bassin made a screwing motion, turning his hand. "As an opened valve allows gravity to empty a canal lock's water."

Bassin saw the universe as a civil engineering project, which was what we were counting on. He said, "This Mousetrap. We would have the opportunity to sculpt an entire world."

When Bassin said "we," the Duck beamed.

All I had to do was, as Nat Cobb would say, keep my pie hole shut. Instead, I cleared my throat. "Bassin, building the Locks on the Marin may have been difficult. You need to understand, this may be impossible."

"When I took up the queen's commission as a colonel of engineers, I learned a saying. 'The difficult we do immediately. The impossible takes a little longer.'"

Ord smiled at me. Combat engineers thought alike.

Navy Seabees a starship flight away lived by the same slogan.

Bassin shook his head, smiling. "You really can show us how to cut rock with knives of light?"

Howard said, "The moonlet's mostly iron and nickel, not precisely rock. But, yes, we can cut rock with light beams. Much of the tunneling will be labor intensive."

Men still died digging sewers under Newark. Carving the Pearl Harbor of space in vacuum, light years from anybody's home, before the scourge of the universe arrived on the doorstep, was going to be more than "labor intensive." Yet Bassin was not just going our way, he was racing ahead of us, like a rich kid chasing new tinker toys.

Bassin watched me frown. "Your concern touches me, my friend. But Jason, I'm a responsible adult. I understand the undertaking, and what it means for my nation. Don't worry that you've cheated some bumpkin for the price of a baseboard cap."

I said, "You don't understand everything. And will the kids in the pits understand when outside their gloves the temperature is just above absolute zero? Will they understand when one of Howard's light knives beheads a friend?"

The Duck's eyes burned into me, and I clamped my jaw shut.

Bassin eyed the ribbons on my chest. "Will Sergeant Ord tell me you knew every single thing that those would cost when *you* enlisted? Jason, I find myself blessed with an unexpected peace, and cursed with an unalterable social contract. This project will provide work for freemen and freewomen who aspire to more than washing rich men's clothing. Those who succeed in this adventure will return with self-respect and the gratitude of their society. They will create the core of what your books call a middle class. Owners who emancipate enlistees will be paid for it. Emancipations will rise. Your Mousetrap lets me begin to cut a cancer from Marin. If I'm doing you a service, you're doing me one, too."

I turned to the Duck, and raised my palms. "Fine. Howard's rathole is now the Peace Corps. All I care about is we get it done before the Slugs come back."

Whump. Whump. Whump. Ike shook enough that coffee in Bassin's decaled souvenir cup sloshed.

He frowned. "What's that?"

The Human Union couldn't defend all the Outworlds. But it sure as hell could shuffle the fleet so that one locked and loaded cruiser was at all times orbiting above the sole source of propulsion-grade Cavorite known to mankind.

Therefore, every moment that we talked, a Starfire simmered in each of the three launch bays designated as *Ike*'s Hot Bays. Each fighter was fueled, armed, locked on the launch rails, and crewed by a pilot and systems officer so strap-down ready that they had to pee into bags.

"Early bird special." Ord frowned, too. "All three launched at once."

There was a rap on the wardroom hatch, but before we said anything, it opened, and a pop-eyed ensign poked his head in. "Sirs? The Captain sends his compliments. He requests that I escort you all to join him on the bridge."

I was already out of my chair, but Ord beat me to the open hatch, with Bassin, the Duck, and Howard following in our wake.

The ensign race-walked ahead of us, as speakers in the

passage ceiling oogahed general quarters. Three ratings dashed toward us, slowed, scooted sideways around us, then dashed aft. One kid looked back over his shoulder at Bassin.

The captain wanted the strangers on his ship where he could see them, not wandering around distracting his crew, when things got hairy. Which evidently they had.

THIRTY-FOUR

ALONGSIDE THE HATCH that opened onto the bridge, a bosun fingered the little electronic whistle that hung around his neck. It squealed, then he announced, "Attention on deck! Visitors are on the Bridge!"

Fifty feet away, at the opposite end of the *Eisenhower*'s red-lit bridge, between two facing rows of swabbies bent over control consoles, the captain stood, his back to us, arms folded. He watched the floor-to-ceiling, wall-to-wall forward display.

The red light was a hangover from the days when it was thought to preserve night vision, in case the crew had to step off the Bridge, into the salt night air, or at least the bathroom. The whistle was even older. Navies, wet or vacuum, clung to their traditions. Churchill understated when he said those traditions were limited to rum, sodomy, and the lash.

The captain turned a shoulder in response to the bosun's pipe, saw us, then waved us to him, through the aisle between the consoles.

"What you got, Jimmy?" I asked.

A flashing red dot near the screen's top crawled toward

a solid green dot in the screen's center. Three flashing green dots, labeled EB 1, 2, and 3 crawled away from the solid one, toward the red one, but so slowly by comparison that they scarcely seemed to move.

"Inbound bogey winked as we rounded. We popped the early birds. Sorry to disturb your meeting."

Behind me, Ord whispered to Bassin, "As this ship circled Bren, an unknown approaching object appeared, no longer obscured from view by the planet's mass. That's the red dot. The three moving green dots are smaller ships we've launched—those launches were the lurches you felt—to investigate, and defend us if necessary."

Bassin nodded.

I asked, "Trash?"

The captain shook his head. "Point six."

Ord whispered, "The object is traveling too fast to be a shooting star or similar natural object. Almost two thirds as fast as the flash from a lightning bolt."

I said, "Too slow for a Viper. Trolls crawl, and there'd be a spread."

"Yep."

Ord said, "The object is moving too slowly to be a particularly destructive type of high-velocity Pseudocephalopod projectile. And if the object were a Pseudocephalopod invasion transport, it would be moving much slower than this ship, and it would have deployed protective escort vessels ahead of it."

I asked, "Spoofing?"

The captain pointed at a large red set of numerals in the screen's lower right, spinning down toward zero, then shrugged. "Closure in two."

Ord again. "Two minutes from now, the distance between the first of our small investigating ships and the approaching object will have closed enough that the small ship can determine whether the object is a Pseudocephalopod vessel, imitating the speed and movement pattern of a cruiser like this one."

Bassin asked, "What if it is an enemy warship?"

I faced Bassin. "Based on our historical performance versus the Slugs, your reign will be very short."

THIRTY-FIVE

THE DUCK WHISPERED over my shoulder, "Can we get His Majesty into a downbound transport?"

I shook my head. "First thing I thought of. The three hot birds were Starfires. Fine in space, but bricks land better. All the other bays will have Starfires loaded, too, by now."

Whether it was a flaw, or a deliberate pistol at the troops' back, a cruiser's design forced its captain to choose early whether to stand and fight, or to man the lifeboats. Not that it mattered. Jimmy Wethers was a gunfighter, not a lifeboat coxswain.

"That Scorpion thing I heard about would come in handy," said the Duck.

Not so long ago I had been watching my godson fly rings around Paris. Now I was watching a gunfight that might kill me.

The countdown timer reached zero.

The Bridge fell so silent that I thought I could hear hearts beating. In addition to my own, which seemed to boom.

The captain asked a swabbie who sat at a console, shoulders scrunched, "Well?"

"Pings are away, sir. Waiting."

The timer started counting up, now, in red numerals. It reached plus fifty seconds when the tight shouldered swabbie pressed his earpiece with his fingers, and held it.

The swabbie's head tilted back, and he exhaled. Then he said, "It's *Emerald River*, sir."

"You're sure?"

"It's Mean Green alright, Captain. Early One pinged her twice."

The captain sighed, then he looked up at the ceiling and spoke to nobody. "What the hell are they doing here? And wouldn't it have been nice to let us know they were coming?"

The swabbie, who didn't seem to know a rhetorical question when he heard one, said, "I guess you can ask Admiral Ozawa that yourself, sir, in a couple hours."

I looked around at Howard. As usual in situations like this, he looked away.

THIRTY-SIX

WE REMAINED ABOARD *Ike* so Bassin and the Duck could enjoy the show from the observation blister, as the three Early Bird Starfires returned, spun a few vacubatics to burn off fuel, then snuggled back into their launch bays. Howard waxed eloquent about the red moon, its uniqueness as a polar-orbiting intragalactic stranger, and any other irrelevant curiosity that might divert attention from what he knew about *Emerald River*'s unannounced appearance.

But Mean Green was enough of a distraction all by herself. *Emerald River* was the newest of the new *Bastogne*-class cruisers, and the only one named for a military victory that occurred *off* Earth. And on Bassin's planet, to boot.

Nickname aside, she wasn't green, but reflective white, which made her look as big as Monaco, with both Bren's white moon and its red one inching, at right angles to one another, across the blackness behind her. Bren spun by, slow and blue beneath us, but Mean Green hung dead still, relative to *Ike*, and a safe two miles away. It normally took hours for cruisers to match orbits, but Mean Green had a woman driver who could parallel park.

We swam down from the blister, which was a bubble on *Ike*'s prow, at the zero gee centerline. Then we made our way back to rotational gravity, and then to a launch bay that was being cleared to receive a transport from Mean Green. Ord towed Bassin, and I towed the Duck. Some people puke their first time swimming in zero gee, but they both grinned like kids in the baby pool.

When we reached the wardroom again, I pulled Howard aside by the elbow, and pressed him against the bulkhead with my forearm across his chest. "What the hell is going on, Howard?"

"I don't know. Honest."

I rolled my eyes. Howard plus honest created an oxymoron. "But you suspect."

"There was some talk before we left Washington." He eyed the far hatch like a roach spotting a baseboard. "Shouldn't we catch up with the others?"

I pressed my forearm harder against his chest. "Howard, I have ways of making you talk. Just tell me it isn't Slugs."

"Worse. It's politicians."

THIRTY-SEVEN

———

TWENTY MINUTES AFTER Howard and I rejoined our group in *Ike*'s cleared receiving bay, the inner bay doors slid open, and *Emerald River*'s transport hissed down the rails and locked. The transport had slid up in *Ike*'s shadow, so it was cold enough that frost had condensed on its hull, and cracked off when its hatch opened.

Twenty-one passengers wearing VIP coveralls wobble-kneed out of the hatch onto the receiving platform. Twenty of them started to mince one at a time down the thirty-foot left-hand ladder, toward the deck.

The twenty-first passenger swung onto the right-hand ladder, then straddled the ladder rails with her feet along their outboard sides, and slid the thirty feet to the deck, swabbie style, like a firefighter down a pole. When she touched the deck, she turned, grinned at me, and said, "It's like riding a bike." Munchkin hugged me, then pulled back. "Aren't you surprised?"

"Almost." Howard had told me a half hour before, in the wardroom, under threat of an Indian burn, that a Joint House-Senate Task Force, a blue ribbon panel, had been charged to investigate "certain undifferentiated and/or restricted line items" in the Defense Department budget. In other words, they were going to pry up or crawl under the loose floorboards, rocks, and mattresses beneath which Howard hid the Spook money.

The rest of the delegation trickled onto the bay floor-plates, and got introduced around.

Every single one was a household-word–famous former senator, representative, or governor. Former because not even a senior sitting senator can take as much time off as a boondoogle like this "fact-finding mission" would take. And not even famous politicians turn down the equivalent of a taxpayer-financed round-the-world cruise that included live tyrannosaurs.

Munchkin and I stood aside together while the legislators got presented to Bassin.

I whispered to her, "They all look sick. The transport ride was only two miles."

"They didn't expect the local monarch to meet their plane. This was supposed to be a surprise inspection. They're worried somebody leaked."

"Oh, it was a surprise. Jimmy Wethers launched three hot birds. Mimi knows better than to risk a friendly fire incident."

Munchkin widened her eyes, and poked my belly. "You used hot, Mimi, and friendly within ten words. That's Freudian."

"Don't start."

The flight deck hatch opened, and the pilot swung onto the ladder, then slid down like Munchkin had. Mimi was a rear admiral, so she had to salute me first. Then she knuckle-bumped with former Congresswoman Munchkin. Fighter jocks and machine gunners don't hug and kiss the air.

I began with a charming pleasantry. "Jimmy Wethers launched three hot birds. Are you on dumb pills?"

Mimi tugged off her pilot's helmet and ran fingers through her hair. The helmet had pinched her ears so they looked like delicate pink sea shells. She said, "My orders were run dark 'til we got pinged. Now I've been on the radio with Jimmy, and he understands." She snorted. "Orders. Do Spooks even bother with those?"

Munchkin grabbed my elbow, and said, "Oh-kay. Jason, come with me and meet the Chairman."

As Munchkin steered me away, I hissed to her, "I'm no goddam Spook. What's that woman's problem?"

"Maybe it was you accusing her of stupidity bad enough to get her relieved of her command." We approached a tan, trim, familiar figure, and Munchkin whispered, "This time, don't be so charming."

Thomas Warden had gotten elected governor of New York by jailing white collar crooks. We shook hands, as Warden said, "We don't want to get in your way, General. But we will have to insist that you suspend whatever you're doing for the duration of our investigation."

"What do you think we're doing?"

He smiled, and slapped my shoulder. "If I knew, I wouldn't have to investigate, would I?"

"How long?"

"If you demonstrate absolute candor and cooperation, we should be out of your hair in three months."

I shook my head. "Sir, I don't think—"

"Then we write our draft report, Congress considers it . . . you're back in business in two, three years." He smiled again. "Unless you're in Leavenworth."

I turned to Munchkin, and pointed at the man. "Does he know—"

The chairman stopped smiling. "I know misappropriation of government funds is a felony. So's suborning human rights violations. And this panel is empowered to detain any witness or hold him in contempt." He smiled again. "Not that we need those powers with you and Colonel Hibble." He looked around the bay, then walked over to look at the Starfire on the other side of the revolver. "I've never seen one of these in person."

I took Munchkin's elbow, jerked my thumb at Warden, and whispered, "And you say *I'm* not charming? Is Warden a fool?"

"Jason, if he's a fool, he's not a lonely one. In case you didn't notice, Congress has given him one tenth of the Fleet, just to investigate Howard. The Spook budget exceeds Portugal's, but Congress outside of the Defense, Intelligence, and Appropriations Committees is kept in the dark about it."

I sighed. Secret defense projects' budgets had been buried in innocuous-looking budget line items at least since the A-bomb was identified as the Manhattan Sewer District. Howard's creative accounting made the stealth fighter budget look like a paper airplane, but rank-and-file congresspersons could hardly claim shock to learn that such things were going on.

Munchkin said, "The non-defense members of Congress don't question the Black Ops budget. To a point. But you've been coddling slave traders and fomenting anarchy, and that's just the stuff people know about. Be glad Howard has one lousy friend on this panel."

"Howard's future is the least of the problem. That's

the reason you joined this fiasco? So we have one lousy friend?"

"It's not a fiasco. Secrecy is un-American."

I rolled my eyes. "Were the Manhattan Project, D-Day, and the stealth fighter un-American? And if you say the only reason you joined this panel is to expose secrets, you're lying."

Munchkin crossed her arms, looked away, then exhaled.

We both knew rotational gravity made her barf. Only one thing would get her back into space.

She said, "I miss Jude so much my gut has been aching for a month." She looked around the emptying bay and her forehead creased. "Where is he?"

We downshipped that evening, I got Munchkin tanked on Casuni mead, then I told her that, after all she had put herself through, her baby was still light years away. She still cried until the sun rose.

THIRTY-EIGHT

FOR THE FIRST MONTH, the Duck and Howard buried the inquiry panel under tourism. The panelists got holo'ed sitting on duckbills, traveled with caravans across the Highlands to see Cavorite come out of the ground in the Stone Hills, sailed the Marin to the falls, and watched scouts trick-ride the Tassin dunes on wobbleheads. They visited the Millennium Wall, got snorted at by chained wronks, and shopped the bazaars of Marinus on Bassin's tab. They got wined and dined on His Majesty's Royal Barge, flown to the Emerald River battlefield, and over the North Pole.

Meanwhile, Bassin raised a pick-and-shovel army of freemen, freewomen, and newly emancipated slaves, for which Ord developed and oversaw modern combat engineering training.

Eventually, Howard and the Duck exhausted the sideshows, and hearings commenced in the Rotunda of the Great Library. The Marini love their domed ceilings, and you could punt a football without scuffing the Rotunda's.

After two months of hearings, I stood alongside Howard, as we looked down from the Rotunda's second-floor balcony, leaning on its gilt balustrade. Through windows opposite us, we could see the Summer Palace, but the panelists down on the Rotunda's floor couldn't. Every hour and twenty minutes, a transport from the *Eisenhower* lifted off from the palace Courtyard. Ten minutes after each lift-off, another transport feathered in and landed, replacing its shipmate.

The twenty-one panelists sat around the rim of a crescent-moon table, which surrounded a witness table.

The Duck was the last witness.

Questioning had begun in the morning, from the panelist at the crescent's left tip, and proceeded counterclockwise. As the afternoon sun threw shadows across the Rotunda, questioning wound down to the panelist at the right tip, a chubby, pale former Representative who apparently did her hair with a grenade. She ran her finger across a line on her chipboard. "One last thing. Two hundred seventy-six Kodiaks were recovered from Tressel. Two hundred seventy-five were inventoried when we arrived aboard the *Eisenhower.*"

The panel had actually been taken on tour and shown the Kodiaks in the *Ike*'s centerline bay immediately, on the day they arrived. That was partly to demonstrate absolute candor and cooperation, and mostly because Howard didn't have a sock drawer big enough to hide the Afrika Korps.

The Duck, hands folded in front of him, leaned toward the witness table stenobot. "Armament was stripped off one unit. It was transferred to the Department of Agriculture's books because it was appropriated for agricultural demonstration, Congresswoman."

"What kind of agriculture?"

"Animal husbandry. Livestock herding."

A gray-headed former senator paused, then peered over his turn of the century bifocals. "That's a big sheepdog, Mr. Muscovy."

"They're big sheep, Senator."

The congressperson with exploded hair tapped her chipboard's keys as she paged ahead. Then she leaned forward, past the gray-headed senator, and turned to Thomas Warden, six seats down. "Nothing further for this witness."

The chairman looked left, then right. "The panel will take this matter under advisement, and prepare its draft report during its return voyage." He rapped his gavel. "We stand adjourned."

I leaned toward Howard and whispered, "If we go through with this, and we live, we'll both spend the rest of our lives in Leavenworth."

He shrugged. "If we don't, there won't be a Leavenworth."

THIRTY-NINE

───────

AT THE MOMENT that the chairman dropped his gavel, across town, on the other side of Marinus, the last of two hundred seventy-six Kodiaks, downshipped from the centerline bay of the *Eisenhower*, was towed into dead storage in the old royal laundries beneath the Summer Palace.

At the same moment, four hundred miles overhead, the fortieth of forty-one Marini boring machines crash-built to royal specifications drawn by Howard and Ord was lashed into place in *Ike*'s vacated centerline bay. Thirty thousand Marini combat engineer volunteers were already packed into the rest of the bay, camping like a Boy Scout Jamboree, and into billet space designed to accommodate a ten-thousand soldier embarked infantry division. Quarters would be cramped, but Mousetrap was just one Jump away.

FORTY

THAT NIGHT, Bassin hosted a dinner party in the Summer Palace Courtyard to bid farewell to the Task Force, who the next morning would reboard the *Emerald River* for the voyage back to Earth. There they would write a report to Congress, and, in a year or two, Congress would reauthorize Howard to do most of what he had been up to. They thought.

If they, and the thousand other guests, had realized that a hundred feet below the woven carpets where they stood was a panzer division parking garage, the evening's ambiance might have differed.

Most people's idea of a dinner party on Bren is a duck-bill haunch as big as a crocodile spitted above a bonfire, surrounded by drunken ogres, or by indigo-faced nomads smoking janga in water pipes. National Geographic viewership increases for Plains Clan holos. The Marini are too, well, normal.

To dine with the Marini monarch was more like an outdoor reception in the south of France. The chamber music instruments sounded woodier, the canapés were reptilian, the torches that flickered on the granite battlements were fueled by sauropod tallow, and two crescent moons sailed above them, but the panelists seemed so at home that most of them wore black tie or evening gown.

Governor Warden, all tux and teeth, stood near a carved gold fountain as I approached. He raised his silver wine flute, toasted us, and grinned like a rube.

On his home turf, with staff, Warden, or any of the other panelists, would have tumbled to our amateur coup in hours. But three hundred light years from home, disoriented by surroundings so alien that even the moons in the night sky added up wrong, Howard, the Duck, and I were poised to get away with it.

Warden spread his arms. "Hah? Did I keep my promise to be out of your hair in three months?"

"So can't we just go back to work, Tom?"

"Jason, that's not my decision. And I can't say there were *no* problems. But I promise you this." He pointed with one finger that he unwrapped from the stem of his glass. "I'll get Colonel Hibble's projects back to active status by the end of next year. If I have to beat down doors all over Washington."

By which time, if we waited on my new best friend, Tom, and Congress, the Slugs might be the ones beating down doors in Washington.

A late-arriving guest caught my eye as she whispered to the footman at the courtyard gate. He rapped his halberd on the pavement, then announced, "Rear Admiral Ozawa."

With *Ike* already on guard above Bren, *Emerald River* had been too valuable a chess piece to leave idling in orbit. As soon as *Emerald River* had dropped off Warden's panel, she had departed Bren, laden with Cavorite,

Casuni mead, and a National Geographic holo crew just back from the boonies, for Earth.

Emerald River's absence had been critical to our little plot, because her crew couldn't have missed the excess traffic to and from *Ike*. We counted on Mimi to be dead-on schedule, always a safe bet, and not return until today.

I'm a sucker for a woman in uniform anyway, but in dress whites, by torchlight, Mimi looked to me like Cinderella with medals.

As Mimi joined us, Warden smiled at her. "Our ride home. Right on time, Admiral."

She smiled at him, and inclined her head. "My crew tells me you're on schedule, too."

"Jason's cooperation had a lot to do with that."

Mimi stared at me, always a pulse-raising event, and smiled longer than conversational politeness demanded. "I can just imagine."

Deep in my brain, a tiny klaxon hooted, which I mistook for lust.

I turned back to Warden. Hoodwinking the Congress, no matter the justification, had kept me awake for months. I had to know. "Tom, hypothetically, what if, when you arrived, a guy like me had just blown you off. Carried on with what he was doing. You're just twenty-one civilians, months away from supervening authority."

Warden cocked his head. "Well, Jason, in the first place, then he wouldn't have been a guy like you."

A guilt pang pinched my gut. "Sure. But you must have come up against crooks who wouldn't back down."

He shrugged. "Plenty of 'em. Seriously? Well, we are just twenty-one politicians." He glanced over at Mimi.

"But I've got a *Bastogne*-class cruiser and I'm not afraid to use it."

"Of course, the crooks wouldn't have a good reason."

The old prosecutor stuck out his chin. "What reason could be good enough to break the law?"

I nodded. "That's what I thought you'd say."

The frizz-headed congresswoman who had questioned the Duck waved Warden to her conversation group. I sipped my wine, wondered when I had grown old enough and cynical enough to lie convincingly, then looked around for Mimi.

I spotted her fifty yards away, strolling alone beside the wall of the castle's main keep.

The castle rose above a rock knob so that it overlooked Marinus. It was, well, a guarded fortress, and so a perfect place to hide two hundred seventy-five large objects. The battlements were guarded, as were the various locked gates in the walls. The doors to the keep, the royal apartments, the kitchens, the royal library, the observatory, were not only locked but guarded by stone-faced Household Guards in polished armor.

However, the vast caverns beneath the castle, the cold, stone laundries, hadn't been used for a century. That was what made them a great place to squirrel away the Kodiaks. It also made them a place nobody cared about enough to guard, or to lock off. And if we had started now, somebody might have wondered why.

Mimi stopped in front of a plain, maid-sized archway in the stone wall. It didn't even have a door, much less a Household Guard. The opening was dark, but not so dark that I couldn't make out downward-curving stairs just beyond its opening.

Mimi glanced around at the crowd, and then, it seemed, stared at me for a blink. Then she stepped through the doorway, and disappeared, circling down into the dark.

My heart thumped, and I walked to the doorway, as fast as I could without drawing looks from guests or guards, peered into the gloom, and waited for my eyes to adjust.

FORTY-ONE

THE STAIRS WOUND down in a tight spiral, not pitch dark, but not light enough to spot Mimi's snow-white uniform. If it was there. I paused and listened for heel clicks on stone. Had she been wearing stilettos? What the hell *did* female dress-white shoes look like?

I heard nothing, except the distant drip of water onto floor cobbles.

With one hand along the cool, curved stone of the stairwell, I felt my way down. I counted steps as I went.

Maybe she was just having a look around. Maybe she was searching for the ladies' room. Maybe she just needed to adjust something. I had to stop and shake my head, to clear the image of Mimi hiking up her skirt to straighten a stocking.

No. Her smirk about me cooperating was no flirt. Maybe Jimmy Wethers ratted us out? Jimmy had been a junior rating aboard *Excalibur*, one of the handful of survivors. He didn't take chances where the Slugs were concerned. He had thrown in immediately. But would one cruiser commander keep secrets from another?

By my count of steps, I reached fifty feet below the

courtyard. The laundries were supposed to be down a hundred feet, but I really had no idea whether this stair even led to the laundry cavern. The Kodiaks had been hauled in through an old laundry wagon entrance I had never even seen.

My heart seemed to echo in the stairwell as I descended.

What if she knew? More probably, what if, for some reason she suspected, and at the bottom of these stairs her suspicions got confirmed?

Talk her out of it? Mimi flout authority? There had been the business with the Armada, but it was a different time and a different imperative.

No, Warden had a cruiser—Mimi's cruiser—and he wasn't afraid to use it.

If I couldn't talk her out of it, she was tough, but she was little. I could tie her up—I had to shake my head to clear away another image—until the panel left.

Abduct the captain of a capital ship and expect no one to notice? Ridiculous. And even if they didn't notice, the *Emerald River* wouldn't take the panel away without her.

The stairwell narrowed, and my sword scraped the rock wall.

I stopped. Then I snorted, and said out loud to myself, "Don't even think about it!"

But I did. I lost count of the steps.

It seemed like I had descended halfway to hell when dim light began to flicker off the wall stones.

I paused. Silence. Maybe I would get to the Kodiaks, and she wouldn't even be there. Maybe there had been a side passage and we had parted ways.

Fifteen steps farther down, my forward foot met rock

when it should have met emptiness, and a faint breeze stroked my cheek.

I shuffled forward down a brightening passageway that opened into rank after rank of low-ceilinged vaults, divided by hewn-stone columns thick enough to support a castle. Flickering torches on wall sconces lit the rows of still, armored hovertanks, which faded to burly shadows in the distance.

I blinked, even at the dim light, and saw no movement.

Then, fifty feet away, a figure stepped into view from behind a hovertank hull. Mimi had her back to me, as she stepped out of the shadows, and stared at the nearest Kodiak.

I stared down into the dimness, and realized that my hand rested on the pommel of my sword.

FORTY-TWO

"THE POINT OF the sword kills so personally," Mimi said, without turning around.

"What?"

She ran her hand along the Kodiak's armored flank. "Armored formations. The point of the sword. I never get closer to my enemy than lighted dots on a glass wall. You fight down in the mud. With these big, brutal things, and with rifles and bayonets and bloody fingers."

I stepped closer, as she turned and faced me.

She said, "But I thought infantry could track people. I've been waiting for ten minutes."

"What?"

"You saw me come down here."

"You knew these were here?"

"I knew one was, at least. I just took the first available down staircase, to confirm what I think's going on."

"And what do you think's going on?"

"When we unloaded cargo at home, we took on a load of enormous containers for us to bring back here. Unspecified supplies addressed to Xerxes Data Processing. Which has been a Spook cutout for years. I had a container opened. And what did we find but pieces of a disassembled Subterrene borer. Bren mines Cavorite, so fair enough. But the containers weren't to be down-shipped. The *Eisenhower* would send transports to tow the containers back to it. What was going on aboard *Ike* that Howard didn't want anybody from our ship to see?"

Her eyes shone in the torchlight. Mimi was adorable when she was curious, even if she was painting me into a corner.

She said, "So I got us back here a few hours early. Our downlooking optics caught the last Kodiak sliding off the *Ike*'s transport and onto a ramp leading under the Palace. Howard—with help from you and Muscovy—is playing an illegal shell game, just so the *Ike* can get the Mouse-trap project started right away, instead of waiting years for Warden to get clearance from Congress."

It raised my eyebrows a bit that Mimi knew about Mousetrap. "That's not enough reason to you—"

"Anybody who lies to Congress just to accelerate a construction project probably should go to jail."

"But—" Good secrets, like Mousetrap, which Mimi knew about, weren't enough justification. And the bad secret of the Weichsel incursion she didn't know about.

She nodded. "But since the Slugs greased Weichsel, anybody who slows down Mousetrap should be shot for treason against the human race."

My jaw dropped. "You know about Weichsel?"

"Otherwise you'd be in my brig already. And Howard, and probably Ord, and that duck-lipped State Department weasel Muscovy. So help me."

"How did you find out?"

"What cruiser do you think found that De Beers dredge?"

"Oh. So now you're ready to bend the rules, again?"

She said, "Weichsel changed the rules."

I felt myself relax, and Mimi breathed out. She said, "So the military business is finished, for the moment."

I frowned. Evidently some other business remained unfinished.

Then I pointed at her. "You were coming back from Weichsel when you picked us up from Bren last time. Carrying the news. That's why you were mad at me for being late."

"Partly. I've been mad at you for a long time, Jason."

"Since when?"

"Since you almost got yourself killed playing hero in that Troll."

It was an odd remark between professionals. "You were there, too, Mimi." I paused, then swung my hand around the cavern, at the hovertanks. "So what about the Kodiaks?"

She widened her eyes. "Kodiaks? All I see is a GI who looks good in a mess jacket."

My heart flickered. "Since when did you notice what I look like?"

She looked into my eyes. "Since the first time I saw you. Jason, after the Armada business, why didn't we . . ."

The evening was taking another unexpected turn. Apparently for the better.

I smiled, and stared down at my low cuts. "I don't know. Ever since then, Munchkin's been saying I should make a pass at you."

She stepped close enough to me to take my lapel,

where it covered my straight-hanging medal row, in her fingers. I looked down at them, and noticed her medal row. Female officers' medals don't hang straight, and *vive la différence*. In fact, hers were rising and falling like a soft wave.

She turned her face up to me as she stroked my lapel, and said, "But you haven't."

"You might smack me."

She smelled like flowers. Orchids, I think.

"I might not." She closed her eyes.

"Jason? Are you down here?" The voice, and clattering footsteps, echoed from the passage that led from the stairwell.

Mimi's eyes flashed open.

I sighed, and said, "What is it, Howard?"

FORTY-THREE

AS HOWARD SCURRIED out of the passage and into the torchlight, his whisper boomed in the chamber. "Thank God you got down here! It sounds like Mimi Ozawa has been sticking her—"

Mimi stepped in front of me, not so much to announce herself as to obscure developments south of my cummerbund from Howard. It was the kind of intuitive reflex that made her the pilot she was. However, matters there were returning to normal rapidly, anyway.

I waved my hand, palm down. "Pipe down! It's okay, Howard. Mimi's fine with it."

Howard stopped like he had walked into a plate glass window. "She is?"

Mimi said, "I thought this through, Howard. You could have told Warden the whole truth as soon as we got here. But what if he shut you down anyway? For all you knew, I'd have backed him up. We could tell Warden now, but if he still objects, what do I do? Throw him in my brig? The safest thing is to keep the panel in the dark. We need to get them back aboard *Emerald River* before you two amateurs screw up another lie."

I cocked my head. Nobody had ever accused Howard of being an amateur liar. Nor accused Mimi of being indecisive.

Mimi pointed toward the stairwell. "Let's go. I'll tell them everybody needs to return to the *Emerald River* right away I'll think of something. After all, it's my ship."

The night was young, and Mimi smelled wonderful. But I knew she was right.

I also knew that she was headed light years in one direction, while I was headed light years in another. And there was a war coming that neither of us might see the end of.

The three of us climbed the stairs back to the palace courtyard in the dark, with Howard in the lead. Halfway up, I felt her hand feel for mine. She squeezed it, all the rest of the way. Once, she raised my hand, so my fingers touched her cheek. It was moist. So was mine.

The next morning, the panel and Mimi, aboard the *Emerald River*, departed for Earth, minus one deserter. The day after that, the *Eisenhower* departed for Mousetrap, plus one stowaway.

FORTY-FOUR

ONE MONTH LATER, I floated in the *Eisenhower*'s observation blister again, along with two other people. Twenty hours earlier, *Ike* had completed the jump into the Mousetrap bottleneck.

Ahead of us, like a poppy seed circling a beach ball, Mousetrap orbited Leonidas, an orange gas ball of a planet as big, and as useless for a human base, as Jupiter. Leonidas was named for the Greek general who blocked two hundred thousand Persians with three hundred Spartans, at the bottleneck of Thermopylae in 480 BC.

"Planetoid" ill-describes Mousetrap because it sounds spherical and robust. "Moonlet" sounds too warm and fuzzy. Mousetrap was a nickel and iron lump, festooned in ice and rock leftovers from a Precambrian fender-bender with a comet. It looked like a twenty-mile long unshelled peanut that had rolled through curdled milk, though actually it had been captured by Leonidas' gravity, the way Mars captured its moons. Mousetrap rotated around its long axis like a top, so the peanut's ends formed Mousetrap's north and south poles.

Howard touched my uniform sleeve, as he pointed

at the big planet. "I had you in mind when I named it Leonidas."

"Nobody cheers up a commander like you, Howard." Earth history says Leonidas was a hero. However, at Thermopylae the Persians riddled him with arrows, beheaded him, then crucified his body.

I turned to the other person in the bubble, who was blissfully ignorant of Earth history. "But you're in command, Gustus."

After he died in 1232, Richard the Lionhearted, another hero, spent thirty-three years in purgatory. So said the Church of England, which Earth history presumes had inside info. Maybe Richard got hard time because he spent ninety-five percent of his reign crusading outside England.

Bassin was a hero, too, but he had a country to reform. So, unlike Richard the Lionhearted, Bassin delegated the crusade on Mousetrap to Gustus.

Gustus the Armorer was the ranking Marini on this project. The Marini equivalent of a Major General, he was pugnosed, with curly black hair, and wore gold wire spectacles. Gustus was more a logistical Henry Ford than a Leonidas.

He shook his head as he floated, clinging to a side rail. "That object is in command of us, until we change it."

Six months later, Gustus and his engineers had changed Mousetrap, or at least made a beginning.

The Spooks' vision for Mousetrap, which Gustus and the Marini were making into reality, wouldn't change its surface, much, at first. The massive mining machinery that Mimi's ship had handed off to the *Ike* would bore enormous tunnels through Mousetrap from north pole to south, so starships could float through them to be reinforced after jumps, like Electrovans through a car wash.

Then the engineers would core Mousetrap like an apple, from the inside out, and construct under the armor of its nickel-iron skin vast barracks and training grounds.

But Mousetrap wouldn't just shelter and nurture the Human Union's war machine, Mousetrap would build it.

At the turn of this century, Earth produced one thousand million metric tons of iron ore each year. At that rate, a single nickel-iron asteroid a fraction of the size of Mousetrap's core would yield well over a million years' worth of iron and associated structural and exotic metals. And most of Mousetrap's metals would be scooped out of its gut nearly pure enough to hammer into swords and plowshares. Mousetrap's rock and water "impurities" would provide the remaining needed building blocks.

In the soon-to-bloom factories within Mousetrap, a shipwright could breathe. But in Mousetrap's tiny gravity, he could lift a ton. A metallurgist could begin with purer materials, and manipulate them in as much vacuum as he cared to use. Mousetrap's finished products would come off the line already out here on the frontier, where they were needed, and minus the cost of shipping them across a galaxy.

So Gustus and the Marini were also constructing within Mousetrap smelters, shipyards, armaments factories, all the infrastructure necessary to build fleets and equip armies.

Mousetrap would be more than mankind's fortress and its crossroads. Mousetrap would be its forge and its armory.

Subterrenes, smuggled from Earth by Howard, were U-boat-sized nuclear reactors that would melt their way through Mousetrap from pole to pole, like gargantuan moles.

Lesser bores were to be made by colossal machines that the Marini had used for decades, to dig everything from aqueducts to castle basements. They resembled the massive monsters Earth's engineers used to bore beneath the English Channel and under the skyscrapers of Manhattan. Marini tunnel borers were like steam-powered freight trains, two hundred yards long. Their locomotives were cylinders tipped with rotating, bladed disc cutters, and stood as tall as houses. On Bren and Earth, boring machines cut rock with carbide steel, scarcely harder than the nickel and iron fabric of Mousetrap, or with corundum.

But Howard and Bassin designed cutters that used crushed industrial diamonds set in a matrix, which would scour through Mousetrap's nickel iron like it was lard. On Earth or Bren so much bort would have been a fantasy.

But Weichsel's first and perhaps last contribution to the Human Union changed that. The wrecked dredge that Mimi Ozawa and the *Emerald River* returned from De Beers' camp to Earth contained ugly-but-abrasive industrial-diamond, "bort." On Weichsel, a child could dig gem quality diamonds by the cup. But a test dredge could suck up bort by the ton.

Much of the transformation of Mousetrap was being wrought by massive machines.

But some was the product of down and dirty pick and shovel miners. During the first months, the miners had worked in pressure suits, to seal a billion years' worth of nooks and crannies. Meanwhile, the engineers had installed a system of pressure tight doors, which could hold air in Mousetrap like a twenty-mile long submarine.

The day that job was finished, a hundred of us, all dressed in pressure suits, gathered in a room on Level

Twenty for the pressurization ceremony. From that control room, every door and hatch in Mousetrap could be opened, or, on this happy day, closed. Gustus, rotund in his pressure suit, depressed a red pad—I suppose more accurately a button—that sealed Mousetrap. We applauded, but made no sound. That underscores why pressurization was a big enough deal to merit a ceremony. But more importantly, we mounted a memorial plaque inscribed with the names of the fourteen Marini who died during construction.

After that, workers and machines could work in tunnels and caverns pressurized with an air mix extracted from Mousetrap's cometary ice patches.

Now, the mining crews dug more "delicate" passages, often up to just beneath Mousetrap's surface. The miners bored conduits to carry power to be generated by solar arrays, dug anti-ship weapons emplacements, hacked out launch ports for defensive spacecraft. Hard rock mining is nasty work. Growing up in Colorado, I had a summer job as a gofer in a half-ass gold mine. It had almost been enough to make me study for SATs.

Many of the crews comprised female soldiers, whose smaller size advantaged them in cramped, claustrophobic conditions, and whose lesser upper body strength scarcely disadvantaged them in Mousetrap's low gravity. Female tunnel rat crews' dug tonnage routinely exceeded the totals of male crews. The Head Rat would tell you that at the drop of a mead flagon.

Which brings me back to the deserter and the stowaway, who were the same stubborn person.

FORTY-FIVE

"GOD, JASON!" Munchkin's headlamp beam reflected off white spikes and splinters that had been one of her miner's humeri. The skin through which they erupted glowed in the light, pale and bloody. A pulsing, baitbox-large night-crawler wrapped around the bone shaft. It was a vein.

Munchkin jerked away from where we knelt together, flung herself across a boulder as big as an old TV set, and vomited her guts out into the dark.

When it was all gone she gasped, as I wiped tears from her eyes and drool strings from her lips.

The Marini girl was conscious now and screaming so loud that I was afraid more of the roof would come down.

Munchkin twisted back, and tried to smooth her palm across the girl's forehead. "Easy, babe. You're fine."

The girl thrashed her hand away, then squeezed her temples between her palms and whimpered. "Make it stop! Make it stop!" She sobbed. "Is my arm off?"

Munchkin turned her light away from the girl's face.

"Is it?"

Munchkin turned back again and drew a breath so

her voice wouldn't quaver. "It's still on, babe." That was the trouble. The angular iron boulder that had collapsed, crushed the girl's arm, and now pinned it, was as thick as a heating duct. On Earth, it would have weighed more than a truck. On Mousetrap it weighed no more than a tree trunk, which was enough. The rubble that came down with it surrounded us.

Munchkin shone her headlamp up into the blue-black cupola the rock fall had opened above us, glimpsed movement and flinched. Something whacked my helmet, then thumped my shoulder as it went by. I looked down. The toaster-sized boulder rocked on the drift's floor. The roof creaked. The rest of it would come down in minutes. We had to get the girl out.

The other crews were working a stope too far away. It was just the three of us.

I knelt and pushed my shoulder on the boulder until my muscles quivered, and swore at myself for not wearing armor. This had begun as a casual visit so Munchkin could brag about her miners, the transferred objects of her maternal affections since Jude was light years away.

Munchkin coiled back on her knees, growled and slammed herself against the boulder. It barely twitched. Rock rattled down. The girl screamed, then passed out.

I slid my light along the boulder, to where it angled back into the wall, and swore. It was all connected. If the beam-shaped rock moved, everything came down.

I crawled to the crew toolbox, rummaged, then sat back on my ankles. My breath made fog in the light while I heard the two of them breathe. Smells of machine oil, dust, and vomit mingled as I thought about what we had to do.

A hand touched my shoulder, and I jumped.

"You said the miners were staying away from the fracture cones."

She turned her head. "It was easy tonnage."

I pointed at the girl, and whispered. "That could be you! Screw your goddam tonnage!"

"It's bad enough I screwed up. Don't yell like that."

The girl stirred and moaned.

I took Munchkin's arm, pulled her ten feet up the drift, and cupped my hand around her ear. "Her arm's hamburger. And pinned. That boulder's not budging. The roof won't last ten minutes. The cavalry's too far away."

I tilted my head, and my lamp beam glinted off the hacksaw's blue-steel blade. "I got it from the toolbox. Bone's softer than steel. I've got cord to make a tourniquet above the break."

Munchkin pushed the saw away. "She wants to be a surgeon, Jason."

Our breath puffed across our interlocked light beams.

The girl sobbed.

I dropped the saw, and sighed. "Go back up where this drift intersects the adit and get a jack. And cable. And those two sheets of corrugated." I held my hand flat and level with my eyes. "The ones about yea high."

"A jack? You move that timber and that roof's coming down on whoever's jacking." She punched her palm. "Bam! Right now!"

I tilted my head, so my light painted her brown eyes. Ice cold.

"Move!"

She ran like hell in the dark.

By the time Munchkin staggered back, the iron jack

in one hand and the two rusty sheets of corrugated steel trussed with the cable across her bent back like a shawl, the roof was creaking worse. It was a constant forty Fahrenheit in here and still I sweated.

I had been busy. A three-sided wall of stacked rock, open toward us, surrounded the girl where she lay, like a sarcophagus in a tomb. Another sarcophagus rose next to the fallen boulder.

I looked up from where I knelt alongside the boulder and waved Munchkin forward with wiggled fingers. "Hand me the jack. Put one sheet of tin over her like a roof. Tie the cable under her armpits."

I tossed a last rock on my pathetic fort, straightened and gasped. "Once I get the jack snugged underneath the timber and I'm laid down alongside it put the other tin sheet over me. Then take the end of the cable and get back a safe distance. I'll yell when I get her leg jacked free."

I pointed at her. "You haul like hell and don't stop for God. Got it?"

"Keep off a rock fall with tin sheets? And who hauls *you* out? What the hell kind of plan is that?"

"The only one I got." I lay down between my stubby stone walls and began setting the jack.

Munchkin said, "You're too big."

I looked around. I had swept together every cobble and boulder within range, but she was right. My little fort was too small. I would be crushed.

Munchkin pushed me aside, and laid down beside the jack. "I fit."

I nodded, then I stood, and tied the cable. As I laid the sheetmetal across the girl, her eyes widened like I was nailing the lid on her coffin.

Munchkin had the jack in place below the elongated rock, and had her hands on the crank. I laid the tin sheet across her back. "Munchkin—"

"Later."

I backed off, turned around and looped the cable around my waist. Munchkin lay facedown in my flimsy, flat-roofed doll hut, the girl on her back in hers. Iron squealed as Munchkin cranked the jack.

Rock pattered against the metal shields. Like the start of a storm. *Clack. Clack clack.*

"Now! Now, Jason!"

I leaned all my weight back on the cable. The girl moved inches and screamed.

Falling rock thundered on the tin. I strained and my boots slipped against the smooth floor rock. The girl wasn't moving. I yelled, and pulled harder.

Munchkin swore in Arabic.

The roof collapsed.

FORTY-SIX

IRON DUST BLINDED ME. I choked on the metallic taste of it and spat into the dark. My ears rang. The cable cut into my palms as tons of rock tried to tear it from me. I had told Munchkin not to stop for God. God didn't seem to be here, anyway. I pulled my guts out. I had stumbled backward. One step. Two?

The darkness got silent. I coughed a fit, and gradually tears washed out eyes I had no hand free to wipe. I kept inching backwards.

My lamp penetrated farther and farther into settling dust. Where there had been space there was sharp-edged iron rock. Mountains of it.

I pointed my light beam down. The girl lay in front of me. Her head. Her torso. Her hips. Her thighs. Then rock. I loosed the cable, staggered forward, tripped and swore.

I tore rock away until I saw the girl's leg. Then both legs. Her broken arm looked like a snapped, bloody Q-tip but it was still attached. I bent, laid a hand in front of the girl's mouth, and breath tickled my palm. My plan had worked. Halfway.

I looked back at the rockfall. "Munchkin?"

Nothing.

"Munchkin!"

I stepped forward again, lifted rock and threw it aside. The big ones I levered with a shovel handle. I moved rock until my back screamed and inside my gloves my fingers slipped in blood and sweat.

Even as I sweated, I trembled. I had torn away fallen rock like this a quarter of a century before, to reach a buried, crushed drop ship cockpit on Ganymede. And part of me had died there. It couldn't be happening again.

I panted, "Munchkin?" every few minutes but I no longer paused for the reply I knew wouldn't come.

I grabbed a dusty rock smaller than a bread loaf. It was attached to something and wouldn't come loose. I looked closer. Munchkin's boot!

I threw and pushed and heaved rock until the edge of the sagging corrugated sheet became visible. I must have swallowed a pound of dust. I screamed, "Munchkin!"

The boot moved. No, it didn't.

Yes. It wiggled. The other moved, too. Munchkin inched herself backward, belly down, from under the sagging, corrugated tin.

She was out as far as her belt line when I heard her, muffled. "What took you so long?"

I slapped her boot sole. "Goddamit!"

Then I cried.

Ten minutes later, from far up the adit, a voice echoed. "Hang on! We're coming!"

I played my light on the adit walls, their hewn surfaces reflecting with the plaid crisscross Widmanstatten crystalline pattern of meteoric iron. Solid.

But the area of the rock fall resembled similar infirm

spots the Rats had been finding. Mousetrap's solid iron skin turned out to be pocked every few surface acres with hundred-foot deep, radiating conical scars, where the iron had fractured in place into shatter cones, as though the planetoid had suffered a drive-by shooting.

I crawled toward Munchkin, but she coughed, and waved me toward the girl. As I adjusted the tourniquet that stopped the miner's bleeding, I said to Munchkin, "I think they can save the arm."

Munchkin didn't reply.

I turned, and saw that she was crawling across the new rockfall, her light beam jerking from ceiling to floor as she moved. Above her, the ceiling opened huge, now. The iron that had filled the space lay in a heap, fractured into sharp-edged fragments.

I shrugged as I said to her, "This could've turned out worse."

She stopped, and shone her helmet light beam at an iridescent, blue object atop the new-fallen rock. She said, "Maybe not."

FORTY-SEVEN

HOWARD CAUGHT UP with Munchkin and me at the *Eisenhower*'s infirmary, where we sat, gowned and facing each other, on Plasteel tables in an examination bay.

He raised his eyebrows at the bandages on our faces and exposed limbs. "Evidently peacetime doesn't agree with either of you."

It certainly hadn't agreed with Munchkin, who had jumped ship from the blue ribbon panel before it left Bren, half from boredom, and mostly because from Mousetrap she could hitch a jump to Tressel to see her baby.

The surgeon who had been working on Munchkin's miner stepped toward Munchkin. "She's sedated. We've reduced the fracture."

"How's the arm?"

He shrugged. "Lot of rehab. But little fine motor loss, long term, I think." He shook Munchkin's hand, then left the three of us.

Howard watched him go, then frowned as he turned to me. "You're sure?"

I nodded. "It's a Football, alright. What's it mean?"

The Slugs might use a million different complex machines, but we only knew about a handful. As Howard would say, the Slugs didn't need to invent much. If the Cro-Magnons had discovered Cavorite, mankind might not have bothered to invent the wheel. So far as we knew, they had no toasters, sportscars, or lawnmowers. What they had included one kind of gun that came in three sizes, from anti-personnel rifle to a cannon big enough to thump a cruiser. They had two kinds of starships, U.N. phonetic designators Troll and Firewitch. They had big kinetic projectiles to blow up cities, and smaller, faster ones to blow up towns. And, finally, they had indestructible little early warning sensors that looked like iridescent blue footballs, which they sprinkled on, or shot into, planetary surfaces.

Howard said, "Well, the first thing it means is that the Pseudocephalopod knows where Mousetrap is. But the fact that all It did was fire a few hundred sensors into the planetoid in passing suggests that It doesn't actively watch Mousetrap. We're lucky you two were there. Marini miners might have ignored the Football. Far as we know, this is the first Football we've disturbed. We were lucky again, that we worked from the inside of Mousetrap outward."

"Right. Lucky." As far as we knew, Footballs weren't all that smart. Unless you disturbed one pretty good, it just sat there. But once you woke a Football up, things went to hell fast.

"You think it sent a signal?"

Howard chewed his nicotine-substitute gum. "Yep. We monitored a microburst." Add one more invention. The Slugs apparently understood radio. They didn't use it much, so far as we knew. Howard pointed out that a unitary organism wasn't too concerned about talking to itself.

"How long do we have?"

"The Pseudocephalopod's a creature of this universe. It's bound by the same physics we are. It can't communicate faster than light, so it probably communicates across Temporal Fabric Insertion Points about the way we do. It depends on how many jumps exist between the Mousetrap and its central ganglion. Likely months or years."

"So we keep working?"

"Faster, harder. It will know we're here. It could still come via Weichsel, but now more likely straight here."

"Boom? Just blow Mousetrap up, with Projectiles or Vipers?"

Howard shrugged. "The Pseudocephalopod didn't blow up Ganymede, Earth, Bren, or even Weichsel. It preserves physical environments in which it perceives value. It may soften us up first, but then expect It to try to take Mousetrap in one piece."

So we sent the bad news to Earth by drone mail and redoubled our efforts.

Digging, then digging some more, for months, when it's too hot, too cold, too dangerous, too lonely, and too boring is part of being infantry.

The other part is worse.

FORTY-EIGHT

"WHOA!" Munchkin tugged herself along in vacuum, floating ten feet above Mousetrap, as she hand-over-handed along a line strung between stanchions screwed into Mousetrap's smooth, black iron surface. Her suit was tethered to the pull line, and to mine, so neither of us would be spun off into space.

Mousetrap was dense enough and big enough that it originally had tiny natural gravity, enough to hold you down, unless you sneezed inside your suit. But that was before Howard and Gustus, with a boost from Cavorite, goosed Mousetrap's rotation a little, so people and things would stick to the skinward-facing floors of the spaces we were creating inside.

Correspondingly, if a person was now on Mousetrap's outside, up was the new down. A person not tethered to the surface would be flung out into space, to become a floater. It wasn't a death sentence. We were wearing Eternad armor. Eternads look like what people expect of a spacesuit, and can serve as one in a pinch. A patrol from one of the cruisers on station above Mousetrap would retrieve a floater, theoretically. But if the pull line in my hands had been a snake, it would have been strangled long ago.

In the blackness above our heads, the *Eisenhower* showed as white as a tiny moon. Equidistant from Mouse-trap, the *Nimitz*, another *Metzger*-class cruiser, hung in space, a black dot silhouetted against Leonidas, as the planet rose huge and orange above Mousetrap's tiny hori-zon, which seemed to curve as sharply as a watermelon's skin.

Ahead of me, Munchkin paused, her legs paddling in nothing, and pointed at the engineer crew a hundred yards away. Her voice panted in my earpiece. "Almost there."

"Munchkin, we *are* there." In the sense of "complete," for the mining phase.

Therefore, as we did for the pressure-up phase, we convened a short ceremony to mark the end of the digging phase. The crew was installing a plaque on the surface, a memorial to the miners who lost their lives over the past eighteen months of construction. Today the primary excavation phase ended.

I tugged my tether to be sure I was fastened to Mouse-trap, then pointed at the *Eisenhower*. "When *Ike* gets relieved, you need to be on it."

"I don't report to you. Combat Engineers report through Gustus."

I raised my palm as we floated. "You're a supernumer-ary volunteer. Gustus can't give you orders either. You can leave whenever you want."

"You want me off Mousetrap because you think it's dangerous."

Mousetrap was dangerous, alright. There were sixty-three names on the newest memorial plaque. But Munchkin meant, and I understood her to mean, the Slug assault that was going to hit Mousetrap sooner or later.

"You came here so you could hitch a ride to Tressel, to be with Jude. You did more than your share, already. So hitch your ride."

"When I came here, we didn't know this was the front line."

"We still don't. The Slugs could hit Tressel first for all we know."

"Stop rationalizing. I'm not running out on my troops."

"Ord and Howard went back to Earth. Nobody thinks that was running out."

"That's a business trip. They're coming back."

I chinned my audio mute so she wouldn't hear me sigh, and my faceplate was dark enough that she couldn't see my eyes roll. Munchkin had no troops, though she and her Tunnel Rats would die—and too many of them had died—for one another. In the grand tradition of Lafayette and the American Colonies, the Flying Tigers in China, and the Eagle Squadron in the Battle of Britain, Munchkin was a noble foreigner who joined the fight against a common enemy. And her job was well and nobly done.

But she was right. I wanted her gone for selfish reasons. In my gut I knew the Slugs weren't going to hit Bren or Earth or Weichsel first. The little maggots always knew where we were vulnerable, and they always smeared us when we needed it least. If there was a Pearl Harbor moment to hit Mousetrap, this was it. The humans the Slugs had used for mining for millennia had just finished mining out a neatly situated asteroid. But the humans hadn't begun emplacing all those defensive armaments, yet.

To guard against exactly that vulnerability, fully three cruisers were now dispersed in the space around Mousetrap.

Above us, silver flecks drifted toward the larger speck of the *Eisenhower*. *Ike* was recovering her patrol fighters, then she would take in the last few transports from Mousetrap. Then she was off, bound for Tressel.

Tressel had lately been quiet, albeit troubled, and by all calculations was distant and non-strategic to the Slugs. It was jumps away from everywhere except Mousetrap, and its one attraction to the Slugs, Cavorite, had been depleted for millennia. If there was a safe haven in the human-occupied universe right now, it was Tressel. I wanted Munchkin together with Jude, and I wanted both of them as far out of harm's way as possible.

As I watched, the last of the fighter flecks merged with *Ike*'s bigger speck.

A frown flickered across my face. For a brief window, now, Mousetrap would be a little exposed, until *Ike*'s replacement emerged from its jump and arrived on station.

Munchkin said, "Maybe you're right."

As I watched the *Eisenhower* float against the black fabric of space, something flickered. So fast that I couldn't be sure I had seen the red streak appear, it began from nowhere and ended at the speck that was the *Eisenhower*.

The fleck bloomed into a white flash, then the flash faded to blackness, leaving behind an expanding sprinkle of tiny light points.

I grabbed Munchkin's arm, and dragged her as I yanked us along the line, back to the airlock hatch that could get us back inside, sheltered from vacuum.

She said, "What happened to the *Ike*?"

My earpiece squealed as Mousetrap called itself to General Quarters.

I pulled faster toward the airlock. "Viper, probably. Hurry up."

Without a sound in the vacuum of space, the *Eisenhower* had exploded into a halo of bits and pieces and human beings. Jimmy Wethers, his kid bosun on deck with the little whistle, all gone.

There hadn't been much we could do to prevent this, that we hadn't done, I supposed.

Nobody had ever actually seen a Viper. Mankind had only experienced one. Which had left me with two organic prosthetic fingers, and Earth defenseless. Viper was just a U.N. phonetic designator for a presumed velocity weapon that substituted size for speed. Before the Spooks knew about Cavorite, they estimated that Vipers traveled at .5 light speed, almost one hundred thousand miles per second, and academics said the Spooks were nuts. Actually, the Spooks estimated low. Current best guess was Vipers flashed in at one hundred sixty thousand miles per second. So a Viper could be small, the Spooks estimated no bigger than a refrigerator, if it was made of dense enough material, yet pack a punch.

That meant that a Viper could also loiter, undetectable in the vastness of space, waiting for a Football to send a signal, then accelerate to a target close by. A fire-and-forget homing mine. The Spooks suspected that Vipers and Footballs might have the Slug equivalent of delayed action fusing.

The airlock was twenty yards away, now. I glanced over my shoulder. Munchkin was five feet behind my boots, pulling like an Olympic swimmer in armor. Forty yards behind her came the Engineer crew.

Maybe the Viper that had just destroyed the *Eisenhower* was just a long-forgotten booby trap, scattered out here by the Slugs for nuisance value, thousands of years ago. They could be perverse little worms. In that case, we weren't facing an impending assault. This was a tragedy, a disaster, but not a crushing blow.

I was five yards from the airlock when I glanced up at the *Nimitz*, floating against the glowing orange disc of Leonidas. All around the *Nimitz* flashes sparkled.

Munchkin said, "Jason, *Nimitz*' fighters are engaging ship-to-ship!"

So much for an isolated nuisance. Chemical-fueled Starfires weren't fast enough to engage Vipers. Probably Scorpions weren't either, and *Nimitz* hadn't even been refitted with Scorpions yet.

The black dot that was the *Nimitz* popped into a bright, white disc.

I looked toward Mousetrap's north pole, as a Firewitch popped over the horizon, and skimmed toward us like a spinning spider, mag rifles ablaze. Mousetrap's skin ahead of me erupted, in a volcano of shattered, black iron. I spun off into space, clutching a tether that was no longer attached to anything but me.

I called into my helmet mike, "Munchkin?"

FORTY-NINE

I SPUN, feet over head, and drifted in silence above Mousetrap's enormity. I was far enough away now that I could see its curvature, and the hummocks and craters of its slowly rotating surface. The fifty-foot by one-hundred-foot solar panels of Mousetrap's power array lay below me, already as small as a game of dominoes. I could make out the gash where the airlock, and the plaque pedestal, had been. I couldn't see people, much less determine whether Munchkin and the engineers were dead or alive. I could see two other scars, hundreds of yards from the one that had severed me from Mousetrap, where other Slug rounds had torn additional rents in Mousetrap's skin. It appeared the Slugs, as Howard had guessed, intended to take over our handiwork, not just blow it into rutabagas.

I called Munchkin once more, and got silence back. I twisted as I floated, but couldn't see her. I switched to command net and heard nothing, though my display showed my radio was in the green. My armor was equipped with a transponder that could be homed on, if anybody had the time or inclination to search for it, but otherwise I was tumbling off into nothing, my arms and legs splayed as helplessly as a gingerbread man's.

Yes, Eternads can imitate a spacesuit. They're body armor, but they're pressure tight against chemical, biological, and radiological agents. They're pressure tight, but they aren't much better at resisting the pressure differential between their inner, atmospheric pressure and real vacuum than a party balloon. They generate heat that will keep a GI comfortable in the Antarctic winter, but in the two-hundred-below shade of space, they popsicle their wearer in an hour or so. They generate and regenerate breathable oxygen, but their joints will brittleize, and fracture, so their wearer will boil in his own blood before he runs out of air.

I made sure my transponder was blipping, cranked up my headlight and set it to flash, cranked down my heat as low as me and the suit's joints could stand, and started repeating a distress call, switching from frequency to frequency. I didn't care whether a fighter jock, an intercomming supply clerk, or a rescue vessel heard me, just so somebody did.

But it seemed everybody had their hands full.

Only one anti-ship turret on Mousetrap was operational, and it spun and arrowed out streams of depleted uranium cannon rounds. Another Firewitch, mag rail rifles outstretched like tentacles on a blue-black squid, swooped across Mousetrap's surface a hundred yards high, at probably a leisurely thousand miles per hour, firing glowing, purple Heavy rounds.

Before I could see whether the turret gunners hit the Firewitch, I rotated away from that view, and faced space.

A Starfire augured toward Mousetrap, jinking left, right, up, down as it bore down on the Firewitch. And on me.

In the holos, the shot-down ace dangling in his parachute can tug his shroud lines, and maneuver. Thrashing my arms and legs against vacuum did nothing but make me spin worse, and pant harder. In space, a body—mine—remains in motion until and unless acted on by an outside force. Also, lack of apparent weight doesn't equate to lack of mass. If the outside force that acts on the body in motion is a forty-ton spacecraft traveling six thousand miles per hour, the effect is about like getting hit by a speeding train. Except the splat sound dies in vacuum.

I switched to fighter jock frequency and screamed into my mike.

The Starfire jinked, released a missile, and peeled off high right. The missile lit, corkscrewed past me, and penetrated the Firewitch amidships.

The Slug monstrosity sailed on, then, a mile or five beyond me and Mousetrap, it lurched, then it flew apart in all directions.

I hooted, then punched vacuum, which made no sense considering my circumstances.

Dogfights raged all around me, and the Starfires were faring better than the antiques we fielded ship to ship against the Slugs years before. But there were more Firewitches than last time. Lots more.

Most of the Starfires that barreled and swooped past me bore the red and yellow MCC-2 fuselage flash of the *Nimitz*. The *Farragut* was supposed to be out there somewhere, and she could recover *Nimitz*' orphans. If *Farragut* survived, which seemed unlikely. Below me, Mousetrap itself offered a haven for the fighters, but they would have to fight their way to the North Pole inlet doors, and things on Mousetrap would have to remain stable enough that somebody could let them in when they knocked.

As for me, Starfires were no more able to pluck a floater from space than an Earth jet fighter could pluck a castaway from the sea. I was going to die in a few hours. That was pretty clear. I switched off the fighter jocks' frequency—they needed no distractions—and screamed incoherently into the rescue band for four minutes straight.

I wasn't babbling, just mad as hell. It wasn't like we hadn't done what we could to protect Mousetrap. Of a dozen operational cruisers, two were in transit to relieve others on station. Three were dispersed around Mousetrap, a beefed-up two were orbiting Bren, a pair were laying for the Slugs near Weichsel, and three were arrayed above Earth. We finally had ship-to-ship thermobaric weapons that, as I had just seen, worked against Slug ships. Firewitches and Trolls are one, or a few, large chambers inside, filled with air at Earth sea level pressure. So one penetrating warhead that disperses, then ignites, flammables inside a Slug vessel scores a kill. Yet still, the little maggots had done it to us again.

I cranked my thermostat down until I lost feeling in my toes, and tried to take smaller breaths, for no good reason.

Forty minutes later, Mousetrap looked about the size of a misshapen pumpkin. I couldn't see any Starfires, except one drifting with a stub wing off. More Firewitches than I cared to count drifted in a loose cordon around slowly rotating Mousetrap. As I watched, more drifted up, from all directions, slow and lazy, moving no faster against the starry blackness of space than airliners on final.

I twitched my arms every few seconds, to keep the Eternads kinetic energy capture system recharging the batteries. I shut off my heads-up display, to save a little more juice. All the news it could display was bad anyway.

When I flexed my arms this time, something crackled like cellophane. My armor's pressure membrane was brittleizing in the cold. The end of my life was a pinhole away.

I tumbled so my view changed again, from Mousetrap to space.

In the distance, a blue-black spider drifted toward me.

FIFTY

SURELY, the Firewitch would simply pass me.

But the closer it got, the more heads-up it remained on me.

What were the odds? I was like a castaway in the mid-Atlantic, getting run down by the *Queen Mary*, approaching at five hundred knots.

The Firewitch had its array spread, so it really did look like a blue-black tarantula coming to gobble me up. The purple, visible-spectrum part of its inner illumination shone out through the hundred-foot wide, transparent blister centered between its six outstretched arms. At low speed, its array wouldn't brush me aside, like debris it encountered near light speed. I would splat against its purple dome like a gnat on a windshield.

The Firewitch bore down on me, so close now that I could see crusty lumps in its array arms.

I stared into the big purple eye, waited for the train wreck, and said, "Crap!"

The eye flashed yellow. Then it burst like a brittle balloon. Then the Firewitch exploded silently into pieces that tumbled in all directions, not least toward me. A metal triangle bigger than a piano pounded my gut, and I began to spin in another direction, twice as fast as I had been tumbling, so I couldn't distinguish what I saw, except alternating dark and blinding brightness.

I thought a voice said, "It's over."

Shadowy, curved pearly wings appeared around me, then slowly enfolded me.

Then there was only darkness.

FIFTY-ONE

———o———

I DIDN'T FEEL DEAD. I felt with my chin, and restarted my visor display. Outside temperature had climbed to a toasty zero Fahrenheit. Outside pressure existed, equivalent to plus-one mile above sea level. I lit my helmet lamp, and saw ribs. Not Leviathan ribs, like I had been swallowed. Perforated, curved, metallic ribs like the inside of a fuselage.

"I said, your tumbling gave me fits. Over."

I replied, "What?"

The voice seemed to speak to someone else. "I have the floater, over." Then, to me, it said, "Who are you?"

"Who are you?"

"Lieutenant Kenneth Arroyo. But I asked you first."

"Wander. Jason. Major General, United States Army."

"No shit? Sir."

I twisted around. The dark space I floated in was a tube six feet in diameter, and twenty feet long.

"Sir, there's a weapons rack clamp on the top center of the bay, back there. You might want to feel around, then grab it tight."

I twisted further, until my light flicked across an angular metal arm. A yellow canvas telltale ribbon, the sort that remained after a weapon had been released, dangled with one end free, in zero gee. I inched to it, twisted the telltale around my wrist like a subway straphanger, and said, "Done. Why am I doing this?"

"I assume this is your first Scorpion ride, sir. It gets a little hairy, even *with* a gee suit." The voice rose an octave. "We got company. Hang on, sir."

I blacked out before I puked.

FIFTY-TWO

I SMELLED RUBBING ALCOHOL. The next thing I saw was a cocoa-skinned man with salt-and-pepper hair, who bent above me as he fingered the touchscreen of a monitor alongside me. He wore medical scrubs, embroidered with a frog clenching a threaded needle between its cartoon teeth, and with the words "Mean Green Sewing Machine." His name plate read "Wallace." Red-brown stained the surgeon's scrubs, and his eyelids drooped like he hadn't slept in a week.

I noticed that burn dressings covered his forearms. I found out later that Doctor Wallace had crawled into an orphaned fighter that had limped into one of *Emerald River*'s launch bays, through flames, then dragged the fighter's unconscious pilot to safety. Then, the surgeon had crawled back in, and dragged out the wounded Wizzo, too.

Doctor Wallace whispered into a Stenobot mike pinned to the scrubs, then said to me, "Aren't you a little old for this sort of thing?" Then he patted my shoulder, and was gone.

I turned my head, and saw, on a Plasteel-framed bed

alongside me, a kid in a transparent burn bag that enveloped him neck-to-toes. Through the gel, I could make out his limbs, legs, and torso, all angry red and purple and black. His pilot buzz cut had been shaved on the left side, around a stitch row that marched across his skull like a line of ants.

I said, "What's your ship?"

"*Nimitz*. Was. Bastards caught *Ike* with all her eggs in the basket."

"The *Farragut*?"

"A log, last I saw her." A cruiser that had stopped rotating, and lay in space like a log, was usually dead. He cried, the console beside him clicked, clicked again, and dope sent him back to Shangri La.

I looked around. The two of us lay in a narrow bay of the size common in cruiser infirmaries. Burn cases were normally segregated to minimize infection risk. If I was stacked alongside this kid, this flight was way overbooked. Or I was in worse shape than I felt. Or both.

I looked down at my right hand. The fingertips were frostbite black, and white-taped to my palm, so my thumb rested above its button, was a Clikit. The bug-shaped wireless transmitter let a patient call up his own dope. It meant I was better off than the kid next to me, who got juiced automatically, but bad enough off that I needed Big Medicine.

My left side began aching, and I ignored it for about an hour, though the wall 'Puter said it was three minutes. The ache metastasized into the conviction that someone had dumped a cutlery drawer into my rib cage, and now a linebacker in cleats was stomping on it. I gritted my teeth for another hour, which the 'Puter claimed was two minutes. Then I clicked my button, again and again, until life became just a bowl of peaches.

Sometime later, Mimi's face stared down at me.

I said, "Will you marry me?"

An orderly leaned between me and Mimi, so close that I could see the stubble on his chin, and said to Mimi, "Get in line, Admiral. He proposed to me an hour ago. I'm cutting his dosage." A transparent IV bag swung across my field of vision, and I proposed to it.

Twenty-two days after the Slugs greased Mousetrap, *Emerald River* settled in to parking orbit above Tressel. From conversations I overheard among the swabbies, the only thing more remarkable than the gentility with which Admiral Ozawa parallel parked was that she had backed *Emerald River* out of Mousetrap in one piece. It was impossible to slingshot a cruiser through a second jump without an intervening overhaul.

I sat in a lounge of *Emerald River*'s infirmary, in a padded chair, wearing a peek-a-boo gown that barely reached my knees. I clutched a walkable medication stand that was tubed to my forearm. Across from me sat she who had done the impossible, crisp and perfect in Class A skirt and blouse. Her head was cocked, her arms and legs crossed. There was probably Visible Thigh, but I didn't even notice.

Mimi asked, "How're you feeling?"

"Bad."

"They tell me the ribs are mending. And the lung is regrowing nicely."

"It was the real one I had left, too." I wheezed and consulted the medication timer on my walking stand. Two minutes until relief. Frostbite in the extremities, a dislocated shoulder, and "undifferentiated soft tissue trauma" rounded out the package. I said, "When you visited before, I said—"

Mimi blinked. "Nothing anybody would remember."

I paused, and closed my eyes. "How bad was it? They won't tell me squat here."

"They want you to concentrate on healing."

"Heal for what, Mimi?"

She sighed. "I know. We lost *Ike*, *Nimitz*, and almost certainly *Farragut*. The Slugs control the Mousetrap. *Emerald River* won't be jump-worthy again for months."

"There were survivors."

"Pilots and systems officers from orphan fighters. You're the only floater we picked up."

I squeezed my eyes shut. Munchkin was gone. "What about Mousetrap?"

Mimi shrugged. "We jumped a drone back into the Mousetrap last week. It hasn't come back."

"Earth? Bren?"

She shrugged again. "We're five jumps out. Maybe we'll know something in a couple months." Maybe Ord and Howard and Earth were building and planning a comeback. Maybe Mousetrap would be just a setback. But maybe we here, on and above Tressel, were the last survivors of the human race. I longed for one of Howard's hunches. Hell, I longed for Howard.

I stared at the floor, and shook my head. "I should have done something."

"Stop feeling sorry for yourself." Mimi's eyes flared, and she pointed at the wall, in a direction that could have led light years to the Mousetrap, wherever in the crow-flies universe it actually was from us. "I abandoned my friends! I left our dead behind!"

"You saved the strongest capital ship we have, maybe the only one, to fight another day. Dead and dumb wouldn't have helped." Swabbie rumor had it that Mimi would get decorated for her actions. That presumed there was somebody left to decorate her.

She stared at the wall, with the fingers of both hands knit beside her thigh, and her eyes glistened. "Still. My heart feels like your lung."

My heart did too. "So, what do we do now?"

Mimi pretended to scratch her nose so she could wipe her eyes. "Heal. Start over. Make it right."

Whatever was happening light years away, what had already happened on Tressel, one thousand miles below us, didn't make healing easier.

FIFTY-THREE

———

I SAT TOGETHER with Jude in iron chairs beneath an arbor grown over with green vines that shaded us against the noon sun. A crystal pitcher of fern tea sat untouched on a table between us. Iridescent dragonflies buzzed in the near distance, above acres of cultivated, teal moss lawn.

We sat silent for ten minutes, then Jude stretched. "Pretty place."

Sanitorium Iridine was Tressel's finest convalescent center. Its grounds encompassed rolling countryside, five miles outside the Iridian capital. The main building looked like Versailles, and had escaped shelling during the war. The sun shone often, the staff anticipated a convalescent's every need, and the chefs were terrific.

I said, "I hate it."

He smiled. "That's the broken ribs talking. You just hate the guest list." True, between morphine withdrawal and "undifferentiated soft tissue trauma," I was still as irritable as if I was wearing broken glass, four months after Mousetrap. But the fact was that if you were a Social Republican, or vouchsafed by one, you convalesced at *Sanitorium Iridine*, at government expense. If you were

Iridian, your accommodations differed. Few medical fa-
cilities in the former Iridia had been rebuilt since the Armistice. But few Iridians needed them. Most chose to live
in government-established relocation camps. The government assisted them in making the choice.

Jude shot the cuffs of the crisp uniform shirt beneath
his black jacket. "Jason, Sergeant Major Erdec's killing
was just the beginning. The Iridians have tried to kill the
members of the Prime Ministrate six times in the last year.
They're animals."

"The Iridians, or the Iridian separatists?"

"Who can distinguish fish in the sea?"

I flexed my shoulder, and rolled my eyes. "You even
talk like them."

"Now who's prejudging? You know Audace Planck.
You know me. But what do you know about Tressel since
the Armistice?"

An orderly peeked around the arbor, pointed at the
pitcher, and raised his eyebrows. Jude shook his head. I
visited with the orderly every day. He was a physician by
training, an Iridian by ethnicity, and an outcast by the "I"
medallion on his smock.

"I know Nazis when I see them."

"This nation was chaos when the Social Republicans
formed a government. The highways are already better
than they were before the war. So's the opera. A man can
have a job, now, if he wants it, and his paycheck won't
bounce. His kids can go to school without dodging street
gangs."

"Unless he's Iridian."

"The restrictions are temporary. Every day, Social Re-
publicanism makes us freer."

I rolled my eyes. "Who writes that crap? Joseph Goebbels? You didn't get chauffeured out here to brainwash me. Something's up."

"I didn't. Ord and Howard are here."

I looked around.

"In orbit. Aboard the *Yorktown*. It's a new B-class. It floats a full Scorpion wing."

I sat forward in my chair. "Well?" The very fact that a ship other than the *Emerald River* still existed was like a Christmas present. But it wouldn't have just brought back Ord and Howard from Earth, it would have brought the first news since Mousetrap.

"Other than—you know—the only other place the Slugs came through was Weichsel, again. The *Powell* and the *Marshall* fought them to a draw."

"With Starfires? It was just a feint, then."

Jude nodded. "Considering what happened at Mousetrap, that's obvious."

"I really meant, you know . . ."

The silent, two-ton scorpion lurking at every conversation between Jude and me was Mousetrap. If we didn't talk about his mother, she wasn't gone.

Jude shook his head. "I'm commissioned in an allied army, now. I only hear through the grapevine." We were speaking English, translators off, and it was a joke. Tressel wouldn't have grapes for a few hundred million years.

I grasped my chair arm, set my jaw, and stood. I was ninety percent recovered, physically. I grimaced, and Jude jumped up, took my elbow. "What do you think you're doing?"

"Leaving." I pointed at the pistol he wore on a broad,

polished leather belt. "Unless I'm shot attempting to escape."

It was Jude's turn to roll his eyes. "Stop it, Jason. My driver's packing your stuff right now. We're meeting Ord and Howard in Tressia." He fitted his black cap with two hands. Above its visor was a cast silver crest, a skull, wrapped by a twisted scorpion.

We walked across the spongy moss to his car, long, low, and black, with segmented chromed side pipes as thick as a woman's thigh. Jude's driver held the rear door open for us.

Jude was the closest thing to family remaining to me in this universe. He was young, impressionable, and, so far as I knew, he functioned strictly as a military-to-military liaison between Earth and Tressel. He knew, I hoped, no more about the SR's "social reforms" than any of us gleaned by comparing SR propaganda sheets to what trickled off the grapevine. The drive to Tressia would take two days, even over the SR's admittedly slick new highways. The journey with Jude could provide what the afternoon-holo shrinks called "quality time" with my godson. Unless we spent it staring out windows in opposite directions.

I pointed at the limo, then at his cap, and forced a smile. "Why do the bad guys always get the cool stuff?"

He shrugged. "Clothes make the man?"

I settled into the backseat, taking my weight on my right hand. "I hope not."

FIFTY-FOUR

THE U.S. CONSULATE in Tressia had moved into bigger quarters since the Armistice, an antiseptic stone box among the sterile limestone boxes with which the Social Republicans had reconstructed Tressia's rubbelized West End. The box was as neat and tidy as the fresh-paved boulevard beside which it rose, and it housed the ten staff I knew from before the Armistice, plus twenty more the new Ambassador had brought with him.

He needed the extra bodies, because not only had he been upgraded to Ambassador, and the facility to Embassy, the place served as the United Nations Mission to Tressel, and the local office of the Human Union. International lip service notwithstanding, the facility was as American, and as ambitiously misnamed, as the World Series.

The Ambassador met Jude and me in the lobby, grinning, and wearing no flak jacket. Social Republican society was orderly. So was Nazi Germany.

I shook his hand and patted the shoulder padding of his suit jacket. "Congratulations on the promotion, Duck."

"You too." Before I could ask what he meant, the Duck

peeled Jude off, then waddled me to a conference room
where Ord, Howard, and two colonels waited, seated
around a polished stone table.

After ten minutes of howdies, one colonel, wearing
the striped-shield brass of the Adjutant General Corps,
slipped a black velvet box the size of Howard's cigarette
pack from his briefcase. The colonel smiled as he said to
me, "Sir, I was posted up here as Embassy staff military
attaché. But my first job is to present you with these." He
flipped open the box. On the interior velvet lay three-star
Lieutenant General's brass.

Most officers who survive to my age, possessed of my
sparse formal training and of my lack of tact and common
sense, were Majors. Events and misfortune had bounced
me uphill from one exotic, screwball job to the next. Most
recently, I had freelanced my simple, advisory assignment on Tressel, and then Bren, and then Mousetrap, into
a cluster hump of galactic proportion. To be fair, fate, the
Slugs, and human stupidity had screwed things up more
than I had.

But handcuffs for me would have been more likely than
promotion hardware. I frowned, and looked first to Ord.

He said, "Consistent with your new assignment, sir."
He smiled, and an unsergeantly softness crinkled the skin
around his eyes. "Congratulations."

Few Drill Sergeants saw a trainee of theirs, who barely
graduated Basic, get a third star. For a moment, I got a
lump in my throat.

Then I narrowed my eyes at Howard. "What about
Warden's report? We lied to Congress."

Howard waved his hand. "Constitutionally, the executive branch has gotten away with worse in other wars. We worked matters out informally."

I stared at him. We both had taken an oath to support and defend the Constitution, not to weasel around it in the name of expedience. But the scourge of the universe was on mankind's doorstep. I'd think about the Constitution tomorrow. I paused at my own thought. I was beginning to wonder whether the pressures of politics, of attacks from all sides, had driven Aud Planck down the slippery slope from soldier to Nazi. Was this how it started?

The AG Colonel closed his briefcase and left.

I looked back at Howard.

He said, "We're going back to Mousetrap. It's your show."

Panic drowned my internal debate. "What?"

Howard popped the conference table holo, loaded a chip from his briefcase, and summarized as the orders scrolled by. "A joint strike force of ten cruisers—"

"We don't have ten cruisers, anymore," I said.

"We will. And then some. Each cruiser will carry a full wing of Scorpions, and an embarked division."

I looked down at my hands. They quivered. Not with fear. They quivered the way, I supposed, a racehorse quivers in the starting gate.

Mankind had come a long way back since the Blitz. We fought the Slugs on Ganymede with one ship, so crude that we painted the unfinished bulkheads during the trip out, with old-fashioned bristle brushes. We fought with cobbled-together antiques, and with a single division. After that, the Armada blew our ships into scraps. And we had kicked the Slugs off Bren with swords, last-century rifles, and armies of nomadic cavalry. For decades we had fought outgunned, outquicked, and outnumbered.

I didn't hate the Slugs. How could I demonize mindless blobs? I didn't even fear them anymore, except in the way that I feared familiar but dangerous instrumentalities like chain saws or hot stoves. But the prospect of finally flat kicking the Slugs' collective-minded ass made my heart pound.

The strategic reason to embark divisions was sound. A fleet like Howard described could stand off and pummel a planetoid into pudding, but Mousetrap was valuable real estate to mankind, even as a fixer-upper. So, eventually, infantry were going to have dig the Slugs out, hole by bloody hole, like we always did.

Countries dispatch infantry for strategic reasons, and infantry believes in them, mostly. But I knew why I was going back, and so would every one of the kids who was going back with me, as soon as the first round flew. I asked Howard, "What about the people we left behind?"

"The colonel will cover that." Howard nodded to the remaining colonel, who wore the Intelligence rose and compass. Then Howard said, "Ten divisions is an Army. So you get the third star. It also evens your rank up with the Fleet Admiral."

It hadn't been so long ago that I wasn't fit to command one division. Now I was going to have responsibility for ten. I would need rank to hold my own with some aging, dirtside swabbie. "Does my counterpart have a clue what we're up against?"

"Absolutely. Specialized experience was a paramount selection criterion. Obviously it wasn't maturity and management skills."

"Thanks, Howard."

"But Mimi has the whole package."

My jaw dropped even as my heart thumped. I hadn't even seen Mimi in the four months since I downshipped from *Emerald River* to convalesce. But I had plenty of time to think about her, including parts of the package that Howard wasn't talking about.

I looked away, at the conference room's granite wall. Mimi and I were obvious choices to command this operation. But mutual proximity could prove distracting. Not for Mimi, I supposed. The female libido is more easily controlled. At least *my* dates never seemed to have a problem.

Howard turned to the Intelligence colonel. "Show him."

Mousetrap's slowly rotating image replaced Howard's document. The Intel colonel said, "We recovered this from one of *Emerald River*'s drones four months ago, after it passed through the Mousetrap. Apparently *Emerald River* sent the drone for a look-back after it withdrew to Tressel, but the Slugs chased the drone, so it popped out on the Earth side. It didn't take us long to figure out what happened."

I nodded. That explained Mimi's missing drone, and why Earth had a plan by the time Howard and Ord got sent back here.

On the holo above the table's center, the surface scars of the Slug attack looked minor, and a few solar panels hung askew. Firewitches swarmed the surrounding space like flies around a water buffalo. Four enormous Troll incubator ships drifted in the distance.

The Colonel said, "We sent in another drone, from our

side, before we left, and recovered it on this side, when we arrived here. The other four Trolls are still drifting."

I nodded.

I said, "Those other four Trolls wouldn't be sitting there, backed off, for months, if the maggots had Mousetrap."

The Colonel nodded. "Consensus inference is that Mousetrap may still be resisting."

I said, "But all we can *see* is a big rock. They could be fighting. They could be captives. They could be dead. What kind of radio traffic did the drone monitor?"

The Colonel shook his head. "None."

"There are automated beacons, transponders all over Mousetrap. There had to be—"

"None. Not the first drone or the later one."

I looked to Howard and he shrugged. "It doesn't mean they're all dead. Captives couldn't transmit. Mobile guerrillas inside Mousetrap wouldn't."

But we weren't limited to reliance on inference consensus, or on what we heard broadcast from Mousetrap. We could see what was inside. "Show me the interiors."

"Sir?" The Intel colonel shook his head, slowly.

"The drones dropped TOTs. Show me what they found inside." Tactical Observation Transports were the highly-evolved products of the robotic aircraft revolution of the turn of this century. Most were designed to support Earth ground forces, to fly in atmosphere, then crawl through windows or into caves or whatever it took to snoop. But I knew the Spooks had modified some of the latest models to operate in space.

Howard said, "Jason, TOTs have been nuclear powered for years."

I nodded. "Crap." One reason we cored Mousetrap

from the inside out was that the initial, monster bores were made by Subterrenes—bullet shaped nuclear reactors that melted their way through rock. We had planned for the Subterrenes to start their work immediately, and to finish early, because if the Slugs showed up early, everything nuclear mankind had, from warheads to the nanoreactors that powered modern TOTs, would shut down.

We had learned that lesson the hard way clear back during the Blitz, when we tried to nuke incoming Projectiles. Howard's Spooks called the technology "neutron damping." That sounded informed, but the Spooks no more understood how the Slugs froze nuclear devices than I understood the female libido.

So we had no TOTs to snoop inside Mousetrap.

I said to the Intel colonel, "I understand we can't just blow Mousetrap apart from space, even if we had workable nukes. We need Mousetrap more than the Slugs do. But I need to know the friendly status inside."

If it came to it, strategic considerations would require that we go in blind. But if we were going in blind, it would be after a massive prep that would slaughter any friendlies as surely as it slaughtered Slug warriors. But fifty thousand possible friendlies was a big number. It was bigger to me because I had bled with Munchkin's Tunnel Rats. I had seen Mimi cry over survivors she may have left behind.

I asked the Intel colonel, "Could we sacrifice a drone? Just barrel it in there?"

The Intel colonel shook his head. "Sir, you've seen the Slug fleet surrounding Mousetrap. Maybe if we mounted a massive diversion we could sneak something as small as a drone down to the surface, but it would be too big to get inside."

"Other options?"

He shook his head, again. "Actually, an old, non-nuclear TOT would have been perfect. We even researched it. The last J-series in DOD inventory was dismantled for parts, eight years ago." He shrugged. "They're not the kinds of things somebody kept for war souvenirs."

I turned to Howard and raised my eyebrows.

His eyes twinkled. "I stopped by your place before I came back here."

FIFTY-FIVE

IN DOWNTOWN TRESSIA, Howard, Ord, and I bunked in with Jude. Unlike his Earth counterpart twenty-something junior officers, Captain Jude Metzger of the SR roughed it in an eight-bedroom, three-story townhome that overlooked a park. Breakfast was served each morning in a sunroom with floor-to-ceiling windows. The sunroom was furnished in gilt and crystal, except for a burgundy silk back wall, across which marched unfaded, picture-sized rectangles, each below a downlight that lit nothing.

The upstairs maid, who apparently came with the place along with the downstairs maid, the cook, and the gardener, refilled my tea cup, as I peeked around the table's candelabra and asked Jude, "Whose place was this?"

"Not was. Is. A surgeon's family. They'll get it back as soon as their papers clear. Meantime, the SR is renting it from them at market plus ten percent. It's practical. Walking distance to my office."

"Which is convenient for your chauffeur. Where's the surgeon's family 'til their papers clear?"

Jude paused with a butter knife in one hand, and a muffin in the other. "Stop trying to make something out of everything. With the mobs after the Armistice, people were happy to leave town."

"So I read in the *Voice Republican*." I pointed my silver spoon at the newspaper on the tablecloth, then at the back wall. "Did the surgeon take his oil paintings along, to brighten up the barracks?"

Jude wiped his lips while he rolled his eyes. "The SR stored displaced persons' valuables for them."

"How thoughtful."

Three stories below, we heard the Tressen door chime, which sounded like a music box with a bad cold.

Jude chucked his napkin onto the tablecloth. "I hope that's Howard and the Sergeant Major. Because you're a pain in the ass for a houseguest."

It was. And I suppose I was. But I wasn't sure whether Jude was naïve about his employer, or he wasn't. The latter possibility scared me worse.

Jude and I met Howard in the townhome's parlor, with their baggage. As we entered, the downstairs maid scurried out, eyes wide.

Howard, his uniform as wrinkled as his face, sucking a nicotine lollipop, was scary enough. But on his shoulder perched a six-legged Plasteel and Ultratanium cockroach as big as a turkey.

Jude elevated his elbow, and Jeeb telescoped out his wings and fluttered over to settle on Jude. Jeeb's diagnostics purred as Jude stroked the antique TOT's radar-absorbent ventral fuzz. Early TOTs were so expensive that the J-series numbered just six units, identified "A" through "F." The second unit deployed was J-series B, thus and forever Jeeb.

Jeeb wasn't obsolete just because he relied on solar

panels for power. Brain link robotics got scrapped years ago, but not because they didn't work. Their radio transmissions, TOT-to-Wrangler, were effectively unjammable. A Wrangler effectively saw and heard everything the TOT did, and the TOT responded to the Wrangler like a virtual extension of his body and mind. Which was the problem. A Wrangler who lost his TOT in combat was like a GI who lost a leg and a brain. The Wrangler suicided on the spot, or spent years in therapy.

All robotics texts will assure you that the relationship didn't wash back the other direction. TOTs were non-self-aware machines, period. Claims that they imprinted their Wrangler's personality were anthropomorphic rubbish. But I saw Ari Klein in Jeeb every day. When I overpaid the Department of Defense for Jeeb's salvage title, I was really adopting an orphan, and all that remained of my friend.

Jude scratched Jeeb behind his optics, which looked like a pair of shiny Oreos. "How could you leave him home, Jason?"

According to the texts, Jeeb couldn't have cared less. But I had cried the day I left him, and the guy I left him with 'mailed me that Jeeb's diagnostics whined for twenty-six hours straight.

I said, "The only person left on Earth who knows how to maintain a J-Series is a retired veteran in Philadelphia."

Ord handed me a chipboard, which showed on its screen the manifest of personality transported aboard the *Yorktown*. "You have to thumb for Jeeb, sir."

I did.

Ord scrolled down, then handed the reader back to me. "And for these."

I read the line item, then glanced at Ord. "More of your antiques, Sergeant Major?"

"I believe they could be useful, sir."

"Four hundred of them?"

Ord shrugged.

I thumbed, then I handed Ord back his reader.

I extended my own elbow, and Jeeb hopped from Jude's shoulder to my bicep, using four of his six legs. I scratched the joint where his sensor lobe joined his carapace, like it was a kitten's neck. Jeeb had no nerve endings that could feel my fingertips, as any wiring diagram proved. But when I scratched him, his diagnostics purred.

I smiled. "He looks good, Howard."

"Ed in Philadelphia overhauled him before we left," Howard said.

Jeeb preened his antennae with his forelimbs, as I sighed. "My friend, all things considered, you'd rather be in Philadelphia."

My next task for that day considered, so would I.

FIFTY-SIX

"THERE WILL STAND the Prime Ministrate." Later that morning, our guide, a scrubbed teen girl in the sunshine-yellow uniform of the Young Social Republicans, pointed across the fresh stone bowl of the Stadium of the Republic to a podium set above the opposite wall, and shouted over the murmur of a crowd of a half million. The Social Republicans needed a new venue for political rallies. The *Voice Republican* pointed out that all political parties would have equal access to the new stadium.

Jude, Howard, Ord, the Duck, and I leaned forward to hear her over the squeal of cranes lifting the SR insignia, a carved stone medallion twenty feet tall, into place behind the podium, which cast the equal-access rule in a different light.

The Slug War had forced each of mankind's three developed worlds to remake itself. The new Earth sought for humans the very opportunity to be. The new Bren sought for humans the opportunity to be equal. The new Tressel sought opportunity for humans, by declaring Iridians less than human. Could this crowd, and perhaps my godson, distinguish the first two from the last?

The guide led us along the curving, stone top tier of the stadium, and I looked out across the treeless, blocky capital.

The guide led us downstairs into the dim corridors beneath the stadium.

The Duck and I brought up the rear. I said to him, "Look, do we really need Tressel?"

"It's four jumps from anywhere. Isolated from our enemy, like the oceans isolated the U.S. last century. The arsenal of democracy."

"Isolated? Mousetrap's one jump from Tressel."

"That won't matter once you recapture Mousetrap."

"Then Mousetrap can be the arsenal of democracy."

"Democracy needs a bigger arsenal."

"Arsenal of democracy loves totalitarian dictatorship. You're a regular cupid, Duck."

The Duck faced me, hands on hips. "Were you this sarcastic at the Pentagon?"

"More."

Planck was at this new stadium to dedicate it, later that day. We met with Aud Planck, one-third of the ruling triumvirate of Tressel, in a conference room beneath the Stadium. Even the Duck, an Ambassador, got frisked by Planck's bodyguards before we got within fifty feet of Aud.

Aud Planck was fifteen pounds heavier, and wearier in the eyes, than when I last saw him. We shook hands, then he pulled me to him, and patted my back. "It's good to see a friendly face."

Aud's comment was as upside down as everything else since the Armistice. When I left Tressel, most faces on the planet were friendly to Aud Planck. Now, theoretically, they all were. In the last election, ninety-nine point six percent of the electorate voted Social Republican, according to the *Voice*. If so, there weren't enough opponents left to throw a decent assassination.

Aud motioned us to sit, then turned to the Duck. "You requested this meeting, Ambassador?"

The Duck nodded, then folded his hands in front of him. "Sir, the Human Union has appreciated your government's cooperation in military affairs—"

Aud waved his hand. "You mean you're here to present the bill for ending the war in Tressen's favor."

I hid a smile. If Aud had patience with anything, it wasn't with diplomacy.

The Duck made a tiny shoulder shrug. "If you like. Sir, we are preparing an operation—"

"To retake the Mousetrap. You may stage the operation from Tressel. We will contribute two infantry divisions. You will train them. General Wander will have operational control of embarked forces, including the Tressen divisions. Overall control will reside with Tressel."

The Duck's mouth hung just a bit. Staging rights. Two divisions. Exactly what he was supposed to ask for. Gentlemen don't read other gentlemen's mail, except in police states. The Duck stiffened, then cleared his throat. "Sir, I don't have authority to cede overall control."

Maybe the Duck didn't have authority, but it wasn't so odd for the tail to wag the dog in coalition operations. Rommel had run the North African theater during World War II, even though much of his army and logistic support was Italian, and even though Rommel reported through the Italian *Commando Supremo*. During the same war, the British accepted Eisenhower as the supreme commander of the invasion of Europe, even though the invasion was mounted from their soil, and the Brits committed more ships and troops to the landings than the Americans. Aud had been my friend. But based on the society that had festered under his leadership, I wasn't so sure Tressel should be in charge.

Aud smiled at the Duck. "Of course. It's a question that doesn't need answering today." Aud stood. "I have to make a speech." He shook hands all around, then was gone.

The stadium walls, even its ceiling, shook all around us with the crowd's roar.

The Duck chuckled. "He's a better politician than you give him credit for, Jason. He could have received us at the Capitol. He wants us to know that Tressel's strong enough that it doesn't need us. We need it."

"You think your bosses will agree to Tressen control?"

"I know they will. I already have that authority, off the written guidelines. I just wanted Planck to think he got *lagniappe*." The Duck shrugged. "You said he's a good general. So is there a problem?"

FIFTY-SEVEN

EIGHTEEN MONTHS AFTER THAT DAY, the Human Union had built up not only new cruisers, but Scorpions for the cruisers to carry into battle. These had made their way around the horn via Bren and the other jumps to what we hoped was the safe harbor of Tressel.

Troops, my troops, were trained and embarked. Aud Planck got the control he wanted, and decided to lead from the front, as always. Mimi and I remained at arm's length. Jude was detached from the SR to command the Scorpions.

We built, we planned, we worried. We worried that if we went too soon, we would fail. We worried that if we went too late, the Slugs would beat us to the punch.

When the fleet finally jumped off for Mousetrap, we weren't ready to go. But we weren't ready to stay, either.

FIFTY-EIGHT

———

WHAT'S IN A NAME? If the name is Union Humane Star Ship *Emerald River*, everything, and nothing. To maintain harmony with the French aerospace industry back home, the diplomats changed the primary spelling of "Human Union" to "Union Humane."

On *Emerald River*'s Bridge, harmony was real enough. Mimi, Aud Planck, Howard, Ord, and I stared into the Bridge's holo display. The older *Metzger*-class cruisers made do with flatscreens, which seems strange since every living room in America's had holo for years. But what you see in your living room, or at the Holoplex, lacks the reliability and freedom from linear distortion required in a modern combat display. Whatever. All I know is that I would love to watch the WorldBowl from Mean Green's Bridge.

Mean Green's display filled the Bridge's center space, ten numbered, winking red dots hovering in front of a purple doughnut. Actually, they tell me that if you put the dots under a microscope, you would see the ship itself at the center, so perfect that you could read hull numbers. The doughnut was the Temporal Fabric Insertion Point that would spit the ten red dots of the fleet out, a few hours' flight away from Mousetrap.

Mean Green's dot was numbered "1." Theoretically, there was enough room to pass multiple cruisers through a TFIP simultaneously. But the tiniest fender bender would be terminal, and Mimi was too smart to risk it. That meant the cruisers would jump one at a time. The most recent drone to peek and return showed nothing but empty space on the other side, immediately inside the Mousetrap. Nonetheless, we would pop out on the other side newborn-naked. Mean Green would spray thirty-five Scorpions from its bays immediately. Unless we were butt deep in Firewitches, these Scorpions would loop beyond Mousetrap and make a pass at it from the side opposite the TFIP entry point. This would draw off Slug interceptors.

More importantly, it would distract the Slugs so that the Scorpion in Mean Green's thirty-sixth bay could squirt out direct to Mousetrap itself. Nestled in the stinger of the thirty-sixth Scorpion was Jeeb. Jeeb flew great in atmosphere, by flapping wings like a hummingbird, but he was helpless in vacuum. The thirty-sixth Scorpion was to deliver Jeeb onto Mousetrap's surface, then beat it. From there, Jeeb would do what TOTs did, crawl into the first nook or cranny that would get him inside, then snoop around.

Jeeb couldn't send out the information suite he could to a brain-linked Wrangler, but we would get rudimentary audio, which was more than we had now.

Mimi asked her executive officer, who stood alongside the console nearest her, "Status?"

"All in the green, ma'am."

"Take us in, Mr. Burke."

"Aye, ma'am."

The only way you knew a cruiser was moving was to watch the sidescreens' display of space. The stars around us began to slip behind us, then they became streaks, as the cruiser accelerated into the Temporal Fabric Insertion Point and the TFIP's core mass began to suck in even starlight. Then the stars went out altogether, as the light itself was sucked in parallel to us.

The ship groaned around us. Planck looked around, his eyes wide. I'd like to say mine weren't, but they probably were.

Then the light—different light—came back, first in streaks, which resolved into new stars in the new space we now shot through.

The first thing I did was check the display for the red dots of objects moving toward us within threatening range. Our green number-one dot was the only thing floating in the display.

Emerald River shuddered, as her thirty-five Scorpions launched from her bays.

A heartbeat later, a smaller shudder rippled beneath our feet as the Scorpion bearing Jeeb launched.

Only moments later, the display got measles. Red Firewitch dots, too many to count, swarmed toward our Scorpions.

A swabbie's voice quavered. "Hell, how many are there?"

"Eighty-three," Mimi replied, her voice as flat and soft as billiard-table felt.

I looked down at the threat counter in the display's lower right corner, at the winking red "83" and smiled.

Mimi said, "Put Tactical on speaker."

"It is on, ma'am."

The Scorpions' ship-to-ship chatter should have been crackling like cellophane on the Tactical frequency. There was only static.

Mimi frowned. "Try the alternate push."

"Nothing, ma'am."

The Scorpions' green dots didn't seem to be maneuvering in large groups, but breaking into duos of leader and wingman.

Mimi swore. "They don't have radio contact, either." She turned to Howard. "Is this why the recon drones didn't pick up any chatter? The Slugs have learned to jam radio?"

Howard said, "Looks like it."

Mimi swore again.

We never knew what the maggots would learn next, except it would usually be something we didn't expect, and something that gave us fits.

She turned to Ord, who held an olive-drab canvas bag that looked a century old, and pointed at the bag. "You think that thing will work?"

Ord made a tight smile. "One way to find out, ma'am." The Slugs' epiphany about radio jamming was an unpleasant surprise, but not entirely unanticipated.

Mimi turned to her executive officer. "We still have intercom?"

The XO fingered his earpiece. "Yes, ma'am."

She stepped toward the hatch that led off the bridge and forward, and said over her shoulder, "Mr. Burke, you have the ship. The Flag is displacing to the observation blister."

Mimi's legs are short, but I could barely keep up.

FIFTY-NINE

SPACESHIPS DON'T NEED WINDOWS, passengers do. But that's not why every cruiser has a hemispherical, fifty-foot diameter crystal dome on its nose. The observation blister on every cruiser carried forward from the first ships, not so long ago, because the designers wanted to provide the crew a means to navigate by the stars if the navigation system tanked.

But today, the *Emerald River*'s blister was bent to another purpose. Mimi was going to command her fleet like Nelson led his Fleet to victory at Trafalgar, watching the action from his quarterdeck, and sending silent, visual signals.

Mimi plugged in her headset to the forward rail, as Ord emptied his canvas bag, and plugged in the thick cord that ran from the bottom of the pistol-grip handle of a brass cylinder like a squat coffee can.

Mimi looked to our right, where the *Yorktown* floated in the distance. She held lenses to her eyes, and sighted on the *Yorktown*'s observation blister. Even without lenses, I saw a light flicker our way.

Mimi nodded. "Good. Flash an acknowledgment, Sergeant Major?"

Ord's surplus-purchased Aldis Lamps were a century old. Their principal advantage over signaling in Morse code with a flashlight was that an Aldis had a telescopic sight that allowed its beam to be directed where the receiving party could read the dots and dashes. After our landing debacle on Tressel, Ord had acquired on Earth, then distributed among the fleet's cruisers, lead Scorpions, and transports Aldis Lamps like the one he signaled with.

He had also made few friends by forcing pilots, weapons officers, and communications swabbies to learn ancient Morse code.

It was hardly state-of-the-art radio, but it worked. Besides, the Slugs saw in the infrared spectrum, so they probably didn't even know we had beaten their jamming.

Mimi also plugged in a mini display, which gave her an electronic view similar to what she had on the bridge. But the battle between our Scorpions and the much larger Firewitches was easy to see, unaided.

The Scorpions darted around and through the Firewitches, which kept together in boxy formations so one ship's mag rifles could cover another's tail. But where a Firewitch could twist fast enough to hit a Starfire, none could lay a glove on a right-angling Scorpion. As a Scorpion would pass above, below, or to left or right of a Firewitch, a flash would flicker as the Scorpion dropped a missile out of its stinger tail pod, the missile homed, lit, and punched into the Firewitch. In moments, the missile's thermobaric would ignite, and the Firewitch would explode in a silent, purple puff.

Mimi gave commands to the Scorpion wings, and Ord relayed them in Morse to the Wing leaders. But I couldn't imagine that a Scorpion pilot, optics or not, would have time to find and decipher those tiny flashes. It hardly mattered. As I watched, more Firewitches joined the fray. Still the hundreds of tiny white Scorpions twisted and danced around the ponderous, blue-black squids. I glanced down at the threat counter on Mimi's mini display. It read sixty Firewitches, down a net twenty-three, and kept dropping, even as more Slug ships entered the battle.

The Slugs were losing so fast that, if this were a boxing bout, they would throw in the towel.

Suddenly, my gut got cold. We had never seriously thought about what might happen if things went too well for our side, because they so rarely did. Slug warriors would drop dead if cornered, unless they could take you with them. We nearly captured an intact Slug Projectile during the Blitz, but it blew itself up, and nearly took Howard and me with it.

I leaned toward Howard. "What do the Slugs do when they know they've lost?"

"Die."

"Exactly. Would they blow Mousetrap up, and themselves with it?"

"To deny it to us? Probably."

"How do we stop them?"

"I can think of one option."

"So can I. But it's bad."

SIXTY

TEN MINUTES LATER, Mimi moved her Flag, again, this time amidships, to the launch bays, with me, Howard, and Planck in her wake. Her executive officer had taken over directing traffic from the observation blister, as new cruisers popped out into the radio-silent Mousetrap, then poured their Scorpions into a massive dogfight no remote commander could meaningfully direct, anyway.

The first of *Emerald River*'s Scorpions was returning to rearm, and Mimi wanted to be on the flight deck, where she could be sure they re-sortied fast, and where she could extract immediate information from pilots while they were back aboard.

We came through the bay hatch into choreographed chaos. The Scorpion, shimmering white, with its ceramic canopy already open, was backing down the hissing launch rails, away from the resealed inner doors.

The hemispheric bay, vast and crowded at the same time, looked like the globe of a gumball machine shaken by a giant. The Bay Boss and Pushers hung above everything in a hovering oversight gantry, pointing and signaling with yellow-gloved hands, wearing yellow vests and helmets. The clamshell doors of the Scorpion's stinger pod, like the doors that had enfolded me when the Slugs first hit Mousetrap, yawned, while swabbies in red armorer's vests hoisted missiles into the Scorpion pod. The green-vested launch rail crew reset the Scorpion to return to the fight, and purple-vested Grapes, the refueling crew disenfranchised by the Cavorite-powered Scorpion, bounced among the others lending hands where needed.

By the number on the tail stinger, this was the Scorpion that had been assigned the most determinative action of this early phase of the battle, and had performed its mission unarmed and vulnerable. It had been assigned to deliver Jeeb to Mousetrap's surface. Its pilot stood, helmet visor up, eyes wide, sweating while he gulped a Coke plasti and watched the armorers reload his ship so it could rejoin the battle as a fighter spacecraft.

Mimi asked Jude, "How'd it go?"

He panted between gulps. Sweat streamed down his face. "Firewitch can't maneuver fast enough to track its rifles on us. S'like stealing, skipper."

I asked him, "Did you deliver the package?"

Jude nodded, but he wouldn't look at me. I still didn't know whether he blamed me for his mother's death, or whether he was afraid that if we acknowledged one another we would finally acknowledge her loss.

He stared at the armoring crew, as he replied to nobody in particular, "Jeeb was crawling around the surface when I backed out."

Mimi asked, "How's the ordnance performing?"

Jude nodded. "One shot, one kill. As long as the Slugs run out of targets before we run out of missiles, we'll control the envelope around Mousetrap."

That was always the problem with the Slugs.

The Bay Boss waved Jude back to his cockpit, and the canopy closed over my godson. The Scorpion slid forward on its launch rails until the inner doors closed behind it, then the hull shuddered as he rejoined the battle.

Howard furrowed his brow, and said to Planck, who, for all his inexperience, was in command of his first space firefight, "Sir, we assumed we'd have greater difficulty in these initial phases. I think it's likely, if things continue, that the Pseudocephalopod will destroy Mousetrap while it still has enough control of the moon to do so."

Planck said, "How do we prevent that?"

"Abandon plans to land forces on Mousetrap. The Pseudocephalopod can't keep up with our Scorpions. If we saturation bomb Mousetrap with penetrating thermobarics, we would scour every living thing out of the interior. Right now, It can't stop us from doing that."

I said, "But we still don't know whether the humans inside Mousetrap are alive."

Planck said, "These Slugs are ruthless. You've said it yourselves. They've been in control of Mousetrap for years, now. The garrison were engineers, not combat troops. Jason, be realistic. There's no one left inside to save."

Certainly there were no Social Republicans inside to save. "Aud, the whole reason to insert Jeeb inside Mousetrap was to resolve that uncertainty."

Mimi said, "The Slugs are jamming everything. As far as we know, Jeeb didn't even find a way in. I didn't want to say it to Jude, but Jeeb's moot."

Howard shook his head. "Jeeb's brainlink transmits outside normal bandwidths. The Pseudocephalopod reacts economically once it reacts. It may jam only frequencies it's heard us use a lot."

The brainlink frequency was so exotic that I wore the only receiver that could hear anything Jeeb transmitted, anyway. But I hadn't heard a thing.

"I won't lose this campaign by delaying for a maybe." Planck turned to Mimi. "Admiral, recover and rearm all the Scorpions, in turn. When we're ready, scour every living thing out of Mousetrap."

Mimi said, "Yes, sir."

Harsh reality may have turned Audace Planck into a dictator. But it hadn't undone him as a commander. I didn't like what he was ordering. But I couldn't disagree with it, either.

Emerald River began to shudder as, one after another, her Scorpions returned to take on penetrators that would enable us to fry every Slug inside Mousetrap.

I recalled Ord by intercom, and met him in the adjacent bay. As we watched, the bay inner doors opened, and a Scorpion slid back in down the launch rails. Armorers scurried toward its stinger pod. Within minutes, the Scorpion would be ready to re-launch. On the revolver's opposite side a troop transport sat cold on the rails.

I pointed at the empty transport. "If we knew there were friendlies inside Mousetrap, we would have landed troops in Mousetrap. What did we project? Thirty percent casualties?"

"Low side, yes, sir."

"Now the embarked divisions may take zero casualties. Overall, this result will be better than our best case. So why do I feel like shit?"

"Heroes get to choose the ditch they die in, sir."

If any humans remained alive inside Mousetrap, they would never have had a choice.

Hydraulic whine echoed, as the armorers lifted a thermobaric toward the Scorpion in the bay.

"Jeeb, is that you?" It was a whisper.

I turned to Ord. "What?"

He turned to me, frowning. "Sir?"

My right earpiece fed me whatever I dialed up. Which, lately, was nothing but intraship chatter. Forgotten in my left ear was the old-fashioned bud that was supposed to have brought me Jeeb's transmissions from Mousetrap.

I pressed the left piece closer.

A voice said, "Jeeb, can I transmit through you?"

I recognized the voice. My heart thumped at the whisper.

I switched my throat mike to Jeeb's frequency, then whispered back. "Munchkin?"

"Jason?" Her voice cracked. "I thought you were dead."

"I thought you were dead. What happened?"

"I hung on to a tether. After you floated away, I got back inside. We can hear activity. What's going on?"

"We?"

"Six thousand of us here, barricaded inside Level Twenty. I don't know how many more. How did Jeeb find me?"

"He was supposed to get inside. If he recognized somebody . . ."

Munchkin asked, "What happens next?"

Ord was staring at me. I motioned him to follow as I ran toward the Bridge. As I ran I thumbed my mike back to intercom.

SIXTY-ONE

MIMI AND AUD faced Ord and me as the bosun piped us onto the Bridge. Mimi asked, "How many?"

"Munchkin says six thousand with her. Barricaded on Level Twenty. The Slugs have been content to wait for them to starve."

Aud Planck frowned. "We can't risk the mission for them."

They weren't Aud's troops. They weren't mine, either. They were mostly Marini. That didn't make them less valuable to me, and I hoped, in spite of Aud's transformation, to him. Humanity aside, if Earth and Tressel turned their back on the Marini, we could lose the ally that supplied our Cavorite.

I said, "We have to try."

Aud looked at Mimi. She stood with her feet planted, arms crossed.

Aud nodded. "Alright." He turned to me. "I'll authorize landings. But if we get any indication that the Slugs are going to destroy Mousetrap, the Scorpions go in."

Mimi spoke into her mike. Within minutes, we felt

the hull shudder as revolvers rotated the Scorpions out of launch position, and replaced them with troop transports.

Ord and I armored up, because I was going in with my troops. We returned to the bays, and watched as troops boarded the transports, then we headed forward again, to the observation blister.

I switched back to Jeeb's frequency. "Munchkin? What's the situation down there?"

"You guys have stirred the Slugs up."

"Meaning what?"

"Meaning they're pounding down our passageway barricades with Heavys. Jason, we won't last an hour once they get through."

I held up one finger to Ord, and raised my eyebrows.

He looked at me, and shook his head. We wouldn't even be able to get our landing transports close to Mousetrap in an hour, much less relieve Munchkin's survivors. As we swam into the observation blister, I relayed the bad news to Mimi on the Bridge.

"Mousetrap's visible now, General." Ord tapped my armored shoulder, as he pointed through the observation blister.

Ord grunted. "The real estate hardly looks worth the price, does it, sir?"

"Location, location, location, Sergeant Major."

Ord and I pushed back from the observation blister's forward wall, to head aft to our troop transport. I glanced at the time-to-drop countdown winking off my wrist 'Puter. Two hours. Too long.

Ord sighed. "A hundred thousand GIs don't buy what they used to, General."

Whump.

The vast hull shuddered, tumbling Ord and me against the observation blister's cold curve.

Hssss.

A thousand feet aft from us, thirty-six launch bay hatches resealed as one.

A tin voice from the Bridge crackled in my earpiece. "Wing away."

I turned to Ord, wide eyed. "What the hell, Sergeant Major?"

Ord turned his palms up, shook his head.

Through ebony space, thirty-six sparks flashed past us. In a blink, they dispersed toward Mousetrap, leaving behind thirty-six silent, red streaks of drifting chemical flame.

For one heartbeat, we formed the hub that anchored those thirty-six fading, translucent wheel spokes. It was as though we spun at the center of a mute, exploding firework. To our port, starboard, dorsal, and ventral, identical fireworks blossomed, gold, green, blue, purple, as the Fleet's other cruisers launched their own craft, each ship trailing its mothership's tracer color.

The ships weren't chunky troop transports. They were Scorpions, their stinger pod racks packed with liquid fire. One order from the Bridge had rotated troop transports out of the bays in fifteen minutes, like cartridges in old-fashioned revolvers, and replaced them with Scorpions.

I torpedoed my weightless body hand-over-hand down the rungs that lined the center tube, back toward the Bridge. "If those bombers fry Mousetrap, our POWs die."

I shook my head at Ord. "If this fleet kills Outworld

POWs, the Union's dead. If the Union dies, the Slugs will wipe mankind out. Did Mimi lose her mind?"

Ord paddled up alongside me, and shook his head. "Admiral Ozawa wouldn't launch bombers, sir. She wouldn't even consider it without consulting you, first. But there is a ranking civilian authority aboard this ship. If he ordered her to do it, she couldn't—"

The two of us 'frogged along toward the Bridge, gaining weight as we moved away from the rotating cruiser's centerline.

Bad enough that Planck was willing to sacrifice Munchkin and the other survivors. My godson—Munchkin's only child—was as cold as his master. And Jude was out there, presumably commanding the bombers that were about to kill his own mother. And he didn't even know she was alive inside Mousetrap.

Crack.

A side-tube pressure valve released, like a rifle shot, and my heart skipped.

A minute later, the bosun piped Ord and me back onto the Bridge.

SIXTY-TWO

I STALKED TOWARD MIMI, Aud Planck, and Howard, their faces bathed in red as they stood staring into the holo display. I pointed at the red swarm that marked the hovering Scorpions. "That's it? You just gave up? You're gonna blow the survivors to hell?"

Mimi drew back, stared at my clenched fists, her jaw slack. "Jason, have you lost your mind?"

"No! Have you?" My heart pounded, and I trembled. A military decision, even one I disagreed with, no longer made me lose my composure. But piled on to Munchkin's resurrection, her current plight, Jude's complicity in the impending murder of his own mother, six thousand others, and, apparently, Mimi's betrayal, I had lost my mind.

Both aisles of swabbies stared up from their consoles at us. Raging battle or not, if a male lieutenant general was going to slug a female fleet admiral half his size, nobody wanted to miss the show.

Aud Planck stepped between us, took my elbow. "Change of plans, Jason."

Mimi straightened herself, and tugged a uniform cuff. "If the survivors inside really have an hour, there's no time to land transports." She pointed at the green dot Scorpion swarm. "We reloaded and launched Scorpions so they can engage and draw off all the interceptors."

I wrinkled my brow. "But we can't land transports."

"No." Mimi waved the display to a cutaway of Mouse-trap that her intel jocks had enhanced. It showed the center tunnel, six hundred yards wide and twenty miles long, which ran down Mousetrap's centerline from the camera-iris entry doors at the north pole to the similar exit doors at the south pole. Level Twenty, where the survivors holed up, adjoined the centerline tunnel fifteen miles south of the north pole doors. A tiny orange beacon blinked within level twenty.

Howard pointed to the beacon. "This is the central access-control facility. Where Gustus punched the button to close the hatches and pressure up Mousetrap. Every airtight hatch on Mousetrap, including the north and south pole doors, is controlled from there. Vacuum kills unprotected Pseudocephalopod warriors as dead as it kills humans. And we've never seen a warrior protected by any sort of pressure suit."

We had rejected the blow down alternative early on, because wc couldn't fight our way to the Button fast enough. But now we didn't have to. We were already there.

I thumbed my throat mike. "Munchkin? Did you guys think about blow down?"

"That's why we holed up on Level Twenty. And probably why the Slugs haven't come in after us. They know we're holding a live grenade."

"You could suit up."

"We've got maybe a couple hundred pressure suits altogether. And Level Twenty can't be sealed off separately. If we blow down the Slug levels, we blow down Level Twenty, too."

I turned to Howard. "So far this doesn't sound like a plan."

Mimi said, "Tell Munchkin to get her people ready to move."

"Why?"

"We're gonna bring them a spacesuit, then strangle the maggots."

I squinted at Mimi. "Spacesuit?"

She stamped the deck. "You're standing in it."

She walked toward the exit hatch, then turned to me, and waved me to follow. "Move it, Jason."

SIXTY-THREE

———

WHEN THE TWO of us were alone in the outer passageway, Mimi spun to face me, then stuck out her chin. "I'd give up on those people down there? You think that little of me?"

I turned my palms up. "Mimi I—"

She shook her head, then spun back and jogged toward the launch bays. "There's no time for this. Jason, tell Munchkin she has to get somebody reliable to handle the Button."

"Reliable?"

"Dead-solid perfect."

"Mind explaining why?"

"On my mark, they need to open the north pole entrance, then close it. Howard says the doors are built to take the stress, and a one-second wink won't hurt the interior pressure."

"What happens in the one second?"

"We fly in."

"Mimi, in one second you can't get enough transports through—"

"Not transports. This ship. At fifty thousand miles per hour."

My jaw dropped and I stopped dead in the passageway. Mean Green was as big as three wet-bottom aircraft carriers. Mousetrap's inlet door was barely wider than Mean Green, designed for a cruiser to ease in at five miles per hour. They said landing a fixed-wing plane on a wet-bottom carrier at night was like taking a belly flop in a dark room onto a postage stamp and trying to hit the stamp with your tongue. This would be harder, and failure more catastrophic. "You're kidding."

She stopped, and turned, hands on hips. "Jason, there's no time."

Mimi actually planned to thread a moving needle in one second. If she missed by a few feet, the collision would be like slamming the Empire State Building into Mount Everest at seventy-one times the speed of sound.

"And if you get in? Fifty thousand miles per hour to zero in fifteen miles?" Theoretically, a C-drive cruiser could stop on the proverbial dime, and return change. People inside the cruiser wouldn't even spill their coffee. But nobody had ever tried it, especially not inside a giant sewer.

Mimi said, "We'll pull up to Level Twenty before the Slugs know what hit them."

"Figuratively speaking." If we hit them, or anything, at any significant fraction of fifty thousand miles per hour, everybody's day would be spoiled.

We reached the launch bays, which were empty at the launch positions.

Mimi pointed. "I'll nuzzle the launch bay level up to

the cargo docks on Level Twenty. Then we'll open all the doors and take on passengers."

In some insane way, Mimi was making sense. If we could pull up transports like a row of taxicabs, it would take far too long to board survivors fifty at a time through their hatches. But Mean Green's bay doors were bigger than railway tunnels.

What the hell. If everybody was crazy, I might as well play. I pointed at the bay doors. "The outer doors are eighty feet wide. If we throw out cargo nets, and help people board—"

She smiled. "See? It'll work. Disembark some troops. To cover the boarding, and to help the survivors get in here. They probably aren't healthy enough to move as fast as we need them to move, on their own."

"How fast?"

"Howard thinks you'll be up to your asses in warriors within ten minutes. The Slugs will decide to blow the place in a half hour, unless we kill them before they get a chance."

Mimi might be right. One area where mankind's untidy individual disorganization served better than the Slugs' unitary intellect was initiative. A human commander on the spot could alter plans instantly when the situation changed. The Slugs had to send information back to a central ganglion, and get instructions back. Actually, the Spooks had never seen a central ganglion, but the theory fit the delays we observed in Slug units' reaction times. Of course, once the Slugs all got pointed in one direction, they were ruthless little maggots.

I asked, "What happens when we get everybody aboard?"

"One thing you *have* to arrange is for somebody to put the Button on time delay. We seal up out here, the delay ends, the hatches all open. We fly out the south pole doors, just in case the Slugs can blow the place up. But every cubic foot of void space in Mousetrap should become vacuum inside one minute. Later, we come back and clean out four hundred thousand strangled maggots."

"Four hundred thousand?" I adjusted the pistol in my shoulder holster.

"Howard's estimate. But he says only forty thousand can get at you at a time." Mimi pointed forward. "I gotta go." Then she paused, looked up at me, and squeezed my hand. Her eyes glistened. "Don't be stupid, okay?"

"Drive careful."

Then she was gone.

SIXTY-FOUR

TEN MINUTES LATER, I stood in yet another launch bay, watching troops clamber out of the Transport in the bay, while their officers and non-comms briefed them on the fly. I spoke into my throat mike, to Munchkin. "You understand? You open the doors too late, the *Emerald River* smashes like a bug. You leave the doors open too long, the centerline tunnel decompresses. You all can't cross vacuum to us. If you blow that timing, the *Emerald River* might as well be in Sweden."

"Got it. One second. On Mimi's mark." In the background, small arms crackled, and Slug mag rail rifles sang.

"How hot is it in there?"

"Getting worse."

"Munchkin, how close are you to the access control room, personally?"

"In it. With a few others."

"Any bad company?"

"Not yet."

As we talked, I watched Ord and the captain commanding the company disembarked in this bay. They briefed the kids who sat cross-legged on the deck, their helmets in their laps. They were Pathfinders, with Mohawk haircuts, even the girls. They were better trained to find their way in Mousetrap's interior tunnels.

I said to Munchkin, "As soon as we get inside, your people and mine are trading places. A couple hours' vacuum won't bother us in Eternads. My people are better armed and armored than yours."

There was a pause, and machine gun fire.

Munchkin said, "No shit."

I glanced up at the display screen on the bulkhead. The ready light that had been blinking red turned amber. I said to Munchkin, "I'm patching you through direct to Mimi. No relay on this end. None on yours. You got your finger on the trigger, personally?"

"It's a Button. Yes."

I switched the feed so Munchkin and Mimi were talking directly.

On screen, Mousetrap rotated far below us, its north pole doors closed as solid as the iron they were. In the far distant blackness beyond Mousetrap, sparks and purple puffs marked the battle among our Scorpions, the Fire-witches, and four of our cruisers. Jude was out there, fighting for his life, unaware that he was fighting for his mother's life, too.

Mimi whispered to Munchkin, "Five minutes."

The Pathfinders helmeted up, checked weapons, buddy-checked one another's equipment. Behind them, another company waited, with rope ladders and folded litters slung across their bodies, to drop down and recover survivors. We would be so near Mousetrap's low-gravity centerline that our rescuers would be able to leap small buildings in a single bound. But Munchkin had confided that conditions below had been brutal. Food and water had been scarce, and then grown scarcer. We couldn't expect the survivors to help much with their own rescue.

Mean Green's other bays contained similar groups. How many bays would wind up close enough to Level Twenty's dock to embark survivors we wouldn't know until we got inside. If we got inside.

My heart pounded against my breastplate. A kid handed me an M-40 from armory stores, and I cleared, then locked and loaded it.

Mimi whispered, "One minute."

The ready light on the bulkhead winked green, then kept flashing.

On screen, Mousetrap looked smaller than a raisin. The doors Mimi had to fly this monstrosity through weren't even a speck on Mousetrap's surface.

The kid who had handed me my rifle stood beside me, eyes squeezed shut, while he prayed into his audio.

Mimi whispered, "Ten seconds."

SIXTY-FIVE

"Go!" said Mimi.

"Done," said Munchkin.

I held my breath.

Emerald River went from adrift in space to fifty thousand miles per hour before I could blink. It was as simple as Mimi ordering baffles opened, just so. The pull of the rest of the universe did the rest.

But inside our gravity cocoon, it was like standing in a ballroom, watching a flatscreen film on the wall.

Mousetrap was tiny.

Mousetrap was huge.

The doors were closed.

Before I could flinch, the screen darkened. I hadn't seen the door open, hadn't seen us flash through it.

Screeeeek!

On screen, a tunnel rotated like we were inside a drab kaliedoscope. The dim dot at the tunnel's end was the south pole doors, five miles away.

Booom!

Snuggling a moving skyscraper up against a rotating iron moonlet was delicate, but delicacy was relative.

Mean Green was going to need fifty thousand gallons of touch-up paint, but Mimi had delivered the goods.

The kid beside me opened his eyes, and they widened. "Wow."

I flicked my eyes to the lights above the inner bay doors, as they cycled red, over and over. Only when the outer sensors detected atmospheric pressure outside would Mean Green's inner and outer doors snap open.

I cut myself back into Jeeb's talk loop. "Munchkin, we're in. Doors open in—"

"Jason, it just got hot out there."

On the wall screen, I saw the flash of Mag rifles, as Slug warriors around the edges of the centerline tunnel opened up on *Emerald River*'s bow. Mean Green's forward turrets returned fire. Streams of red tracer poured out, marking the path of forty-five hundred rounds per minute of explosive cannon shells, each bigger than a middle finger and less friendly. The turrets also lobbed flares into the tunnel, at lower rates of fire, that burst and made the drifting gunsmoke glow red.

The kid next to me stood goggle-eyed. "I thought they weren't so hard to kill, sir."

Slug body armor makes a warrior look like a shiny black, man-sized cobra, with a single pseudopod poking out, wrapped around a Mag-rail rifle. An individual warrior looks scary, but even a pistol round cuts that armor like cheese.

Mean Green's turret guns were designed to shoot down incoming missiles, not splatter Slugs like green tomatoes. I said to him, "The flares and the rounds are mostly to raise the temperature out there." According to the Spooks, the closer to human body temperature the air around us got, the more us humans looked as invisible as shadows to the Slugs. Outnumbered by hundreds to one, we needed all the help we could get.

Despite Mean Green's suppressive fire, Slug rounds rattled off her hull like raindrops. She could take rifle fire all day without damage, but if the Slugs were able to bring up Heavys and shell *Emerald River*, we could be stuck in here with four hundred thousand angry maggots, and no ride home.

The faster we got out of this ship and into Mouse-trap's passages, the faster we could shut down the Slugs. I glanced again at the flashing red lights above the bay doors, and hissed between clenched teeth. "Come on! Come on!"

The Pathfinders pressed forward, rifles held across their bodies at port arms.

In my ear, Munchkin said, "Jason, we've got a problem here."

Above the bay doors, the lights turned solid green.

The inner doors hissed back, then the outer doors, with a pop as the slight remaining pressure differential between the interior of Mousetrap and the interior of *Emerald River* equalized.

SIXTY-SIX

ZEEE. ZEEE. ZEEE.

Mag rifle rounds whizzed into the bay through the open outer doors, clanged off the deckplates and bulkheads, and ricocheted off equipment and armor. A round thunked my left thigh, hard enough that I slipped to one knee, but didn't penetrate.

The Pathfinders had fanned out across Level Twenty's dock platform, which was one hundred yards long and fifty yards deep. The collision with *Emerald River*'s hull had wrinkled the platform's thick steel like a tablecloth, and the Pathfinders dropped behind the folds and set a semicircular perimeter.

Behind me, *Emerald River*'s hull rose and curved away, as big and white as a convex hydroelectric dam. In a row above our open bay doors, I could see the black openings of a half dozen more doors, with troops rappelling down toward us.

I ran, crouched, to the Pathfinder captain, and pointed toward an open overhead loading door beyond which a passage led up and away from the centerline tunnel. He had his own map on his visor display, but I had been here before. "That's the way to the Button. Move your people out!"

"Yes, sir."

Something had caused me to lose radio contact with Munchkin, but it wasn't Slug jamming, because close range intercom here inside Mousetrap was working fine.

I switched back to my link via Jeeb to Munchkin. "Munchkin? Do you copy?"

Nothing. I swore, tried again, as I fell in behind the Pathfinders. Fifty feet beyond the loading door, we came upon our first survivors. The two of them hobbled toward us. One held a pistol in one hand, while his other hand held the wrist of his buddy, whose arm draped around his shoulder. The buddy's left leg was splinted, so he hopped on the right one, only. Torn, greasy uniform shards dangled from arms and legs that were as thin as wire. The one with the pistol smiled. "Good to see you!"

The Pathfinder captain stared at me through his visor, as he whispered on command net. "Sir, if they're all in as tough shape as these two—" Which they were, or else hundreds of them would have greeted us at the loading platform, like they were supposed to. "—It's gonna take us a lot longer to load 'em."

Worse, they were all clogging the passages we were advancing through. We would have to pick our way like we were clearing a hostage site, or we'd risk shooting the very people we were here to save.

I tried Munchkin again. Nothing.

I switched my visor display to monitor Jeeb. It was possible he was shut down but Munchkin was fine. I swore. All Jeeb's indicators were in the green. Was Munchkin down? Did the Button still exist?

We had made a hundred yards toward the access control room, and had three hundred to go. Behind us, other troops filtered forward, picking up survivors too weak to walk, pointing the healthy ones back toward the ship.

The Command Net light flashed yellow on my display, and I keyed up Mimi.

"Jason? What's going on?"

"These people are almost too weak to walk out, Mimi. Can you buy us time?"

"I think so. The turret gunners are having a turkey shoot, so I don't think the ship's in danger yet."

The smoke and thunder that had begun from the forward turrets had now spread to the midships and aft turrets, too.

The maggots were coming out of the walls and floors and ceilings all around us. One of the maggots' favorite tricks was to strip their armor, then attack. Like octopi, they could squeeze their boneless bodies through inch wide cracks. They oozed through the nooks and crannies without armor or weapons, but, by the tens or hundreds, they could take down a careless GI, plug off his armor vents and sensors with their slimy little bodies, and eventually strangle, fry, or freeze him.

According to the Spooks, Slugs had no more sense of self than a fingernail clipping had, so the tactic wasn't some noble kamikaze sacrifice. If the Slugs had enough warriors in any battle, they tried it. If they were still trying crap like the squeeze and wheeze, they felt like the battle remained winnable, so they probably weren't going to blow Mousetrap up.

An unarmored Slug dropped from the ceiling, and smothered my faceplate in translucent green. I torc it off, flung it to the deck, and jumped on it with both feet. The warrior popped like a green grape as big as a sleeping bag, I slipped in the goo, and landed on my butt.

Couldn't I ever just command a battle like a real general? Just stand on a hill with binoculars, ordering my staff to order battalions to maneuver this way and that, while my pennant flapped in the breeze? Why did I always end up ass deep in slimy green maggots, who never followed the script?

Ten minutes later, the Pathfinder column halted, took knees, and covered down. I squeezed around the troops, panting into their intercom mikes, until I reached their captain. The passage opened out into a dim, high-ceilinged, wide chamber. So far as I recalled, Level Twenty had no high ceilings. The captain stood in front of a rough iron mass that ran from the passage's floor to ceiling and from wall to wall.

He spread his arms at the mass in front of him. "Sir, we got a bad map or we're lost. This isn't the access control room."

Worse, maybe it was the control room, all that was left of it.

I played my light on the ceiling, then back on the mass that blocked us, and grunted. "Roof caved in." Theoretically, the vibration of the firefights and the impact of *Emerald River* scraping against Mousetrap shouldn't have triggered a cave-in. Theoretically, bumblebees didn't fly.

In a space between fallen, angular iron boulders, movement flickered. A soldier yelled, "Maggot up!" He fired, and sparks flashed as rounds ricocheted off iron block.

I raised my hand. "Hold fire!"

An antenna like a thin, black worm poked around the boulder, then the rest of Jeeb's head followed it.

I ran to Jeeb, peered behind him, and shone my light into the space from which he had crawled. It necked down to a jagged tube in the rocks no wider than a man's leg.

A thin, dirty face appeared at the tube's end. "Anybody out there?" Munchkin called.

SIXTY-SEVEN

I LEANED FURTHER in to the crevasse, and popped my helmet visor. "Munchkin? It's Jason. What's going on?"

She shouted to me, and it was a weak shout, "A half dozen of us were buttoned up here, in the access control room. We started taking fire from Slugs. They got impatient, and knocked the roof down with a heavy. I'm all that's left."

My relief that our action hadn't brought the roof down on her was short lived. "Are you okay? Does the Button still work?"

She coughed. "The Button worked fine to get you inside. I think it's still fine. I'm nicked."

"How nicked?"

"Doesn't matter. I'm not going anywhere."

"We'll dig you out."

"You won't."

"I got you out of the last rockfall. I'll get you out of this one."

"I mean don't even think about trying. If you move this rubble, and a rockfall damages the Button, it's all over."

"There may be a space big enough—"

"Jason, the reason I can't talk to you through Jeeb anymore is because, when the roof fell, Jeeb wound up out there, and I'm stuck in here. Jeeb's been hunting a way back in here for ten minutes. If there's not room for a TOT, there's not room for a person."

This time the command circuit in my helmet didn't flash. Mimi just broke in. Her voice echoed loud enough that Munchkin could hear through my open visor. "Jason, we're gonna have all the survivors boarded in six minutes. Are your people gonna be able to blow the doors?"

"No. Yeah. I need more time."

"I already bought as much time as I could. What the hell's going on?"

I told her.

I rubbed my forehead through my open visor.

Munchkin said, "Jason, it's simple. You leave. I blow the doors. We win."

I couldn't even say, "And you die!"

Mimi said, "Twelve minutes. Not one second more."

"Look, Mimi. You could just pull the ship out of here like you came in. We just won't decompress the whole—"

Munchkin said, "Give the Slugs a chance to blow Mousetrap to bits? And Mimi's ship and crew with it? And if they don't blow Mousetrap up, you have to fight your way back in? I'm one casualty. That's thousands."

Mimi said, "Jason, she's right. Given time, we could bring in engineers and move that blockage. Given time, we could dig the Slugs out of their holes without decompressing everything. But I can't trade my ship, and the future of the human race, to buy time. Not for anybody."

I shook my head. This wasn't Ganymede. We were

stronger now. We were smarter. I was stronger and smarter. I had beaten the Slugs in space, I had beaten the Slugs on Bren. This time, when I had dug Munchkin out, I had beaten death itself. I would do it again, somehow.

The Pathfinders' captain tapped my shoulder. "Sir, we have recall from *Emerald River*."

I waved him away.

Mimi whispered, "Jason, there's no other way. Eleven minutes!"

Jeeb squatted in the rubble, beside me. His optics stared up at me, round and unquestioning. He might not know why, but he knew he would never leave me.

I turned to the Pathfinder captain. "Get your people back aboard."

I heard a tiny exhalation of relief hiss through his microphone. He saluted, started to turn toward the ship. Then he turned back. "Sir? What about you?"

"I'm staying."

SIXTY-EIGHT

—————

NINE MINUTES REMAINED before Mimi would radio in that it was time for Munchkin to open every hatch in Mousetrap. Then *Emerald River* would escape with six thousand saved souls. Every Slug in Mousetrap would die, and it would again be ours, intact. And Munchkin would die.

The whole rock was silent, as though even the maggots were resigned to the end.

Mimi whispered in my earpiece, "Why the hell are you staying, Jason?"

"Somebody has to relay your cues to Munchkin."

"She doesn't need any cues, and you know it. She knows we'll be buttoned up in nine minutes, then she pushes the Button."

"I'm wearing Eternads. I'll be fine." I could have said that the decompression would mean for Munchkin at least a quick end. I could have said a lot of things. But the truth was that my remaining here was irresponsible. I was in command of a hundred thousand troops. There was no rational basis for me to remain with Munchkin. I couldn't save her, and I was delaying the moment when I had to explain my failure to myself.

Across the stillness, Munchkin whispered to me, "How is he, Jason?"

I swallowed back sobs, until I could speak. "He's great. He looks more like his father every day. Flies like an angel. He smiles a lot, now—"

"But . . . is he one of them?"

I paused. Jude might not be. Planck was a hard man, but could I say he was a Nazi? Wasn't Jude more of her than he could ever be of them?

She said, "Jason!"

"No. Never. He—"

Bang.

SIXTY-NINE

I LEAPT FORWARD so far that my helmet wedged into the crevasse. "Munchkin!"

Her face was no longer there. She had shot herself. My hesitation had caused it. If I had answered sooner . . .

The Button was inaccessible, now. *Emerald River* was trapped in here now, surrounded by four hundred thousand Slugs.

Bang.

"Jason! They're oozing through the cracks!"

The openings into the access control room were too small for me, too small even for Jeeb, but plenty big enough for a Slug warrior to squeeze through.

"How many?"

"Lots. Jason, I'm out of ammunition."

I screamed to Mimi, "Munchkin's got Slugs! We gotta blow the doors now!"

"We've got six bays open, with a thousand people in 'em. Find me two minutes, Jason!"

I tugged out my pistol, gripped it in my fist, then thrust my arm into the crevasse. "Munchkin! Here!"

"Farther! I can't reach!"

I stretched my arm until the socket screamed, then stretched some more.

"Jason, you're a foot away." She grunted, and I heard a sound like shoe leather kicking maggot.

My trench knife? Too short.

Throw the pistol? The tube was too narrow, too rough.

I looked around the passage. There was electrical conduit running across the ceiling, which I could use as a push pole, but by the time I ripped it loose . . .

I pulled my arm out of the crevasse, snatched out my trench knife, and pried my armored sleeve loose at the shoulder joint. I could stuff my bare arm deeper into the crevasse than my fat, armored arm.

"Munchkin! Here!" I grasped my pistol in my bare hand, then plunged my arm back into the pit.

I heard her grunt and struggle.

Then I felt fingertips against mine, and the pistol was gone.

I counted eight shots, from the other side. The full clip, then there was silence.

Mimi said in my ear, "We're sealed. Push the Button!"

My armor's arm lay ten feet away, the shoulder seal torn beyond repair. Theoretically, the metal bands at the major joints of Eternad armor would constrict if the suit sensed decompression, like automatic watertight doors in a submarine. Even to the point of amputation. Nobody had ever tried it. At least, nobody who had lived to brag about it. I was out of options.

"Munchkin?"

"Yeah. I'm clear of maggots for about another thirty seconds, in here."

I clenched my teeth. "Do it!"

In the distance, machinery squeaked and rumbled.

She whispered, "It was nice to feel your touch over here, Jason. Take care of my baby. Take care of you."

The hatch at the side of the passageway hissed, then it inched open.

The iron below me trembled, then the distant hiss became a roar.

Jeeb hopped up alongside me, cocked his optics, and peered in through my faceplate.

The roar became thunder, and dust and bits of construction debris stirred, then swirled, then blew away toward the open centerline tunnel.

On my visor display, I watched the outside pressure drop. The band at my shoulder clamped my arm, not too tight, yet. Like a blood-pressure cuff.

The rush of air down the passage was like a hurricane now, and rolled me toward the centerline.

I hooked my armored arm around a stanchion as I rolled past, and clung to it.

The shoulder band tightened around my arm like, I suppose, a python.

Jeeb clung to my armored shoulder. He wasn't helping, but it was good to know he was there. The outside pressure displayed on my visor reached zero, then the numbers blurred, and so did everything else.

SEVENTY

THE SPECIAL NEEDS Ward of New Bethesda Naval Hospital was on the ground floor. The Yellow Ribbon Girl with the pushcart chirped to me one day that this gave us the best courtyard views. But it was really so the convalescents— or, as I preferred to think of us, inmates—couldn't hurl themselves from windows.

I sat in my room chair, waiting for the screaming pain of morning therapy to subside. The sadists strapped my new arm against my ribs after every session, like the uneducated meat it was, which was supposed to reduce post-therapeutic irritation. What would have reduced my irritation was joy juice, but the bastards had weaned me off that months before. They assured me that traumatic amputation—was there any other kind?—resulted in a perfectly normal diminished sense of self, to which I would adapt, with time and therapy. They could give back my arm, but they could never give back family. Jude and I hadn't communicated since I failed to save his mother.

I turned my head toward my unmade bed. Later a therapist would unstrap my arm, and force me to make the bed myself, with as little assistance from him as possible.

He would extol the benefits of routine, of self reliance, and of motor skill redevelopment, while he smiled at my agony. I never spoke to the therapists. In all the months, I had never spoken to anyone.

Locked in the nightstand beside the torture rack was the medal that was awarded to band-aid my failure. They really didn't need to lock it up. They had already sawed the pin off the back. Even the meds in Special Needs were administered without IVs, so us convalescents couldn't manufacture nooses out of the tubing.

On the nightstand by the bed Jeeb perched. Some of my fellow nut jobs preferred companion dogs. Jeeb, however, didn't slobber or poop.

I read News-on-Text off the flat wall screen, waiting for the morning sun to light the courtyard outside my window. Special Needs Ward wasn't fed images, just text. Disturbing images retarded healing.

So, apparently, did news reports, because all Special Needs Ward ever got was a gruel of months-old headlines.

Human Union threatens additional sanctions against Tressel, citing intolerable human rights abuses. Clan hostility again threatens Cavorite. Fleet continues hot pursuit of Slug vessels escaping Second Battle of Mousetrap. By then, nobody on Earth knew how hot the pursuit was. Nobody even knew how many jumps out the Fleet was. Someday, word might wend its way back across the jumps. Unless the Fleet had been destroyed, and she was dead.

"Good morning, General! How are you feeling, today, sir?" Ord stepped through my door smiling like a drill sergeant meeting a busload of recruits, as pressed as ever in antediluvian utility uniform. He stiffened his utilities in some sort of ancient vegetable starch introduced during the laundry process. He smiled every morning, and asked how I felt, even though he knew I never answered.

As he did every morning, Ord pulled a visitor's chair alongside the window, where the light was better, donned his ancient wire-rimmed spectacles, and sat tapping away on his chipboard, plowing through paperless paperwork.

"Good morning, Jason! How are you feeling, today?"

It must have been Friday, because Sunshine Boy number two was also darkening my doorway. Nat Cobb visited every Friday morning. I never answered him, or anyone else, but still he came.

He had new Virtulenses, sleeker, presumably lighter, and he smiled as he drew up a visitor's chair in front of me, and leaned forward, elbows on knees. "No word yet on your retirement paperwork." He patted my knee. "Should come through any time."

He was lying. With my physical disability, retirement papers should have processed in days. Stump Peavey got early retired in hours after his stroke. General Cobb wouldn't admit it, but as long as he kept me on active duty, he could keep me there in Special Needs. Retirees were transferred to VA care, and the VA didn't have much of a suicide watch, whereas Special Needs was a funny farm. Also, as long as I remained on active duty, Nat could, apparently, trump up some job description so Ord could babysit me daily.

Actually, I had thought about self-waxing, in a detached, professional way. I concluded that, despite a soldier's familiarity with firearms and edged weapons, drug overdose would be most efficient. I could task Jeeb to steal barbiturates. This is a hospital. How hard could it be? But the trouble with a robot with personality is that he would probably come back, look up at me, hydraulics whining, and hold out a yellow box of chocolates from the gift shop, labeled "Please get well!"

Nat Cobb said, "We need you back. Jason, *you* need you back."

I looked away.

"I don't know why you stayed behind on Mousetrap. I suspect you don't know, really. It was irrational. But I know that if you hadn't stayed, we might have lost that battle. Instead, we won."

I kept staring at the wall. Why did people like Cobb and Ord keep imprinting merit onto my bungling? My so-called career had consisted of stumbling out of bad situations after the roof fell in—often literally. My stumbling had already burdened the taxpayers with reequipping me with two lungs, two femurs, and undifferentiated soft tissue. Currently it burdened them with the cost of my new arm. Not to mention a minimally camouflaged suicide watch. Worst, my stumbling had killed almost all of the people I loved most.

"Jason, I can teach any officer tactics and management. I can't teach intuition, and I can't manufacture life experience." General Cobb sat with me for ten more minutes. Finally, he sighed, like he did every Friday, then stood, and said to Ord, "A word, Sergeant Major?"

Ord would be gone with him until after lunch, presumably attending to some actual, productive business, instead of nursemaiding me.

Five minutes after they left, I heard in the hallway, "And how *is* the General on this *beautiful* day?" Yellow

Ribbon Girls wore sunshine-yellow smocks that identified them as volunteers. They spoke in italics, like they were on work-release from a home for the terminally perky. They delivered hard-copy mail, parcels, and USO flowers, from squeaking pushcarts.

I recognized the voice. That particular Yellow Ribbon Girl came each Friday. Nat always had chocolates sent up from the gift shop, which always arrived via her cart after he left. She always said, "Well, *well*! We have something *very* special for *you*, today!"

I always faced the wall, and waved her away. Finally, she always sighed, and I heard a metallic clank, as she chucked the chocolates box in the cart's wire bin, to be dropped off in the staff break room.

I heard her cart's wheels squeak as she entered my room. Then I heard paper rustle as she dug through the mass of parcels and mail on her cart.

She cleared her throat. "There's something for you, today."

Well, *well*! Today she didn't bubble. In fact, she had whispered. I waited for her to leave.

Plop.

The cart wheels squeaked, then vanished down the corridor.

I turned, and saw on my bed a Plastek mail bin. I never got mail, but the bin was labeled "Wander," followed by the right room number. Two envelopes angled above the bin's lip.

The first was the pale green of the Army Officers Personnel Directorate. AOPD still issued career-dispositive documentation in hard copy, and required blue ink, cursive signature. I suppose they required that because they were afraid you could steal somebody's thumbprint while they slept. I reached forward, plucked the envelope from the basket with my good hand, and tore it open with my teeth.

The Retirement Request Confirmation's first page thanked me for my service, and directed me to a site where I could research my VA options. The last page required my signature, requested date of separation, and choice of VA facility within the Continental United States, to which Retiree would be transferred forthwith upon separation.

I dropped the papers on the bed, for now. The only pens in Special Needs were welded to chains inside the nurse's station. Sharp objects.

I peered at the second envelope peeking out of the basket, and shuddered. No wonder the Yellow Ribbon Girl wasn't perky. In a nearly paperless age, the one communication in every service that was always hard copied, in fact always written in longhand, was a commander's letter of condolence to next of kin of a decedent. The letters were always written on commander's standard personal letterhead, always mailed in a thick, cream envelope, always hand-addressed.

Everyone associated with the military recognized weep-and-keep stationery, and approached the envelope like it was a cottonmouth. There was no letter any next of kin dreaded more. There was no letter a commander dreaded writing more.

I stared at the personal letterhead envelope's corner for ten minutes. Then I took a breath, and tugged it out.

The envelope was wrinkled, and covered with overlapping, multicolored cancellation place-and-date stamps. Hard copy mail inbound from the outworlds got cancelled each time it transferred ship-to-ship after a TFIP jump. I counted eight stamps. Some of the stamps named jumps I had never even heard of. When there is no transport, letters pile up, but when the chance comes to move mail back home, it flows in lumps. The envelope's earliest, original postmark was months old, barely after I was dragged out of Mousetrap.

I tore the envelope open, unfolded the single page inside, and read the handwriting.

Dearest Jason,
If you are reading this, you are alive, a fact uncertain to me as I write this. Just as you cannot know, or may not care, whether I am still alive as you read this. It is selfish of me to wish that you remain safe, and to hope that we may one day be together, but command leaves so few opportunities to be selfish . . .

There was more, but tears blurred my vision, and I had to set the letter down, to wipe my eyes with my available hand. I did blink my eyes, and cleared them enough to read the signature, "Love, Mimi."

I bent forward to look into the basket. It was filled with commander's stationery letterhead envelopes, identical to the one I had just dropped, and as I thumbed through them I found serial postmarks, one envelope for every day following her first letter.

I picked up my unsigned retirement letter, clamped one corner between my teeth, and tore it in half, then in quarters.

One of the usual therapists, his name was Roy, came in

to administer bed-making torture. When he saw the torn paper dangling from my mouth, his eyes widened.

I spit out the scraps, then spoke to him for the first time. "I'll make it alone, Roy. But first I've got mail to read."

SEVENTY-ONE

I FLOAT WEIGHTLESS in the observation blister on *Abraham Lincoln*'s prow. The spangled blackness glides around me, as the ship rotates. Dead ahead beckons the lightless disk of our next insertion point, its gravity already accelerating us forward. Invisible over my shoulder, the Fleet trails us, a single file of projected power that stretches behind this flagship, over a span longer than the distance between Earth and the moon.

My only companion in here, Jeeb, perches on the blister's handrail alongside me, and one of his legs squeaks loud enough in the stillness that I wince. He stares up at me with polished optics, and I task him. "Accelerate left third locomotor replacement."

In response, his internals click, so faintly that only I would notice, as he reprograms.

I rest one hand on the rail beside Jeeb, and my replaced arm throbs. By now, Jeeb and I each resemble George Washington's hatchet. One hundred percent original equipment, except for six new handles and four new heads.

But Jeeb, for all the humanity I see in him, is so immortal that he can survive a near-miss nuke, and is selfless in the way that only machinery can be. We humans are all too mortal and all too selfish. And that, my life has taught me, is the essence of being us. We understand our mortality, yet we sacrifice everything for others. Sometimes the calculus of sacrifice is simple, one life for six thousand, or for all mankind. Sometimes the calculus is one arm for nothing explicable. I believe that sacrifice won the Second Battle of Mousetrap for mankind. I fear that only more sacrifice will win this longest and broadest of wars for us. I believe that we will overcome the Pseudocephalopod because, in our best moments, we overcome our selfishness.

The Spooks and my life have taught me that our distant adversary is one, single, self-perpetuating unitary intelligence. As the Fleet gets closer and closer to It across the jumps, the Spooks gather their clues, and read their entrails. They say we will find at our enemy's core sentient tissue so eternal, so massive, that it has filled an entire planet, the way that a hermit crab grows to fill a discarded shell.

Despite the experience of most of a lifetime, that's all I know of the future. I think I've earned answers, but all that my soldier's life has rewarded me with are loved ones lost or barely known, and questions.

What else does Howard know that he hasn't told me? Can my old friend Bassin remake a world that exists half slave and half free? Are my godson and Audace Planck complicit in Tressel's evil empire? Does Jude blame me for his mother's death? Can Mimi and I ever be more than interstellar pen pals? And is this universe big enough for us and the Slugs?

From the speaker in the handrail, the bosun's whistle disturbs Wander's Philosophy 101. The whistle's music lilts, but I grumble because it never stops calling me. I sigh, then I somersault, and float aft, in the direction from which I came. "Let's go, Jeeb. We're not done yet."

Acknowledgments

Thanks to my editor, Devi Pillai, and to Orbit's publishing director, Tim Holman, for support and wisdom in making the Jason Wander books possible. Thanks also to Kim Gonzalez for thoughtful copyediting, to Calvin Chu for yet another sparkling cover, to Alex Lencicki, guide to the Internet and fixer of tickets, to Jennifer Flax for perceptive editing and so much more, and to everyone at Orbit for their energy and great work.

Thanks particularly to the many readers who have served their countries around the world and who have written to tell me that my labors have in some small way lightened or validated theirs.

Thanks also to Winifred Golden, agent to the stars and even to me, and, always, thanks to Mary Beth and the kids for sticking around.

extras

orbit

meet the author

ROBERT BUETTNER is a former Military Intelligence
Officer, National Science Foundation Fellow in Pale-
ontology and has been published in the field of Natural
Resources Law. He lives in Georgia. His Web site is
www.RobertBuettner.com.

introducing

If you enjoyed ORPHAN'S ALLIANCE,
look out for

ORPHAN'S TRIUMPH

Book 5 of the Jason Wander series
by Robert Buettner

BLAM-BLAM-BLAM.

The assault rifle's burst snaps me awake inside my armor, and the armor's heater motor prickles me between the shoulder blades when I stir. The shots' reverberation shivers the cave's ceiling, and snow plops through my open faceplate, onto my upturned lips.

"Paugh!" The crystals on my lips taste of cold and old bones, and I scrub my face with my glove. "Goddamit, Howard!"

Fifty dark feet from me, silhouetted against the pale dawn now lighting the cave's mouth, condensed breath balloons out of Howard's open helmet. "There are dire wolves out here, Jason!"

"Don't make noise. They're just big hyenas."

"They're slobbering!"

"Throw rocks. That's what I did. It works." I roll over, aching, on the stone floor and glance at the time winking from my faceplate display. I have just been denied my first hour's sleep after eight hours on watch. Before that, we towed the third occupant of this cave across the steel-hard tundra of this Ice Age planet through a sixteen-hour blizzard until we found this shelter, more a rocky wrinkle in a shallow hillside than a cave.

I squint over my shoulder, behind Howard and me, at our companion. It is the first Pseudocephalopod Planetary Ganglion any Earthling has seen, much less taken alive, in the three decades of the Slug War. Like a hippo-sized, mucous-green octopus on a platter, the Ganglion quivers atop its Slug-metal blue motility disc, which hums a yard above the cave floor. Six disconnected sensory conduits droop bare over the disc's edges, isolating the Ganglion from this world and, we hope, from the rest of Slug-kind.

Two synlon ropes dangle, knotted to the motility plate. We used the ropes to drag our POW, not to hogtie it. A Slug Warrior moves fast for a man-sized, armored maggot, but the Ganglion possesses neither organic motile structures nor even an interface so it can steer its own motility plate. Howard was very excited to discover that. He was a professor of extraterrestrial intelligence studies before the war.

I sigh. Everybody was somebody else before the war.

Howard would like to take our prisoner to Earth alive, so Howard's exobiology Spooks can, uh, chat with it.

That means I have to get us three off this Ice Age rock unfrozen, unstarved, and undigested.

I groan. My replaced parts awaken more slowly than

the rest of me, and they throb when they do. I'm growing too old for this.

"Jason!" Howard's voice quavers. He was born too old for this.

I stand, yawn, wish I could scratch myself through my armor, then shuffle to the cave mouth, juggling a baseball-sized rock from palm to palm. Last night, I perfected a fastball that terrorized legions of dire wolves.

As I step alongside Howard at the cave mouth, he lobs an egg-sized stone with a motion like a girl in gym class. It lands twenty feet short of the biggest, nearest wolf. The monster saunters up, sniffs the stone, then bares its teeth at us in a red-eyed growl. The wolf pack numbers eleven total, milling around behind the big one, all gaunt enough that we must look like walking pot roast to them.

But I'm unconcerned that the wolves will eat us. A dire wolf could gnaw an Eternad forearm gauntlet for a week with no result but dull teeth.

I look up at the clear dawn sky. My concern is that the wolves are bad advertising. The storm we slogged through wiped out all traces of our passing, and, I hope, kept any surviving Slugs from searching for us. But the storm has broken, for now. I plan for us to hide out in this hole until the good guys home in on our transponders.

If any good guys survived. We may starve in this hole waiting for dead people.

We don't really know how Slugs track humans, or even if they do. We do know that the maggots were able to incinerate Weichsel's primitive human nomads one little band and extended family group at a time. And the maggots had rude surprises for us less-primitive humans when we showed up here, too.

I wind up, peg my baseball-sized stone at the big wolf, and plink him on the nose. I whoop. I couldn't duplicate that throw again if I pitched nine innings' worth. The wolf yelps and trots back fifty yards, whining but unhurt.

Howard shrugs. "The wolf pack doesn't necessarily give us away. We could just be a dead bear or something in here."

I jerk my thumb back in the direction of the green blob in the cave. "Even if the Slugs don't know how to track us, do you think they can track the Ganglion?" Disconnected or not, our prisoner could be screaming for help in Slugese right now, for all we know.

Howard shrugs again. "I don't think—"

The wolf pack collectively freezes, noses upturned.

Howard says, "Uh-oh."

I tug Howard deeper into the cave's shadows, and whisper, "Whatever they smell, we can't see. The wind's coming from upslope, behind us."

As I speak, Howard clicks his rifle's magazine into his palm, and replaces it with a completely full one. I've known him since the first weeks of the Blitz, nearly three decades now, and Colonel Hibble is a geek, alright. But when the chips are down he's as infantry as I am.

Outside, the wolves retreat another fifty yards back from the mouth of our cave, as a shadow crosses it.

My heart pounds, and I squeeze off my rifle's grip safety.

Eeeeerr.

The shadow shuffles past the cave mouth. Another replaces it, then more. As they stride into the light, the shadows resolve into trumpeting, truck-sized furballs the color of rust.

Howard whispers, "Mammoth."

The herd bull strides toward the wolf pack, bellowing, head back to display great, curved tusks. The wolves retreat again.

Howard says, "If we shot a mammoth out there, the carcass would explain the wolf pack. It could make an excellent distraction."

He's right. I raise my M-40 and sight on the nearest cow's shoulder, but at this range I could drop her with a hip shot.

Then I pause. "The carcass might attract those big cats." Weichsel's fauna parallels Pleistocene Earth in many ways, but our neolithic forefathers never saw sabre-toothed snow leopards bigger than Bengal tigers.

Really, my concern with Howard's idea isn't baiting leopards. Sabre teeth can't scuff Eternads any more than wolf teeth can. I just don't want to shoot a mammoth.

It sounds absurd. I can't count the Slugs that have died at my hand or on my orders in this war. And over my career I've taken human lives, too, when the United States in its collective wisdom has lawfully ordered me to.

It's not as though any species on Weichsel is endangered, except us humans, of course. The tundra teems with life, a glacial menagerie. Weichsel wouldn't miss one mammoth.

So why do I rationalize against squeezing my trigger one more time?

I can't deny that war callouses a soldier to brutality. But as I grow older, I cherish the moments when I can choose not to kill.

I lower my rifle. "Let's see what happens."

By mid-morning, events moot my dilemma. The

wolves isolate a lame cow from the mammoth herd, bring her down two hundred yards from us, and begin tearing meat from her wooly flanks like bleeding rugs. The mammoth herd stands off, alternately trumpeting in protest at the gore-smeared wolves, then bulldozing snow with their sinuous tusks to get at matted grass beneath. For both species, violence is another day at the office.

Howard and I withdraw inside the cave, to obscure our visual and infrared signatures, and sit opposite our prisoner.

The Ganglion just floats there, animated only by the vibrations of its motility plate. After thirty years of war, all I know about the blob is that it is my enemy. I have no reason to think it knows me any differently. For humans and Slugs, like the mammoths and wolves, violence has become another day at the office.

Howard, this blob, and I are on the cusp of changing that. If I can get us off Weichsel alive. At the moment, getting out alive requires me to freeze my butt off in a hole, contemplating upcoming misery and terror. After a lifetime in the infantry, I'm used to that.

I pluck an egg-sized stone off the cave floor and turn it in my hand like Yorick's skull. The stone is a gem quality diamond. Weichsel's frozen landscape is as full of diamonds as the Pentagon is full of underemployed Lieutenant Generals. Which is what I was when this expedition-become-fiasco started.